PENGUIN BOOKS

THE HUNTER'S WALK

Nabeel Ismeer builds solar power plants across Asia during the day. He spends his nights writing, centred around the question 'What if?'. What if the stone age had a Leonardo Da Vinci, was Lascaux *her* Mona Lisa? What if prehistoric leaders resorted to discrimination when they had no answer to the ice age? What if mitigating climate change can also help reverse inequality and further humanity?

His writings, which include themes of climate change and inequality, have been published in print and online magazines.

The Hunter's Walk is his first book.

T0021047

The Hunter's Walk

NABEEL ISMEER

PENGUIN BOOKS

An imprint of Penguin Random House

PENGUIN BOOKS

USA | Canada | UK | Ireland | Australia
New Zealand | India | South Africa | China | Southeast Asia

Penguin Books is part of the Penguin Random House group of companies
whose addresses can be found at global.penguinrandomhouse.com

Published by Penguin Random House SEA Pte Ltd
9, Changi South Street 3, Level 08-01,
Singapore 486361

First published in Penguin Books by Penguin Random House SEA 2021

Copyright © Nabeel Ismeer 2021

ISBN 9789814914079

Typeset in Adobe Garamond Pro by Manipal Technologies Limited, Manipal

www.penguin.sg

To Shenaz,
Thank you for this dream of ours,
Dreaming dreams together.

Contents

1

The Zarda, the Sanaa, the Gubba

'Why do you protect that fair skin?'

'Why do you attack fair skins? Dark skin or fair skin, our blood still flows red,' Ghar felt the cold wind sting on the sweat running down his back. He felt ready for the fight even though their assailants' advantage, as a larger group, promised certain injury. With a resolve that increased with every moment, Ghar stood firm in front of his friend, Dun, a Gubba, a fair skin.

Ghar, was a Sanaa, a dark skin, born to a fair skin mother, Gharra. *Brown as the earth that made us, brown as the earth we will become*, as the tribal Elders would often rejoice. His thoughtful eyes were speckled brown like a forest floor of leaves. He had a baby-like roundness to his face, which aided his trustworthiness. He was tall but looked shorter because of a slouch, the result of a habitual studying of everything around him. He would stoop to observe a centipede's motion or ponder a butterfly's colourful wings, much to the annoyance of his quick-to-action companion, Dun.

The Gubba he was defending, Dun, was a fair skin, born to a dark skin mother, Adura. As infants, when their skin colour started to mature, the tribal Elders switched them, to comply with the resolution that the Gubba were impure and not allowed to live close to the Sanaa. Adura became Ghar's adoptive mother and Gharra became Dun's.

'Let's see if his blood is really red,' the lead intimidator stepped forward. His loose furs partially revealed his glistening, sinewy arms

1

and legs, and a torso that had been hewn by spear-throwing. His friends took off their pelts, in further acknowledgment of the fight.

Ghar could smell the warm-time sweetness of pine mixed with the acrid smell of long grass—these were usually the smells of freedom, away from the camp, where the Zardan found his true home, but today they smelled foreign and menacing. Ghar found himself distracted momentarily, thinking about how this fight would turn out and what excuse he would give Adura for the new wounds.

Then out of the leaves and the brown tree trunks and the busy birds came the first blow. Ghar dodged part of the fist, but the sting on his brow still took the firmness out of his knees. His eyes briefly met Dun's, accepting defeat—Dun reassuring Ghar the fight would still be won.

Dun stepped in front of Ghar, deflecting the next swing with his arm, unleashing his own fist through his defensive block, finding their assailant's chin.

Some of their attackers retreated at Dun's vehemence. Dun did not have the training that the Sanaa had. As a fair skin, his lessons were restricted to watching dark skin boys be trained by the hunters. He practised with Ghar who was given the formal training in Maraza—the Zardan martial art. But Dun had invented moves, unknown in Maraza, and now used it to his advantage. He was tall among the Zarda, his body showing the first signs of manhood. Strong broad shoulders perched ready on a taut midriff. Calloused limbs and scars told a tale of youthful and brash endeavours. A fringe that refused to be tamed, escaped his secured hair, and playfully bounded in front of his face.

Dun confidently paused, broadening his shoulders in a show of superiority, giving their aggressors a chance to reconsider. Instead, they regained their composure and attacked with their spears. Dun swiftly sidestepped the bigger swings and took the smaller jabs, grunting, while shielding his head with his arm. Each short quick stab he made, each painful blow he took, was accompanied by a step forward. In a moment of advantage, he was upon them, swerving, flexing and lunging, delivering resolute blows with the blunt end of his spear—even in his anger he knew there would be drastic punishment for a Gubba maiming a Sanaa, so he avoided using the sharp, stone tip.

It was over. The fight that had started out as words, ended in bruises. A final brandish of Dun's spear caused a full retreat, their Sanaa attackers scurrying for their belongings, muttering threats of vengeance under their breaths.

Dun watched them flee in the direction of the camp as he opened his fur to tend to the cuts and bumps on his skin. He limped, more from his excited limbs than injury, to check on Ghar.

'Those slimy toads!' Ghar examined the blood that came off his cheek, 'Is it bad?'

'You look different, maybe less ugly,' Dun smiled through his pain.

Ghar looked up at his friend, not amused, 'We had better get moving to the river to catch fish and think of some explanation for our bruises.'

Dun sighed, 'I wish the Elders would believe us when we tell them about this abuse.' He reached behind his neck to soothe his bruises.

'I think even if they saw their beloved Sanaa boys beating us to death, they would still act like it were the will of the Fathers. They might even praise it,' Ghar lamented.

'You keep forgetting you are Sanaa,' Dun reminded his dark skin brother.

'I would rather paint with more colour, not less. Dark skins, fair skins, we should also have green skins and blue skins,' Ghar tapped Dun on the arm, 'You can take away the stars, to make the moon look brighter, but for that the night time sky will be darker.'

'Green skins! Imagine what Das would do to them,' Dun chuckled. He turned serious again, 'But still, when we have to share these bruises, I wish you would embrace your skin colour. You could be training to be a hunter and complete the Hunter's Walk.'

'Dun,' Ghar drew the blood from his brow and offered his hand, 'by my blood, we will complete the walk, by the Fathers, together.'

Dun accepted reluctantly, 'I think it's more likely that we'll be tied to a tree.'

They started to walk through a beaten path. The Narun river was quickly revealed through the thickets, her yellow banks seemed lower every warm-time.

'Listen, whatever we do, whether it is becoming hunters or being tied to a tree, we'll do it together.' There was a sureness in Ghar's voice that he felt at ease in conveying; he knew, deep down in his bones, that this was the right way forward. 'Now let's catch some fish.'

* * *

The Zardan tribal Elders limited the area that the youth were allowed to explore in the forest, but there was no such restriction on how high they could go. Dun urged Ghar, 'Higher, I think I can see past the ridge.' Youthful curiosity was their chief motivator, but there was also the vow of secrecy imposed on the hunters—the only tribespeople to complete the Hunter's Walk. What they did or saw on the journey was not to be discussed, which left the youth of the tribe desperate to carry out the trek themselves.

Ghar's favourite songs about the hunters spoke of young men exploring and learning the forest, memorizing the calls of the animals, the smells of the flowers.

> With the first sprouts of hair,
> The boy, is a boy no more,
> His spirit is given to the forest,
> Watched over by the Fathers by the black caves,
> As he learns how the cold gives birth to the warm,
> And the night gives birth to the day,
> And the dead gives birth to the living,

Be sure his tracks will be different,
But his path will always lead back to Zarda.

Every song ended with the last refrain. Remembering all the songs would help the hunters locate landmarks to help find their way in the disorienting, chasmic forests, but there were also the Zardan ideals that would help guide the tribe back to the way of the Fathers.

Ghar took a moment to entertain a fantasy. Running through the forest, his heartbeat in unison with the prey. In a rush of spiritual simplicity, his spear leaves his fingers to rest in the middle of his quarry's chest. He stands above the creature, the remainder of life trembling out of its body. He kneels to respect his kill and remember the Fathers of the Zarda. He retrieves the spear, the stone tip covered in blood which he tastes off his fingertip. He pauses, trying to find some continuity in this privileged act. Was that all it was? Killing an animal, and then, when the hunger returned, killing another animal?

'You know, maybe being a hunter is not all that interesting?' Ghar tried to quell their enthusiasm.

Dun sighed, 'If I were given the chance, I would take the Walk right now. I wouldn't even need to get food and water; I would do it right now.' He looked out over the ridge, an expanse of Zardan mountains that nestled a trail, beyond which only their dreams could take them.

'But Gubba men are not hunters,' Ghar blurted out, with an immediate pang of remorse.

Dun looked down, 'Ghar, you know why they are not, so don't pick that scab; it might not heal again.' The Gubba were never given the chance to make the rite of passage. There were many edicts from the Elders. Fair skins were deemed impure. The Fathers, angered by the presence of the Gubba in Zarda, took away the prey that the tribe needed.

This struggle was the unlikely source of the boys' friendship. They were switched while they were infants, an order by the Elders, that no dark skin child would be left to the Gubba. However, the mothers of the children could not bear to be without their babies, and secretly spent time with each other. Some Elders had noticed the transgression but, apart from the occasional admonishment, they let the relationship be. Edicts aside, all the tribe understood that the bonds between mother and child were mystical, better left undisturbed.

'We should stop delaying fishing for this daydreaming,' Dun gestured to a setting sun. 'With fish I might still be a Gubba, but at least I won't be hungry.'

* * *

The boys returned to a solemn camp. Ghar had repaired paintings that used to depict the Zarda as a small tribe, when there were only a few tepees around the Grand Cave. There were smaller caves that were initially used as shelter, but later used as stores for dry firewood, dried meat, dried fruit and new furs. All the caves were part of a rock mass that was part giant rock and part boulders. A cave at the back sprung a small brook which gave the Zarda a convenient water source. At the base of the caves, tepees were built to accommodate the increasing size of the Zarda tribe. As the tribe grew, more tepees were built along the brook. The best tepees were close to the brook but also elevated so that they would not get flooded during a rainstorm.

Zardan shelters were constructed around a readiness to change. Although the Zarda had spent the last few generations in the Narun valley, there was a need occasionally to move, due to the increasing needs of the Zarda tribe. The best land was the firm high ground that did not flood.

Ghar could split the tribe into identifiable groups. The main division was through skin colour. Sanaa and Gubba. The dark skins lived closer to the Grand Cave, while the fair skins lived on the outer edge. The rest of the splits were mainly based on tasks: the Hunters, who were only Sanaa men; then the Elders, who spent most of their time inside or just outside the Grand Cave; the Sanaa women, who took care of the camp and the children. The last group was the Gubba who were given the tasks of collecting firewood and keeping the camp clean.

The last few warm seasons had left the tribespeople's faith on the decline. The herds of deer, illustrated on the cave walls, were waning. The hunters would tell the tribe that the long-nose buffalo, giant hornless deer and tree-eating bears were all on the decline. The rains were noticeably less frequent and even the mighty Narun River was surrendering her secrets.

Adura and Gharra explained to Ghar and Dun that these were difficult times for the Elders. Usually they had all the answers. The wisdom locked in the songs was theirs to decipher. But now, after the last cold-time, their advice seemed hollow.

'This is even further from the Grand Cave,' Ghar commented on the recent move of the Gubba tepees.

The floor of the tents was usually packed with furs. In the middle sat an arrangement of rocks, where a soft fire rumbled. The capricious plumes of smoke snaked out through an opening at the top of the tent.

The boys joined Dun's adoptive mother, Gharra, in her tepee. Gharra's infant, Ra, bellowed at their entrance.

Ghar bowed, Gharra was his birth mother, but he could not overcome the barrier of respect. He was much less formal around Adura.

'Gharra,' Dun bowed graciously while offering his catch to his mother. 'There were not many fish today in the river, I hope this will be enough for our meal.'

Ghar joined in, 'Gharra, listen, have this as well, it's the first catch with my new spear, and it would be an honour if you would accept this from me.'

Dun glanced surprised at Ghar, but quickly returned to a pose of deference, 'Is Ra getting better?'

Gharra acknowledged the boys' respect. She moved closer to the fire to inspect the cleaned catch. Ra continued to whimper. Gharra was tall for a Gubba, her arms were taut and there seemed to be a rocky tract hidden under her skin. Adura had stories about a younger Gharra fighting the Sanaa boys exposing lapses in their Maraza fighting style. She had even learnt to hunt herself, catching fish and other small animals, which often ended with her tied to a tree. Her hair was tied back, revealing a large, but feminine, forehead, she had wide cheekbones and dimples in her cheeks that would cool any trouble that the boys were facing. 'Ra is still hot, she might not make it.' She turned to Dun, 'How was your trek today, did you see anything interesting?' She prised out a few stray scales, and lay the fish down to cut and skewer, 'Any sign of the hunters?'

Dun took a moment to answer, he looked despondent about Ra. 'They haven't come back yet,' he didn't try to mask the disappointment in his voice. 'Is there something we can do for Ra?'

'This is all a test from the Fathers to see if we are true to Zarda.' A flicker in her voice betrayed her doubt to both Dun and Ghar, 'Getting fish to eat will help, but please be careful, if Das catches you, I will lose you as well.' She took a deep breath, 'Get some wood, we need some more for the night, maybe we can smoke some of the fish.'

The boys bowed their heads and left.

'Why did you give away your fish?' Dun asked Ghar as they again set off down the trail.

Ghar shrugged and avoided Dun's eyes, 'Listen, you must not let your family know—we have food for the Sanaa. Dried meat and fruit, a small portion every day—'

'Oh! So, that's how Adura gives us a little food every day. She says she steals from the Elders,' Dun interrupted Ghar, 'and that we shouldn't tell any other Gubba.'

Ghar thought about the meagre quantity of the food portion rationed out to him, *is Adura giving away what little she has?* He kept the thought to himself; he knew Dun would feel guilty at the thought of taking Adura's food.

'Wait, does Adura have enough to eat?' Dun asked, a sad realization in his eyes.

Ghar sighed, he shared this guilt with Dun, 'I think Adura and Gharra would do anything for us,' his eyes started to well up, 'even starve.' Ghar looked at Dun, through the tears in his eyes, 'I am sorry Dun, I should have shared my food too.' *But Adura told me not to.*

Dun continued his inquiry. 'Do you have food today? You must have, otherwise why would you give us your fish?' Dun could barely keep his anger in, he quickly wiped out his eyes. 'How could you not give us food, Ghar?'

Ghar took a step back at Dun's anger, 'I would give you all that I have, I am not allowed to; Adura has sworn me against even telling you and the Gubba.' He saw the wisdom in Adura's actions. Dun's anger would not change anything, and the Elders might decide to punish any retaliation. *But shouldn't the Gubba have a say in this, to argue about what they should get?*

'Why do the Fathers let this happen, why do they let us go hungry?' Dun's anger gave way to a sudden sense of helplessness and shame, 'are we not worthy of Zarda?'

Ghar sighed. 'Listen, the Fathers have guided us on this path—' he stopped himself. In his mind he spoke the truth, but the unfair nature of the words escaping his lips betrayed an uneasy feeling, 'listen, let me take back what I just said. I don't understand why they don't share the food.'

Dun collected some firewood that was drying in a cave, 'They will stop us from using the firewood next.'

Ghar knew there was some hurt humour in what Dun said, but the Elders' blocking the use of firewood could be a possibility. 'The Fathers test us, let's try to be patient.' He said it, but there was doubt. He needed to act. Leaving the Elders to lead only widened the ravine between the Sanaa and the Gubba. 'Let's talk to Adura.'

2

The Grand Cave

A starry night sky glistened over the camp. Hearth-cast shadows mysteriously danced on the tepee walls. The forest chirps and drones filled the darkness. Warm-time nights were usually warm enough for light furs, but recent seasons were cold enough to keep the tribespeople inside.

Dun moved stealthily between the tepees to avoid notice. The moon and the flicker of light through the hides of the tepees were the only guides to Dun's steps.

'Over here,' Ghar called, hoarsely. Unaccompanied youth were not allowed out by themselves at night. There had been many incidents of a curious child wandering into the forest and being snatched away by equally curious nocturnal beasts.

'Why did you tell Gharra you wanted to meet me here?' Ghar was about to answer but Dun pressed on, 'this is the Sanaa Elders' land, if an Elder saw me here, I would face a punishment.' Being tied to a tree was the most common punishment, usually done in a well-travelled locale of the camp, serving as a public reminder of the dangers of disobedience. Adults could get more severe punishments ranging from confinement to death by drowning or burning. Zardan punishment did not include mutilations; the Elders decided that crippling an able body in the camp was a disadvantage that could be ill-afforded. Either you left the camp by being cast out or by death or stayed behind to be of use to the camp for lesser offences.

'Keep your voice down, otherwise they'll tie both of us to a tree,' Ghar stepped out of his hiding place to survey the surroundings. He grabbed Dun by the hand and walked quickly towards a tepee.

'*Hera*, we are outside.' Hera was a term affectionately used for an older person.

'Is that you, Ghar?' Adura's voice was muffled by the tent's hide.

'Yes.'

'Come in before Das finds you and ties you to a tree,' Adura warned. Das was the tribal chief.

The boys politely made their way inside. The tepee was temporarily empty because a sickness had reduced the previous inhabitants. The survivors had moved out into another tepee. The softs skins that lined the walls had lost their youth to the many lives that passed through.

'How are you, children? Come closer to the fire, it'll keep you warm.'

'We are well, by the Fathers,' Ghar started with the appropriate greeting of respect. 'Adura, you said you might have an answer to why the Zarda treat the Gubba differently? We give them less food, we keep most of the new furs for our tents and forbid the Gubba from hunting,' Ghar glanced at Dun. 'Why?'

Adura chuckled, 'Questions to start a conversation—' She motioned for Ghar to hold his next words.

Dun interrupted her, 'Adura, are you eating anything at all in the nights? You've been giving your food to us.'

Adura looked at Ghar, 'This is why sometimes silence is better than sound.' She reached over to Dun and stroked the back of his neck, 'You are my son, and I will make sure you have food, even if it is by my own body.'

Dun started to tear up, 'Hera, you cannot do that, you must eat. I will try harder to catch more fish.'

'You can't hunt, Dun. The Elders do not allow it. If they catch you, they will punish you.' She sighed, 'Come with me.' Adura stood up. She lit a brand and walked out of the tent. Ghar and Dun glanced at each other reassuringly and followed.

'Hera, where are we going?' Ghar was hopeful of a nocturnal adventure to quell the sad revelations.

'Be calm like the clouds in the sky. Being patient of the Fathers, they will bring the rain to Zarda.'

Ghar pressed his lips together to contain the anticipation.

Adura, as a maintainer of the Grand Cave, took care of the paintings and the carvings that adorned the Elders' meeting place. She had Dun's small eyes and wide nose. Her long hair that was tied loose, hid her ears. Her hands were stained with the pigments that she used to maintain the cave paintings. Her large jaw had a large scar, the result of an altercation with a hunter, over an argument of her being in the Grand Cave during an Elders' gathering.

As a child, Ghar's artistic skills were hard to pass by. Adura had taught him the use of pigments, and the different methods of applying the paint on walls. But he was not satisfied with merely fixing damaged paintings or helping fill in the colour for an Elder. He would happily leave samples of his work all over the camp, on tepees, rocks, or sometimes even in quelled hearths.

Zarda's Grand Cave was home to a collage of works that portrayed Zardan life. To the spiritually mature, a visit to the cave would be a journey into a different world, the symbolism in the art revealing a different story each time.

Questions from young people generally centred around hunters and their victories. But Ghar had a different palate for knowledge. He was more interested in why flowers had different colours and where all the water in the Narun came from. Adura did not always have the correct-sounding answer, but Ghar still felt satisfied by the discussions. His curiosity could easily be brushed aside by a patronizing disclaimer, 'The Fathers are the holders of all secrets.' But Adura always took time over Ghar's doubts.

Adura led them up to the ceremonial caves where most of the Elders' meetings were held. The entrance to the largest cave, the Grand Cave, held a large hearth, which was waning peacefully in the night air. The sweet smell of burning pine had a slight tinge of dried meat, which came from the nearby caves that were used to store meat.

A guard keeping warm near the fire stood up to investigate, 'Adura, may the Fathers protect us. Why are you here so late?' He stopped for a moment as he noticed Ghar and Dun, 'Why do you bring a Gubba?'

'Who I walk with is of no concern to you,' a strong forceful demeanour replaced Adura's customary mild manner.

The guard was taken aback by Adura's uncharacteristic intensity, 'Please pass.'

As they walked into the cave Adura chuckled to reveal her true persona, 'Sometimes the best answer is no answer.'

Ghar and Dun acknowledged the lesson with a bow, while exchanging grins with each other. Ghar knew that there could be repercussions for Adura later, but she was usually able to talk her way out of it.

Dun had never been inside the Grand Cave; his experience of the shrine was confined to the outside entrance where he, along with the rest of the tribe, would listen to a sermon, or a verdict on some dispute. Dun held on to Ghar's shoulder for reassurance. The boys shared their courage in different situations—Dun, more willing to take on physical risks, while Ghar, more willing to take on authority.

The cave was only lit by the flickers from the fire at the entrance, but Ghar could already make out the cavernous room through the echoes of their movements.

Adura made her way to a massive cold hearth near the centre of the cave and touched the hearth with her torch. A fire, aided by wood soaked in deer fat, erupted streaming beams of light in all directions. The cave walls suddenly came to life in a burst of colour.

'There is an opening at the top, the smoke goes through there,' Ghar explained, noticing Dun looking at the smoke rise and disappear.

For a moment, the splendour of the plush, fur-laden floor and the dazzling motifs distracted them from their troubles.

'Listen,' Adura lit up a cave wall using a firebrand. She moved along the intricate drawings on the wall as if she were looking for something. Adura drew their attention to an image of the Zarda camp, 'I do not have an answer to your question. But I do have a question for your question.' Adura brought the fire closer to the wall, 'Why are Sanaa and Gubba babies buried together?' She stepped back to let the boys take a closer look. 'Looks like a time of failed hunts,' she pondered out loud.

Ghar stepped in closer to study the painting. Zardan drawings had a stylized look, adult figures had long hair, pointy chins and high cheekbones; their heads sat atop strong, slanted torsos and thin legs. Infants were heads on a fur-bundled torso. He studied the drawing of limestone-white and ochre-brown infants buried in the same pits. 'Why would they be buried together?'

Dun realized the curiousness of the discovery, 'Is this real? The Gubba are not buried near the Sanaa.'

Adura held her birth son in her arms, 'It probably happened a long time ago, but if a Gubba can come from a Sanaa, then why shouldn't a Gubba be buried with a Sanaa?'

'I don't really understand this; I just assumed this was how it always was,' Dun said.

They pored over the rest of the paintings. They did not know what they were looking for, they were not even sure why they were looking for something. But they were there, in that moment, wandering through the Zarda's history. It was hard not to digress, exploring the majestic creatures, bears with legs taller than a hunter, wolves in packs that would scare children out of their sleep.

Dun asked, 'What's this animal?'

'Long-nose buffalo,' Ghar answered, 'I have never seen a real long-nose buffalo, only on this wall. I have never seen most of these creatures. Long-tooth cat, tree-antler deer.'

The rumbling fireplace had diminished to a steady crackle. Adura had taken a place beside the fire to nap. Ghar's inspection had progressed beyond the stories to the type of the colour used and symbolism that was repeated in the drawings. He thought the difference between his skin colour and Dun was not as stark as the ochre and limestone on the walls.

'When I look at these paintings, I think the Sanaa and the Gubba look really different.' He compared his arm to Dun's, 'we are not that different.'

Dun nodded in agreement continuing his quest, although the goal of his search was still unclear.

After further deliberation Ghar appealed, 'I am tired Dun, and I think Gharra will be looking for you.'

'Please, Ghar, let me look a little longer. Most of these paintings have a separation between the Sanaa and Gubba, but some don't.'

'But why, what are you looking for?' Ghar softened his tone at the end of the sentence, he had never seen Dun take an interest in the paintings.

'I don't know,' Dun quickly replied to continue studying the paintings.

Ghar perked up when he noticed the positioning of a painting.

'This is not a great place to paint. The surface slants downwards,' he lay down next to the painting and mimicked the imagined actions of the artist. 'I would have to paint from down here.' He clambered to his feet to inspect the others, the discovery cascading into new questions. His eyes came to rest on a darker portrayal. Dead children littered the image.

The commotion broke Adura's slumber, 'That painting has interested me for a long time. There is no blood, so I think those children died of hunger.'

'I think you could be right, Hera,' Ghar inspected the painting, 'It's also not a great place for a painter to work,' he took a pause as the revelation sank in, 'maybe this was painted later?' Ghar felt the piece did not have the attention to detail of the other paintings. He imagined himself as the artist, probably weak from hunger, composing on the wall whatever he could. 'By the Fathers,' he murmured a praise in respect.

Adura put Ghar's thoughts in order, 'The older paintings are on the better walls, the newer paintings are on the bad places to paint.'

As their torches revealed more of the paintings, Ghar noticed a small portrayal at the edge of the wall. 'Why start a new painting here?' The flickering light slowly gave up the image, 'That's a fair-skinned Gubba bowing to a dark-skinned Sanaa, and the Sanaa seems to be gesturing to him to leave.'

'What does all this mean?' Dun asked.

Ghar stood in the middle of the cave, 'If I were painting, I would pick the best part of the rock, somewhere flat, at standing height, with good light from the fire.'

'Away from water drops,' a smiling Adura joined in.

'Yes,' Ghar's eyes came to rest on a depiction he thought was the best place to paint, of the Zarda on the hunt, stalking a deer. 'This might be the earliest painting here,' he contended. 'By the Fathers,' he glanced at Adura prompting her to join him. 'Within the Sanaa group, there is a white mark,' he brought a firebrand closer, 'that's a Gubba, the paint has faded, but it has just not been repaired. And look at these white marks,' Ghar pointed at traces of limestone that seemed to have been painted over with ochre. He flaked off some of the red, which revealed more limestone.

Adura was next to Ghar studying the figures, 'The Gubba in old Zardan paintings have been hidden in the painting.' She tilted her head looking at another interesting depiction of large-chested men. 'Their chests,' she used her fingernail to trace a layer of ochre on the torso, 'this used to be a woman!'

'So, the Gubba and tribeswomen used to hunt in Zarda!' Dun caught up with the discovery.

Ghar looked at Adura, with disbelief, 'Who would do such a thing?'

Adura looked around the cave, 'What if all these other paintings have also been altered?' she took a deep breath. 'I have spent my life covering up lies. I have been asking the wrong question.'

Ghar reassured Adura with his hand on her shoulder, 'We are supposed to repair and create. Another tribesperson altering the paintings is surely not our responsibility. Surely the Fathers do not expect that.'

'Is there a way we can use this?' Dun asked. 'Can we use this story to convince the Elders that maybe there doesn't have to be a split between us brothers.'

'I don't know,' replied Ghar. 'I think the Elders would say that the paintings depict the Gubba's crimes and ignore that we used to hunt together.'

'Or they could just say that this is what the Fathers ordained,' Adura said. 'I'll talk to the Elders when Das returns.'

Ghar took a last glimpse at the paintings while Dun hopefully grasped Adura's shoulder.

'Thank you, my brother,' Dun turned to Ghar, taking a moment to reflect. 'Tonight, I found out who I used to be, and who I can be.'

Ghar felt hope, 'If we hunted together before, surely we can hunt together again.'

* * *

The next day, Ghar and Dun returned early from their fishing to see if Das and the hunters had returned, and if Adura had talked to the Elders about their findings in the Grand Cave. They had discussed and agreed that they should not expect a full reinstatement, but they reserved hope for a start to some improvements to the Gubba: at least a ration of food.

They rushed through the camp, past the Gubba side, and past the Sanaa tepees, even though they were aware they smelled like fish.

As they trudged on the hardened dusty pathway that branched out to tepees on either side, they heard a commotion growing behind them. Joyous cries heralded the returning hunters in the distance. Tribespeople erupted from their dwellings to greet the hunters. Ghar, engulfed in euphoria, forgot about his quest and joined the celebration, with Dun following closely behind.

The celebrations were wrapped in too much joy to notice the despair on the hunters' faces. Slowly the happiness cleared to reveal an unsuccessful hunt. Das, the only Elder to be a part of the group made his way up to the Grand Cave.

He said something to the Elders present, and they retreated to the cave.

Ghar whispered to Dun, 'I think now would be a good time to go.' Das did not look like he was in the mood to hear the appeals that Ghar had prepared in his mind.

As they walked to Dun's tepee, Ghar thought about what the next move could be—send hunters to a different part of the forest, maybe reduce the ration of food. He thought about the much-needed food for Gubba families. A lot of the children were fighting hunger with the hope that the hunters' return would be a reprieve. He knew hope would eventually lose to hunger.

'Let's go back to the river . . . catch more fish,' Dun answered Ghar's thoughts.

As Ghar turned and walked with his friend towards the Narun, he wrapped his arm around Dun's shoulder and whispered, 'For Zarda.'

* * *

The day had proven fruitful, there would be enough food for Dun's family and maybe another.

Ghar looked at his partner, the whole day had passed with only words of the hunt. 'By the Fathers, I hope this is enough.'

In a moment of clarity, Dun imparted wisdom, 'This might not quell the hunger, but it might feed the hope.'

Ghar smiled, 'That sounds like something Adura might say.'

Dun blushed, his fair skin not able to hide his surge of pride at his poetry, 'She is my mother.'

They got to Dun's tent wearing their contentment, only to be unravelled by Ra's inconsolable crying. Gharra knelt on the furs, cradling Ra.

'Gharra, we have done well today, no reason to be hungry, we have lots of fish today.'

The boys did not receive the predictable praise. She looked like her eyes could give way to tears, but were being held back by exhaustion, by thoughts that were not in the moment.

Dun immediately held her shoulders, 'Gharra, what is it? Why are you sad? Talk to me!'

She avoided Dun's questioning eyes. 'The other hunting group came back; they had no food either.'

'But that's all right, we have food, see this fish.'

'No, Dun,' she touched his brow, and nervously combed his hair away from his eyes, 'they are blaming us. The Fathers are saying that this is the Gubba's fault. Adura told me what the Elders had heard from the Fathers.'

Dun cradled her, the son momentarily becoming the mother. Dun looked to his brother for advice, 'Ghar, what should we do?'

Ghar sighed, the weariness of the last days clawed at his thoughts. 'I don't know Dun, let's talk to Adura,' He embraced Gharra, and held her as hard as he could, 'Gharra if you were out there hunting, we would not be in this position.'

Gharra chuckled through her tears.

Ghar found himself feeling very uneasy as they walked back to his tepee. His elaborate plan to discuss the Gubba's position in the camp based on the old paintings, was now like a maimed fish being carried away by the Narun. *The Fathers are saying it's the Gubba's fault. How can I argue against that? I don't speak to the Fathers.*

Dun noticed some men moving from tent to tent. He took Ghar's shoulder and walked by, close enough to garner a sliver of information, but sufficiently far away to avoid alerting the hunters.

Have they already decided? And do they want us there right now? Ghar could barely hear them.

Yes, by the Fathers, leave. Please go there now. The sun is about to leave us for the day.

Ghar looked at Dun, 'An announcement? Let's go.'

Closer to their destination, the crowds grew denser. Meeting Adura in this throng would be a challenge. 'Can you see Adura? Should I maybe go back and get Gharra and Ra?' Dun asked.

'I think Das is about to come out, let's climb those rocks for a better view.'

Das came out of the cave and looked around wearily.

'Dun, there is something different about today, all the Elders are so quiet.' They crouched together for warmth, and to keep their whispers quiet. He looked at the crowd. From up on his perch on the rocks, he realized just how large Zarda was. Familiar faces but still strangers. So many people he did not know at all. He looked back at Das who had started to call out his message.

'My people, my Zarda. The Fathers lead us through many paths, but they all end here in Zarda.'

A gradual murmur of the prayer resonated through the gathering. Members in the back following the crowd in front.

'My people, these are trying times. The herds of animals provided to us by the Fathers are growing leaner. The nights and days are colder than we Elders can remember.'

Ghar was temporarily impressed with the eloquence and clarity of Das's address, but he reminded himself that the words were going to lead to an unkind end for the Gubba.

'My people, these are all signs that the Fathers are unhappy with us, unhappy with the unity of the tribe.' Das lifted his staff, 'We will be cleansed of our uncleanliness, we will unite against separation.'

'Unite against separation?' Ghar whispered, 'Is there hope for the Gubba yet?'

Another wave of prayer reverberated through the camp.

'We have kept our Gubba brethren in Zarda, because of our ties of kinship. But the Fathers are not happy with this,' Das changed his tone from reverence to authoritative. A hunter appeared from the cave carrying what looked like a small animal. Das held it up in the waning light—gasps of horror travelled through the camp.

Ghar stared for a moment. It was the head of a man, a Gubba. He felt Dun shiver behind him.

'The Gubba, our brothers, have betrayed us. We caught a group of them on Zardan land trying to steal our prey.'

A tribeswoman started to wail at the back of the group.

Dun edged closer to Ghar and whispered, 'That's Kuna.'

Ghar whispered back quickly and cautiously in acknowledgement, 'What was a Gubba doing out hunting?'

Dun glared at Ghar, 'I hunt fish.' Ghar quickly realized his lapse and apologized.

'My brethren, the Fathers have instructed our animals away from our grasp, as a test. There is a choice for us, a forked path in the forest to choose from. A path laden with meat and blessings from the Fathers, and a path with untold and unknown hardship,' the pause in Das's speech gave way to worried conversations amongst the camp-dwellers.

Ghar looked out on the camp. The size of the Zarda tribe surprised him again; the immense burden on the hunters' shoulders to feed so many hungry mouths. He turned to Dun, the face he knew most, for a glimpse of confidence, but now he couldn't tell. Stoic courage had abandoned his friend, leaving behind a vulnerable uncertainty.

'My brethren, I have spoken to the Fathers and they have told me what they want.' Every generation of the Zarda had a leader, who was appointed by former leaders to take the highly revered role of being in contact with the Fathers. 'Today is the last day the Gubba spend near these hallowed grounds. I have sent hunters to aid in their move. Tomorrow they will be escorted down the river to grounds outside Zarda.'

Dun let out a gasp, turning to Ghar's look of shock. He skipped down the rock face and ran towards the Gubba side of the camp.

Ghar, to the surprise of the Elders, showed himself and shouted across the tribe, 'The Gubba are our brothers, but you don't give them food and you don't let them hunt.'

Das answered enraged, 'Who is this impudent child, and how dare he interrupt me in matters ordained by the Fathers?'

'I ask you, who are you to send our tribespeople away? The Fathers would never support something to hurt our tribe!' Ghar turned to the other Elders, 'How can you let him tear our family apart? We have seen a painting in the cave where Sanaa and Gubba hunt together.' He turned to Das again 'Where in the Songs does it ask us to cast out our brothers in hardship? The Songs tell us to help each other in troubled times!' Ghar felt the silence he was shouting into, but he missed Dun, like he was already expelled. 'We stopped the Gubba from hunting, then we stopped tribeswomen from hunting, we are just making it harder for ourselves, we need all our people to help solve this.'

'The Fathers have directed me to do so,' Das bellowed. The logic of Ghar's arguments had prised out an answer that was not usually needed. This angered Das, and he walked over to a guard reaching for a spear.

A voice of uncharacteristic vehemence erupted from Adura, 'Get down from there, you disgraceful child!' she tossed a rock in Ghar's direction.

Ghar leaped down the precipice, stopping in the crowd to listen to the remainder of Das's address. A few angry hands berated Ghar's interruption, but the tribe quickly used the break to discuss the revelations.

Das resettled his attention on the tribe, 'My brethren, this will be done, this is the way forward for Zarda.' He retreated into the cave with the Elders.

Ghar raced towards Dun's tepee, his chest felt like it was tearing apart with each step. Dun was the only clear thought.

Dun was with Gharra, Ra tucked in between them, embracing, quietly praying and consoling each other. The intensity in the room was so thick that it stopped Ghar at the entrance. He gazed at Gharra, his birth mother. He wanted to call out to her but realized his place was not here.

The walk back winded him more than usual. The dusty paths seemed to branch out more, and the babbling creek that usually brought cool water to the tribe's thirst, only seemed to remind Ghar that he could not stop events larger than himself; reaching into the flow helped him attain just a momentary solace. It all seemed unreal, the idea that Dun, Gharra, and the Gubba families would be exiled from Zarda. He almost felt comforted that this could only be a nightmare from which he would wake up.

The sight of Adura walking towards him, released the last remaining strength in his limbs, as he stumbled into her arms.

Adura smothered him, 'I am sorry, my beautiful boy, I do not know what to say. I am sorry I threw that stone at you.'

Ghar felt his mother's warmth pass by the cold soft hairs of her hide, and into his grateful arms. He felt like a little boy, who had cut his knee, and the only solace, the only healing, was the gentleness of her voice.

Adura continued, 'This is not fair. Das has always had something against the Gubba.' Her attention went out to Dun and Ghar's birth mother, 'Dun, my beautiful son, and Gharra, my closest friend, I can't believe they are going to be cast out,' she started to sob.

'We have to keep trying, Adura, we have to save the Gubba to save Zarda.'

* * *

Sometime in the night, Ghar had eventually fallen asleep. A restless slumber disturbed by the many ways the next morning would proceed.

He peered through a gap in the tent covers for any activity outside. 'Maybe it was just a bad dream,' he said to himself, hopefully. The Sanaa in the tepee were rhythmically asleep, huddled together for warmth. The fire in the hearth had long been reduced to embers, sleepily trying to stay awake. There was a strong caustic smell that scratched the insides of his nose, from infants that had repeatedly relieved themselves through the course of the night. He looked around for Adura; she did not seem to be there. *She must be in the unused tepee.*

He stepped out into the cold air. A fresh beautiful air that reminded him of the blue sky and the green trees. But Ghar knew its beauty hid the mean prejudiced events that floated in with the wind.

He found Adura in the unused tepee, wrapped up in a hide, staring vacantly through the opening.

'Hera, may I join you?'

Adura smiled faintly. She unwrapped an opening in her fur and gestured for Ghar to get in, 'You are still my little boy.' Ghar felt his cheeks warm up, a welcome relief from the thoughts that seemed to push out from inside his head. 'Again, I am sorry I cast a stone at you yesterday.'

Ghar looked at Adura, 'It is all right, Hera. I should thank you. If I had said anything further, Das would have struck me down.'

'I think he's wrong this time. He usually has Zarda's wellbeing in mind, but I think this time he has run out of answers.'

'But is this order not from the Fathers?'

'Well, I don't think he actually talks to them, like you and I are talking to each other. What's more—the order does not agree with the Songs.'

'That's what I said yesterday.'

'I know. That's why I am out here thinking,' Adura said. 'There is hope, Ghar, some of the Elders have voiced disapproval. They argue that the outcasts might join other tribes and turn against Zarda.'

'Other tribes? You mean outsiders?'

'Tribes that are not the Zarda.'

Ghar had heard of the stories of people whom the hunters had encountered, but it was a new thought that they were not Zardan. 'If they are not Zardan, then what are they?' Ghar asked, 'Do the Fathers guide them?'

Adura smiled, 'So many questions, Ghar, but are these the questions to ask? Remember an answer will only be as good as its question.'

Ghar was exasperated at this revelation. *Who is the outside tribe? Are they Zardan? Do these questions really affect me? What do we do to help the Gubba? Can we still ask the Elders to consider the paintings?* 'We could tell the Elders that Kuna was only hunting because the Gubba are hungry?'

'A hunter told me that Kuna was not violent. It was Das who attacked first,' she looked at Ghar, her eyes welling up. 'I would do anything for Zarda, but this is not my Zarda.'

Ghar leant on Adura and drifted back to sleep with Adura's words on his mind, 'Anything for Zarda.'

* * *

Ghar woke up to an unfamiliar voice. 'Hera, Das requests your presence at the Grand Cave.'

Adura turned to Ghar, 'Patience, my son, we will see what the Elders decide.'

Ghar watched as Adura got up walked out. He clambered to his feet and stood for a while, wondering what could happen, what would happen. 'They must be getting ready to leave,' Ghar thought to himself. He ran swiftly through the forest taking a short cut to Dun's tent, his toes digging in conviction.

'Stop, don't pack yet,' Ghar called out to Dun, who was rolling furs on a splint.

'Ghar, stop. I do not want to think about this anymore. I want to take my family to a place where we can be on our own, safe and cherished.'

'But you can be safe and cherished here, Dun. We just have to fight this. You and I, we can fight this.' The words from Ghar felt unfair and naked.

Dun's eyes wavered. 'We are not Zardan, we never were. From the day they took me from Adura.' He looked away to hide his tears, his hands keeping busy, fastening furs together.

A rush of anger overcame Ghar's inhibition and he grabbed his Gubba brother by the hand, 'Put that down when I talk to you.'

Dun clung on and continued to work. Ghar snatched the furs and threw them to the ground, 'Listen to me, Dun. You are not going anywhere. We are going to talk to Das and any one who will listen.' His anger caved in to reveal his hopelessness. He clutched at their shared dreams, 'We will become hunters.'

The air of despondency that fell over them broke into a commotion. Das, accompanied by the hunters, arrived at the Gubba tepees.

'You have until sundown.' The hunters moved into the further reaches of the camp to convey Das's message.

Ghar had run out of options. He approached Das through the crowd of people that had gathered and fell to his knees, the words coming out in sobs, 'Hera, the Elder who talks to Fathers, surely you can find a better way and keep Zarda intact.'

Das ignored his pleas and continued to bark orders at the tribesmen.

Ghar impulsively touched Das's feet, 'Please.'

'Go back to the Sanaa quarters before I banish you along with the Gubba,' Das kicked Ghar in the head leaving him motionless in the dirt.

Dun reached for his spear but was restrained by Gharra. The lack of anything to lose emboldened him, and he broke free, his fists ready to deliver the message that Ghar's mouth had failed to.

A nearby hunter quickly sparked into action and struck Dun down to the ground. Ghar could just about make out his friend's motionless body covered in dust. His mind fought to hold on to his senses, but the unconsciousness won and his eyelids betrayed his outstretched fingers.

3

The Outsider

The familiarity of the Zarda presented a chance for Dun to appear at any moment. The children playing about, enjoying the remaining warm-time, mothers chatting away as they nestled around the fire—to Ghar, these daily moments were a big part of what the Zarda was to Ghar. Dun was a big part of what the Zarda was to Ghar.

The next few days seemed unimportant to Ghar. He went to the same fishing holes to catch fish, fire-keeping and firewood-collecting duties went on as normal. But there was a limpness to his enthusiasm. Each daily chore was carried out as if shackled by irrelevance. None of these acts could bring Dun back.

Adura noticed the change in his disposition, over meals, and during their time at the Grand Cave. At first, she let him be, but then she started to fear that he would be expelled from the tribe as well, especially after his reaction on the day of Dun's expulsion. 'Ghar, Dun will be all right. Gharra and the Gubba are as strong as us.'

'They don't know how to hunt. They don't know the terrain; they don't know how to avoid predators. They don't know; they don't know anything.' Ghar had been holding back the last question, 'How could you let them go?'

'Do you think I let them go, send my son, from me, out into the forest, among the bears?'

'I am sorry, Hera, I think I'm asking the wrong question.' He knew what the right question was: 'Why did the Elders and Das expel the Gubba?' Ghar did not like that they were powerless, that they were not asked for an opinion about the Gubba's fate. 'Was it to mask their own failure?'

Adura stared at the camp, with a contempt that Ghar had never seen before. 'I think the better question is, who is next?'

* * *

The Narun river had slowed over the warm season. The lack of rain made firewood more accessible, making Ghar's routine even shorter. His walks along the banks each day surpassed the previous trek.

A tree had fallen across the river. The end of the tree extended out almost to the opposite bank. Ghar had never been to the other side, he was caught off guard with the new possibility. What was beyond?

He looked around cautiously, and carefully made his way across. At the tree's end he got into the water, the river still had some strength, but he managed to wade to the shore. He grabbed hold of some grass and pulled himself on to the bank. He looked back at the Zarda territory. It looked different from here. Suddenly he felt alone and vulnerable. There could be other tribes on this side. He might be killed if found.

His curiosity outweighed his fear. He used his spear to cleave a path through the undergrowth but did it with care. These parts were unknown to Ghar, so he thought it best to travel with discretion. Crouched, he crept stealthily into the forest, scanning the area for signs of outsiders. Stopping to examine peculiar-looking plants or out-of-place rocks.

A midday sun made its way down to the mountains. He looked back at the way he had come; Ghar had travelled quite a distance. Disappointingly only the trees were there to celebrate his achievement.

He suddenly realized something: for all the hurt Zarda represented, there was still a sense of belonging. With the evening sun's yellow rays lighting the path back to Zarda, Ghar went home.

* * *

The verdant green of the Narun valley peeled away to uncover a barren, ochre landscape that quelled any hope that the tribespeople kindled. The creek that brought much-needed water to the Zardan tribe had slowed to a trickle, enough for a drink and to wet their skin, but fur washing and bathing now required a trip down the river.

A commotion broke out near the old Gubba camp. A man was seen emerging from the thicket. Some of the Zardan tribesmen sprinted out to resist him. Ghar took up a vantage point on a rock outcrop. *Who is this man? He is not a fair skin; did he want to harm anyone?*

The man bowed down to assuage the flared tempers of the Zardan tribesmen. Surrounded by readied spear tips, he moved cautiously and laid out a fur that was tucked under his arm.

Das arrived on the scene in an unrelenting mood. He grabbed the fur, threw it back at the man and motioned vehemently to leave. Words were unexchanged but the screams and actions communicated Das's intent. The man reluctantly left.

Ghar was curious, *the man was trying to give us something. Maybe it was in exchange for food or something that he needed.* He observed the man's initial direction back into the forest, and quietly descended from the rock and quickly ran back into the camp.

He had been experimenting with sun-dried fish, using smoke and fire to dry out the flesh before leaving it out in the sun, to reduce the amount of firewood that was usually used. He retrieved the fish he had hidden in a crevice near his tepee and hid it in his fur. *Maybe the man will give me the furs for this?*

Ghar caught up with the man, near the Narun, but kept a cautious distance. The man continued down the riverside, intermittently pausing to take aim at a fish.

Ghar could sense that fishing was not the man's strength—many unlucky stabs into the water came out unrewarded.

The spear reaches its target, not by the arm of the Hunter,
Nor by the long training in the art of Maraza in the Ravine of
*   Returning Voices,*
Nor even the Hunter's Walk.
The spear strikes only so that the Fathers may guide,
You back to Zarda,
So teach those who need to be taught,
Feed those who need to be fed,
Help those that need to be helped,
Throw the spear that will lead you back to Zarda.

The song had been on Ghar's mind lately. Zarda had not taught, fed or helped the Gubba. *Maybe I can help this outsider.*

The man eventually gave up and made his way into the forest. Ghar slowly followed. They had walked a short distance when the man called out. A young girl with an infant emerged from the trees and pranced around. He crouched down to the children and handed them a few berries.

Ghar noticed that the infant had a sunken torso, protruding ribs, and bare limbs. The sight made Ghar feel the same emotion that had accompanied the unfair treatment of the Gubba, and a need to announce himself, and more importantly to present the dried fish.

'I am not going to hurt you,' Ghar drew attention to himself to limit alarming the children. He put down his spear and drew out the fish from his cloak making sure they could see his actions clearly.

The man quickly mobilized with his spear and ran towards Ghar, shouting and brandishing his weapon.

Ghar took a step back, manoeuvring away from the blows. He sidestepped the man's efforts to trip him up from behind, but was astonished to find the man still flailing in the same direction. *He can't see very well.* Ghar sprinted a small distance away and shouted to attract the man's attention to indicate he was unarmed.

The young girl called out to the man, her shrieks in a foreign language calmed the man's violent swings.

For a while, the only sounds that filled the clearing were the whimpers of the infant. Ghar began to feel uneasy at the prospect of the man deciding to lash out suddenly. Neither of the options of the children losing their protector, or himself being killed in a scuffle were appealing.

The man monitored Ghar's every action. He motioned his older daughter to draw closer—it seemed to Ghar like she joined the man, probing him, engaging in animated conversation, exchanging views. The girl suddenly went quiet when she noticed the fish in Ghar's hands. She turned to the man, her eyes filling with an expectant hope.

Ghar offered the slices of fish to the girl, as she moved within arm's distance. She grabbed it and without any other gesture, she broke off a piece for the man, and another for the infant. Their faces shone with the relief of a deer escaping his captor. Ghar felt good about it, although this was an unfamiliar feeling, helping people outside the tribe.

The upbeat atmosphere around the camp did not change the man's cautious reaction to Ghar. He still watched Ghar closely, his spear on his shoulder.

Ghar broke the uneasy silence by announcing himself, 'I am Ghar,' he motioned to himself softly. He repeated, 'Ghar,' placing his hand on his chest.

The man was silent for a while. Ghar was about to repeat his introduction, when the man interrupted. He copied Ghar's gesture, and tentatively offered, 'Medar.' He repeated with more confidence, 'Mukaiwak Medar.'

The shadows of the trees were getting longer. Ghar was aware that it would be dangerous to navigate back to the camp without daylight. And he felt curious, and a bit of fear for the younglings.

He decided to stay the night—he would have to concoct a story for Adura in the morning. *Perhaps I was in the trees all night, avoiding a pack of wolves.*

The children had finished eating. They had furs just like the man, pieces of animal skin mimicking their movements. They stretched playfully and wandered around the camp examining rocks and leaves. The girl watched Ghar occasionally, but for a situation that had been extremely tense earlier, they seemed to bond well to their new shared existence with Ghar.

Medar had made his way up a nearby tree and reached into a collection of dead leaves nestled in the branches. Ghar looked on perplexed as Medar extracted cordage that he tossed down.

Ghar picked up the cordage. It was as strange as Medar's language. It had the thickness of vines but the flexibility of animal fibre that the Zarda used. The cords reminded Ghar of birds' nests, with fibres sticking out.

Medar climbed down and smiled at Ghar's surprise. He took the cord in both hands and pulled it apart with a loud snap. It stretched, but the cord remained intact leading to further amazement from Ghar. His disposition towards Ghar had changed quickly from foe to wary friend.

Medar motioned to Ghar to climb another tree and followed after him.

The children picked up on the activity and started to collect leaves and shrubbery. The infant climbed a tree with a similar clump of brown leaves and returned with animal skins.

Up in the tree, Medar, after inspecting the branches, tied sticks around the limbs to create a flat layer. The shrubbery and leaves came on next. He made careful effort to conceal the cords that were visible from the underside. Finally, the skins came on. Medar signalled Ghar to hop on.

Ghar was unsure of its safety, the drop down to the forest floor seemed daunting. He sat up first with most of his weight still on the branch.

Medar grunted disapprovingly, saying something foreign, while pushing on Ghar's shoulders to get him to lie down.

The knots creaked ominously while the thin sticks across the tree limbs sagged. The depression formed by Ghar's weight in the makeshift hammock had a wrapping effect around his body. After the initial fear of falling through wore off, he found it surprisingly comfortable.

Medar and the children were all smiling now. They had made a new friend and judging from the frailness of the little infant, Ghar had come at the right time.

Ghar made his way down and started collecting tinder and dry wood. There was a bit of sunlight left, and it would be best used preparing for the cold night ahead. He started to drill a twig into dry wood.

Medar forestalled him with a look of resignation. He pointed up at the tree berths and motioned to sleep curled up.

Ghar immediately understood. They were in the trees not only because of predatory animals, they were also trying to avoid men.

* * *

The morning sun shone through the trees. Ghar had slept well save for the chill during the night. He felt refreshed beyond his body, his mind renewed. The family was already down on the forest floor, Ghar negotiated the tree boughs to join them. The mixture of decaying leaves and soft gravel had an uneasy hold in the morning dew. Ghar treaded softly to the amusement of the children.

He had thought about the man's struggle in catching fish, with his failing eyesight, and decided it would be useful to teach the younglings to fish. He demonstrated spearing a fish with a leaf and a stick. He thought an actual spear would scare the tribe.

The family looked at each other, they did not seem to understand.

Ghar gave the stick to the eldest girl and moved the leaf in front of her. He tapped his chest, 'Ghar.'

She looked at Medar, and with his approval replied, 'Muna', her eyes widened as she swung enthusiastically smashing Ghar's wrist. Ghar could not stop a yelp escape his throat, to the laughter of the children.

Medar looked unconvinced at first, but after Muna's repeated attempts and Ghar's confident demeanour, he seemed to accept the new-born trust they shared. Ghar climbed his tree to retrieve his spears.

The infant animatedly called out to their father in what Ghar figured was a plea to join in. Ghar gestured to convey that he did not want to move around the river with a baby. He wanted to give Muna quick lessons in fishing, and hopefully some ways to navigate the area, and maybe some good locations to hide. This was Zarda territory.

Medar still did not seem entirely convinced, but he let Muna join Ghar. For the most part Muna did not understand Ghar. He had to resort to acting out what he wanted to say.

Ghar fastidiously showed her the plants she had flattened, or the impression of her feet in the earth. He traced back her steps taking pains to avoid the fragile undergrowth and to hide her tracks.

Teaching Muna to spear fish, in the limited time, with the threat of Zardan hunters arriving at any moment, was going to be a difficult task. He had learned from Gharra in secret, how to pick which fish to go for, how to predict its motion before a strike. It had taken Ghar a long time to figure out the nuances in fish movement.

With the river clearing in sight, he hesitated for a moment, and looked back at Muna—partly trying to figure out a way to get through, and partly assailed by doubts about the challenge ahead. Her curls playfully looped above her brow, and her soft skin and glistening, ingenuous eyes betrayed her inexperience.

At the river he knelt beside her and altered her stance so her shadow was just inside the bank. He followed a fish's route with his finger, prompting her to do the same. Ghar handed her a spear, and smiled encouragement. Her enthusiasm distracted her accuracy and her first attempts only disturbed the fish.

Each time the fish were disturbed, it took time for them to come back and stay still. Ghar went over the steps again, he lined up Muna's arm and shoulder to have the spear tip close to the water edge for aim. He felt like every miss was an extra chance for the hunters to catch them.

Then her spear connected momentarily. It was not a clean strike but was enough to injure the fish. Ghar quickly jumped in to apprehend the startled creature.

She smiled ear to ear at the sumptuous catch. Ghar figured it would be enough for the day. Muna took out a flint blade, and cut through the fish abdomen, carving whenever the skin slowed her. She sliced all the way through to the chin of the fish, and prised out the innards, dismembering the end of the tube from the mouth.

Ghar was quite impressed with her knowledge on preparing the meat, the removal of the gut was critical to make the meat last. *She must have learned this when Medar's eyesight was better, or maybe they were part of a bigger tribe. Maybe they are outcasts like the Gubba.* For a moment she seemed to have Dun's smile.

At the back of his mind, he imagined the kind of panic that his absence was causing back at Zarda. Adura would be worried. When he did get back, he would be in a lot of trouble, might even get a beating, and a night tied to a tree was guaranteed.

He decided to spend only another day with the family. He would teach everything he could, and maybe come back to visit them after his anticipated punishment at Zarda.

As Muna and he approached the camp, Ghar called out to alert the family. He didn't want a repeat of their first encounter.

Medar gratefully accepted the fish, placing his coarse cold hand on Ghar's head. His body had bulk that harked back to better times, the shape of strength was there, but diminished by many hungry nights. He gestured to the children who busily prepared a collection of animal furs. They approached Ghar, hoping he would try on the furs.

Ghar rubbed the infant's hair. The skins were the same as what the family was wearing. They were disparate pieces but somehow moving as though they were connected. On deeper inspection he noticed the small strands linking the sides of the garment.

He started to tie the skins around himself, to rapturous laughter from the family. Muna pulled the skin over Ghar's shoulders, guiding his arms through.

He was instantly taken aback at how comfortably warm it was inside the suit. He rolled his arms around and stretched to test the flexibility of the clothing and was amazed at how well it held together. He pulled apart the fur to show Medar the disappearing and reappearing fibres holding the skins together.

Medar smiled and walked back to a collection of skins. He showed Ghar how he pierced a hole with a pointed bone shard, pulling the fibre through. He repeated the action while holding the furs together.

Ghar felt like he had had an epiphany and everything he had ever done up to that moment was irrelevant. It was so simple, but so unbelievable at the same time. His adulation was only interrupted by the infant's cries, possibly of hunger.

Ghar rotated his arms around again. A thought crossed his mind, *who did this fur belong to?* He looked at the other furs that the children were putting back in the trees.

Muna placed the fish, inside out, on a rock. She smeared some crushed fragrant leaves into the raw meat. Part of Ghar wanted to rescue their meal from this possible ruin, but the curious part of him won.

'Why?' Ghar limited his vocabulary to communicate with Muna. 'Fish cook?' He drew a touch of the mixture to his nose, the scents seemed to create new paths for hunger and enjoyment. Muna cast a confident smile to seal Ghar's trust.

Medar interrupted them, requesting the cooking to start. He motioned to his torso. Muna twisted the portions of the succulent meat on the spit, sprinkling the remainder of the crushed leaves over the it, which instantly released a sweet, mixed aroma of fish and herbs. The more Ghar listened and tried to interpret the conversation between Medar, Muna and the infant, Ghar realized that, as tribespeople, they were just like him, in need of care, in need or companionship, and in need of belonging.

They ate, animated dialogue and gestures filling the silences between satisfying chews. As he crept into his berth, the new flavours still settling in his body, he suddenly missed Adura's warmth. He had a need to share the new abilities he had learned, attaching furs and rubbing leaves on meat, but mostly the idea that the Zardan songs were not the songs of all tribes.

He knew that going back and presenting his reason for absence as aiding Medar would be extremely risky, but deep down he knew it was important he did so. To go back and challenge his tribe and invite them to consider new possibilities. The Zarda had asked the wrong question, sending the Gubba out. *We should have asked: 'How could they help the Zarda?'*

4

The Appeal

His steps were staggered with excitement, happy to be going back and confident that he would be received well. He was glad that there was still some heat from the sun as cold-time beckoned. The journey back seemed shorter; he remembered a song that helped him find a stream that led back to the Narun. From there, he would follow the river's edge until he found the trails of Zarda.

> *A Zardan hunter starts a journey knowing its end,*
> *A step with the foot is only a word in the story,*
> *So, make those steps with intent,*
> *Through the Forest of the Giant Trees,*
> *Find the creek that leads you to the Narun,*
> *Follow the Narun back to Zarda.*

The Zarda were not overly worried about hiding their location. They were a huge camp, and there was always a hunter presence along with the Gubba men—even though the Gubba men were not trained as hunters, they were still expected to defend the tribe. Although now the Gubba men were there no more.

Ghar thought about how he would present himself. The different scenarios branched out like the tree canopy overhead. Some of the trails in his head ended in punishment for himself, but he refused to let that fear deter him from his mission. He would go to Adura first, she would understand. And together they would talk to Das and the other Elders. They would hopefully call a gathering which would renounce the banishment of the Gubba. Ghar knew it would not be that easy, but the thought that Dun could be back in camp made him smile.

He decided to take off his new fur, it would attract too much attention. He stopped to examine his reflection in the Narun to make sure nothing was out of place. Part of him was disappointed that the camp had remained unchanged while he was away. Dusty footpaths erupted in a cloudy trail, and unruly vines crept up the tepees.

His progress through Zarda gradually built up his confidence. His mind focused on the conversation he was going to have with Adura. What was the right question? *Why did I meet the outsiders? Why did I help them? Or why did we send them away without knowing how they could help us?*

Ghar suddenly heard a rush of footsteps behind him, 'Ghar? You're alive!' Adura flung her arms around him, 'Where have you been? I thought you were dead, I just asked the Elders.' Her body began to tremble, 'I asked them to send hunters to look for you.'

Ghar felt relieved in Adura's embrace, but also anxious with all the attention the display was receiving.

'I am well, my mother. I followed the stranger that came to our camp.'

'Why would you do that, Ghar? He could have killed you,' Adura stared at Ghar for a moment. 'I fear Das will try to punish you.'

'So, you found the youngling.' The voice had a frighteningly familiar causticness about it.

Ghar turned around to find Das and a group of Hunters. 'Do you have any explanation for your absence?'

Adura interjected. 'Hera, my son has only just returned, let him rest; he will come and talk to you when he is rested.'

'The boy is ready to be a hunter. He can speak,' Das retorted.

Ghar's thoughts collided and tripped over each other. He could tell Das that he had gotten lost in the woods, that he had been

confused by some of the landmarks. But there was this dimly lit idea
in the corner of his imagination: if he lied now, he could lose his
chance to change the Zarda. Truthfulness was among the highest
virtues of Zardan life.

The fear of not being able to see Dun overcame the fear
of being severely punished, and the words of his tale began to
spill out. 'Hera, he who speaks to the Spirits,' the dialogue he
had prepared on his journey had abandoned him, 'I mean no
disrespect, Hera, but do you remember the outsider? The man of
a foreign tongue.'

Das who, at that moment, was more interested in ordering
around a hunter, stopped at Ghar's introduction.

'I followed the man.' A simultaneous gasp escaped the gathering.
Das seemed unconvinced, even uninterested. Ghar decided there
was no going back, 'Hera, I followed him to see what he was doing.
I knew you were protecting the camp by sending him away, but I
felt . . . I knew he was asking for help.'

'Whatever your intention, you still disobeyed my decision.'

Ghar interrupted Das, 'No, Hera, I would never go against your
decision, please let me finish my story, and then judge.'

Das again acceded, although visibly irritated.

'I followed him to the river, where he tried to fish, but he could
not aim,' Ghar wanted to get to the important part of his story
quickly but was cautious in building up the event. He continued to
explain about how Medar could not see well, how Muna stopped
their fighting, and how they slept in the trees. 'I taught them how
to fish.'

Das's demeanour had changed from stern annoyance to a twisted
scowl, 'You did not go to kill him, or make sure he left? Instead, you
taught him how to fish.'

'Not him, the girl,' Adura chimed in. 'He was only trying to help
the family.' Her eyes betrayed her fear for her son, but she was still
nimble enough to come up with an explanation, 'Helping is the way
of the Fathers?'

'Helping the Zarda! Not outsiders,' Das snapped. He turned back to Ghar, 'You have betrayed the Zarda by teaching outsiders our ways.'

Ghar was hit by the sudden change in direction of the conversation. 'Look, they taught us as well. There are things we know and there are things they know. We can help each other.' He frantically searched for the thin shard that was used to attach the furs together.

'He has already desecrated the Elder's gathering; now he has disobeyed me. Lead this boy out of the camp. He has betrayed the Zarda; he will live here no more.'

'No, Hera, he is just a boy, he made a mistake,' Adura burst into tears, 'He is just a boy, we will help him realize the faults in his ways.'

'I will give you time to pack some supplies. When I get back, you will have to leave,' Das started back for the Grand Cave, oblivious to Ghar's mother's pleas for exoneration.

Ghar stood there, his eyes emotionless, as he stared at the prospect of being on his own. Maybe he would have to join Medar's family. There was a flash of relief; he knew Medar's family needed a new member to take care of and train the infants.

Adura shook him back to reality, 'You careless child, look at what you've done.' She held Ghar close to her bosom, 'Why did you undermine Das?'

Ghar searched his thoughts for a reason, *Did I want to undermine Das? I was curious about the outsider, and I thought I could help him with the dried fish.* He gave up trying to explain, it did not matter. He was being cast out of the tribe. He pushed out of Adura's embrace, and walked silently, trying to keep his body from breaking down in emotion. He really wanted to start crying, but he was a man, supposedly ready to be a hunter. He wanted to be strong.

Ghar sank to the floor in their tepee, in the area where he had slept most of his life. There was a small gap in the yellow brown walls through which he would peer out to see what was happening. As the eldest child of the tepee, maintaining the hearth was his responsibility. He would wake up in the night when the heat blew low. He looked over at the spot where his sister was born, and then to another spot where his sister died.

This place was not just where his life had happened; this place *was* his life. He began to sob, tears accompanied the mostly unpronounced thoughts. He had started the morning with high hopes for change. This was not the change he wanted.

* * *

'Das is here. He wants us outside,' a hunter announced.

Adura however was still turning over her possessions to find anything Ghar would need. She was still whimpering prayers. 'How could we send this little boy out into the forest? He will be killed in the first night. Fathers, protect my son, and let him pass from harm to safety. Let him pass from harm to safety. Let him pass from harm to safety.'

'Das is here, Adura.'

Ghar's adoptive mother scornfully replied, 'Tell Das, that horrible man, to wait a little.'

'Watch what you say, woman. Ghar, let's go.'

Ghar gathered his belongings, and the collection of tools and food his mother had packed. Das was outside, a disposition resolute carved on his face. A branding spear, its ember tip burning, ready in his hand.

'Hera, I am ready,' Ghar's life in Zarda had trained him to be respectful, even at this moment when his chest was flooded with contempt.

'Hunters, guide him to the Yellow Grassland, and watch him walk until he is out of sight.' He turned to Ghar, 'From this day forward, if you are seen on Zardan land you will be treated as an outsider, and an enemy. Hold out your hand.' Das pressed the glowing brand on Ghar's forearm. 'Let the will of the Fathers keep the Zarda safe.'

The pain, combined with the emotional ordeal, buckled his knees. The hunters moved in to lift him to his feet, but Adura intervened.

'Ghar, my son, when you are ready,' Adura put her shoulder under Ghar's, with the other hand on his face, she was sobbing, but her body remained firm.

'The Fathers' will be done,' Das left.

Adura carefully cleaned Ghar's burn mark. 'This will hurt, youngling,' She broke a plant stem that oozed out with sap and applied a cooling layer on the wound.

Ghar's eyes rolled back at the pain. A hunter caught him as he stumbled.

'Keep the rest of the stem. You will need to use it for the next few days.' There was a disbelief in Adura's words.

She then washed off Ghar's Zardan tribal marks, 'When we leave you at the Yellow Grasslands you have to give up being Zardan.'

Ghar looked up at her, tears blurred her face, 'I don't want to give up being Zardan,' he ran a finger around the outline of the symbol on his right shoulder.

'You need to find another tribe. If you find another tribe, find out as much as you can about them, try to see whether they could admit a new member.'

'What if I could find Dun and the Gubba?'

'That would be best,' Adura's eyes cleared, hope filled her cheeks, 'if you can pick up their trail. But even if you can't there is every likelihood a tribe will admit a child, like yourself, un-marked, as a new member. But you must show submissiveness. Observe them from a distance and find out if they will be friendly to you.'

Adura hung the waterskin on his shoulder, 'Keep as much water as you can, and if you find a water root, draw out as much water as you can,' Adura knew that Ghar already had the training and understood what to do. The advice was really a comfort to herself.

The hunters started to pull him away.

Adura started to tremble, she let out a long lonesome howl. Hunters held her back as she started to struggle towards Ghar.

Ghar felt an emptiness grow in him, his feet moved towards her, he was kicking, screaming, but he knew it was futile. He kept his tear-filled gaze as much as he could on his mother, until the forest closed on her, closed on Zarda. He was still being dragged, his limbs had given up, he just stared at the sky—the only part of Zarda he could take with him.

*   *   *

The sun crept shamelessly over the horizon. The hunters were awake, packing their belongings for the trek back to Zarda. The only emotion that stood upon all was the melancholy jealousy that Ghar held, the thought that these men would be going back to their families.

What have I done? What have you done, Ghar? This was not worth it. Endless thoughts crammed into the crevices of his mind, making it hard to hide away his anxiety.

The hunters must have noticed the forlorn look on Ghar's face as they helped him pack, giving him constant sympathy. The moment had marched into the present. 'May the Fathers guide you, youngling.'

He decided not to turn back for a last time like he did with Adura. Maybe he would regret not gazing at Zarda, but he wanted to focus on the task before him. He needed to find his way back to a river or even a stream.

The valley ahead was flanked by mountains on either side and at the far end. At first, he tried to part the waist-high grass with his spear but, after a few steps, his emotion-clouded mind let his feet lead the way. Midway across the field, he noticed a large rock covered in symbols, similar in colour and style to those worn by Zardan tribespeople, but different. *Maybe this marks Zardan land;* he stopped to study them. *I want to ask Adura about these marks.* He sighed, as he remembered he was not here out of curiosity. He continued on through the grass.

A Zardan hunter starts a journey knowing its end, he quietly recited as he started up a mountain. The terrain was different from Zarda, the valley behind him seemed sparse, with few trees and no animals in sight. The mountain in front of him was difficult to navigate, there was no real path, and the most accessible routes only led to cliffs and overhangs.

I wish Dun were here, he would have climbed right up that vertical rock face. He tentatively tried the steep slope, but then decided against it. If he were to get injured, there would be none to help him. Every impasse would only open a little to let in his longing for Dun's companionship. Every corner would hide hope of finding Dun.

* * *

Ghar, this was a good choice, he looked up speaking to himself, starting with the accessible foot holds in the tree bough. He had spent most of the good light looking for a pass through the mountains. He climbed the tree until he was well out of reach of the forest floor, but not mortally high. He suspended his bag, out of which he drew out Medar's roll of cordage. The tree had seemed promising, but now that he was up in its boughs, he realized that there were no branches that were the right fit to lie upon. He picked branches that were tilted upwards, he would have to sleep seated.

Using the cordage, he tied some sticks that he had found on the ground, to the tree's boughs, and then layered his pelts on for softness and warmth. The sun still lingered in the mountains, so Ghar decided to forage in the grass. Maybe there were some tubers and roots he could eat.

As his feet touched firm ground, his attention was drawn to colours on the side of the tree trunk. He walked around to get a better view. He felt a disquieting emptiness. They were coloured markings, like Zardan symbols, possibly territorial marks of another tribe.

The hunger had left him. He scanned the area for any trace he might have left behind and picked up his spears which he had left at the base of the tree. He slotted the weapons in his furs and clambered up the tree. His hunger would make unwelcome company for the night.

* * *

The moonlight slithered with the wind's whispers rustling through the valley. The deep cold distracted Ghar from feeling alone.

He wavered uncomfortably between sleep and keeping a look out. He whispered a song while he warmed his hands on the flanks of his body. He made a resolution to make his sleep furs warmer in the coming nights. *Even if I have to build a fire up here in the trees,* the thought propagated through the biting air, scratching at the tiny gaps in his closed eyes.

'Ghar!' a familiar voice perked up behind Ghar. 'Thank you for standing up for us . . . for me.'

'Dun! You survived! I always knew you were a great hunter, only a great hunter could survive out here,' Ghar felt the surge of happiness warming him up.

Dun continued, 'I know supporting us was not an easy thing to do; you had to leave Zarda, Adura.'

Ghar turned to embrace his brother, 'To win, you had to lose,' Das said in Dun's voice. Ghar shook out of his vision. He felt like his body had forgotten his limbs and fingers. The wind had built in anger, buffeting him with rain, trying to shake his covers off. He peered at his feet. The hide had detached and was flailing in the angry storm. *Why Fathers, why give me rain now?* He gritted his clattering teeth and closed his eyes.

* * *

The morning was better, the cold still gnawing at his skin and somehow from inside his bones, but at least the rain had stopped.

He carefully picked out the shapes in the field below, decided there was no danger, and quietly descended. He took a last glance around before studying the tribal mark on the tree. An ochre and black line crossed over each other. The Zardan mark was a line going through a circle. The line signified the Narun river. *Maybe this foreign sign also meant there was a river nearby.* He broke down the things he needed to do—get a feel for the terrain, get food and water, and find the next place to sleep.

The moist, cold grass uncomfortably scratched at his knees as he started up the mountain to get a better view. His heart despaired at the task ahead; maybe it would be better to take his own life before being torn apart by a bear. The hunters had narrated stories about the beasts, taller at the shoulder than any of the hunters, being able to claw down an entire tree.

Ghar snapped back into reality. Dreaming about the tales of the hunters was a favourite pastime, but right now it was a distraction. 'Terrain, food, and shelter.'

His moccasins slid back a little for every step forward, in the fresh mix of dead leaves, soil, budding plants and overnight rain. *Terrain, food, shelter.* The valley changed as Ghar made his way up the slope. The journey was a painting, Ghar felt as he got higher, he could see the details of the valley below blend into the bigger picture. *Terrain, food, shelter.* Ghar felt the colours merge: *survival.*

* * *

'Ghar, my son,' Gharra spoke softly from behind him. Her warm hand firmly caressed the back of his neck. Ghar knew this was a dream, the nightly cold clawing at his face. He squeezed his eyes shut harder to continue the vision. He turned around to face the tranquil brown eyes in which he had found solace so many times. His embrace was more of a pounce, his arms taut around her shoulders.

Outside in the cold, his lips broke into a smile. 'Gharra, how are you, Dun and Ra?'

'I wish I could say I am well; Ra needs me to be well, we need you to be well,' Gharra trembled, but with a strong mother's voice that comforted Ghar. Ra who was on her side started to walk up the walls of the cave.

Ghar broke into a soft chuckle, 'Ra does some funny things? Is she still sick?'

'Yes, Ghar, the Fathers are spiteful, there is no fairness or mercy in them.'

'No, Mother, the Fathers are our sustainers,' Ghar's tone admonishing her. 'Please don't let our predicament taint your view of the Fathers, they have blessed us so much. If there is somebody to blame, it is the Elders, especially Das.'

'It is good you were born a Sanaa. Wisdom and hunger in the same head might have driven you crazy.'

'I know. Listen, what else is happening? I hope you have enough food,' Ghar could only feel guilt about being a Sanaa.

She paused for a moment, 'I hunt now, mostly fish, but the other day I followed a rabbit to her hole, and dug her out,' Ghar was suddenly next to Gharra, digging furiously.

'By the Fathers, that's already better than being part of the Zarda,' Ghar quickly interrupted. 'Maybe this is how the Fathers help us?'

Her image faded out to the cold wind beating through the moonlight. He again forced himself back into his dream, into Gharra's arms, gazing into her eyes. *Maybe this is how the Fathers help us.*

* * *

Ghar noticed a potential pass through the mountains, that needed a steep, dangerous-looking climb to access it. He considered his options, squeezing his empty water bag. He could either die a slow painful death of thirst and hunger or die quickly, falling from the slope. The perilous pathway was suddenly not quite so unappealing anymore.

The climb was not easy, the rains had left the ground uncertain, and the winds unburdened their vitriolic cold. *How do hunters survive this? I would be keener to be a Gubba and stay in the camp*, Ghar thought cynically.

Hope, more than knowledge, urged him over difficult slopes and across thin ledges. The more he travelled the more he realized the dwindling chance of getting back to where he started. *Maybe I can just live here. Right here on this ledge. I'll just lie in wait for some unsuspecting animal, or maybe even another tribesman, and knock them on the head.* He chuckled at the thought of eating another man. He had never eaten man flesh, but there were stories of outsiders doing it.

The path ended in a tall, rocky, unscalable rock. A dark, shadowy crevice caught his eye. *Surely there is nothing that lives up here. By the Fathers, I have not come all this way to end up the meal of a hungry bear*—he closed in on the entrance and took up a position, high on the incline. If he were to be accosted by a bear, he could at least take the advantage of height. He held a spear in his right hand, and took up a Maraza pose, ready to strike.

His next move was not quite so elegant as he clumsily under-armed some stones into the cave and screamed with all the strength in his voice. His belligerence was only met with the winds whistling and winding through the mountains.

Spear at the ready, he peered into the mouth of the cave, trying to discern movement. The more his eyes reached a far wall, the more he could make out a light. A very faint light, barely touching the rock face. His chest fluttered with hope, but he remembered to compose himself. There could still possibly be snakes inside the cave, or other dangerous creatures who would not respond to screaming.

He carefully crouched in stealth, low and ready to strike, like the wolf described in the songs:

Through the tall pine trees,
You will see Wolf,

Lurking stealthily, not threatening,
But in his final leap a fatal end,
Be sure his tracks will be different,
But his path will always lead back to Zarda.

The light slowly grew to a crevice, that grew into a new forest. At the threshold he reminded himself, *Ghar, you do not know what is out there, look first.* He peered out of the cave. It seemed to look the same as the area he had just left behind. What he hoped, when he looked out, was that there was nothing dangerous, but also that there might be a friendly tribe. *Maybe warm fires, deer meat on a spit, and a warm dry tepee to sleep in,* he hoped to himself.

His stomach rumbled angrily at him, criticizing his decision to support the Gubba.

He picked up a routine, watching out for, *Terrain, Food, Shelter,* that kept him from revisiting his actions in Zarda. He decided he was right to stand by the Gubba, and to help Medar. *Terrain, Food, Shelter.* Dun, Adura and Gharra lead him back to the Songs.

Be sure his tracks will be different,
But his path will always lead back to Zarda.

Ghar responded grudgingly to the reminders from the little light that remained, water became a priority: *Water, Food, Terrain.*

Twilight was hard, the memories of walking back to camp with Dun, maybe carrying out the last prank for the day, the warm chest to chest greetings of his family. They were not just moments to Ghar; out here in the cold, alone, they were integral parts of him.

Ghar carefully picked his way down the mountain, to the valley. In the distance, he made out a mound, perhaps a termite hill. Termites themselves were not considered a meal, but usually the earthy refuges lent shelter to small animals, easy prey for even a novice hunter.

It was a bit far, running the risk of Ghar being on open ground in the dark, but his body was beginning to rebel against his thriftiness.

During the past day, he had found himself on many occasions gazing longingly at his remaining rations: *Maybe enjoy it while I am alive.*

Each step towards the mound, through the knee-high grass was accompanied by both hope and fear. He poked a spear into a hole in the mound, holding the attack spear in the other hand. He patiently scoped the burrow, carefully trying to make out the first glimpse of escape. With this kind of hunt, the animals might quickly make an escape before the spear could come down.

Without warning, a blur of excitement caught his eye. He was late to react, but good fortune found his spear tip into the terrified little creature.

He held the spear down hard, pressed to the ground, the rodent still writhing and yelping pleas for a pardon. He was careful not to stomp on it, the little meat it had would be contaminated by shattered bones and the putrid taste of the innards.

After he was sure of its death, he gathered his belongings along with the kill, and walked towards the trees on the other side of the mountain valley. He found a prospective tree with suitable branches, and he settled his possessions in preparation for his meal.

Ghar rummaged through his belongings to find a small sharp flint. He was still not sure about the presence of big predators in this area, especially bears or wolves. The smell of a freshly killed animal might give away his hiding place, so he thought it best to consume his prize some distance away. He put the flint back in his pouch, and pouch back on his shoulder and took the dead animal to a clearing that still allowed the waning sunlight.

He threw a final look around to make sure he was alone. *Thank you, Fathers, for this animal,* he made a slice from jaw to tail, sawing through some parts, careful not to damage the flint. He collected the guts and left them out on some grass he had prepared. He looked up and scanned for curious eyes.

As he proceeded to skin the small carcass, the thought crossed his mind to cook the meat. But the night was drawing in quickly, and he decided against the attention a fire might attract.

The raw meat was strong to the taste, stronger than he could remember, and much more sinewy. But he relished every roll on his tongue, every give in his jaws. His whole body seemed to celebrate the simple act of chewing.

He picked up the innards from the grass, wrapped them in the fur and buried it. With a few taps on the mound of dirt fill, he walked back to the tree. The small victory had given him some much-needed happiness.

As he rested his head in the tree, and wrapped himself up in the furs, his face broke into a smile, he could feel himself smiling, and that feeling cradled him into slumber.

* * *

'Remember we are with you,' said Gharra and Adura in unison. They sat facing each other knapping flint; every shard on the ground sprouted legs and became little creatures that scurried into Ghar's hand.

Ghar woke up suddenly when he realized there were actual insects in his hand. He tossed them away and climbed down from his tree.

The morning was still peeking lazily over the mountain tops. Ghar stood motionless for a while, gathering his senses, taking in long draws of fresh, meadow-scented air. He was taught, as a child, to control his reaction to the cold. The inclement weather could be a fatal enemy, or it could be a curious unwelcome companion. Instead of overreacting to the cold, he had to accept it, attend to it in small steps.

> *Through the Long Arm Trees comes a Windy Chill,*
> *A true Zardan accepts his invitation to talk,*
> *A long, precipitous walk will visit through the black rocks,*
> *Accept his talk, and he will not harm you.*

The song blossomed in his thoughts as he accepted the inclement weather, and slowly suppressed the urge to react. He kept singing, his mind, blocking out the frosty calls of the wind.

He was about to retrieve and roll his furs up, but then decided to act on a theory he had about his aching shoulders—the weight of the tied furs and his knapsack with the spears caused his shoulders a lot of pain. He had felt it especially during the kill the previous night. He made an incision in the middle of the furs for an opening to put his head through. He decided it would be better to wear all the furs rather than carry them separately. He felt some relief, but he also noticed that there was a loss of dexterity for his arms—his spear-throwing action would be hampered. *Maybe I can hide in my furs if some creature were to become curious.*

He pulled his pouch inside the furs on his shoulder, his spears fastened on cordage on the outside. Ghar continued in the direction from the night before. He tried to imagine Dun, walking alongside him; together they inspected the forest for animal tracks or other signs of danger. Suddenly, out in the distance, a movement caught his eye. He dropped to his knees and tried to hide in the grass. The blurry figure made its way over the ridge.

The animal was too far away to identify, but there was something menacing about its movements. He had never seen a bear or a wolf other than in the Grand Cave paintings. Das wore the skin of a bear, but the hunters judged it to be a baby animal. *This creature walks like a big animal,* Ghar fearfully concluded.

Ghar was originally headed in the vicinity of the animal, now the more tortuous route seemed friendlier. He trudged on carefully. The thought of confronting a large animal, stronger, faster and more agile than himself, weighed on his hopes. He quickly revised his Maraza foot-positioning and throwing action in preparation for an attack, while he looked out. The rest of the afternoon was spent planning every step, locating places to hide in if needed. He felt like he had not made any progress, but staying alive was now his main concern. His night was spent contemplating shadows in the dark moonlight.

* * *

The daylight relieved some of his anxieties; Ghar scaled up a ridge, to check for the beast. But as he looked over the top he was overwhelmed at the blue-white blessing flowing through the valley below. He ran down the precipice, but then stopped himself—the animal was still out there somewhere.

'Ghar, be calm, like the Narun in cold-time,' Ghar tried to restrain his excitement but he eventually gave up. 'Ghar, you did it! you managed to find a river! A big fish would be nice right now—I feel like I could eat a whole fish, and still have space for another.' He reached into his pouch for his remaining dried scraps.

Ghar carefully made his way to the river's edge, he took the water in his palms, watching it hop down the riverbank. It tasted especially invigorating, clear and lively, softening the dry rocky outcrops on his lips. There were fish darting about in the water, a possible meal. A doubt still lingered about the menacing figure he had seen earlier, but he decided that he would stay here near the riverside, to regain his strength and rekindle his spirit. The taste of fish began to uncoil in his mind.

I should stop here and build a home in the trees; nobody would ever find me out here. He thought for a moment about his needs. *Ample fish in the river, maybe the occasional rabbit or squirrel, nothing too big. And I could paint, paint great depictions of all the bears I will escape.*

The lonely air stirred for a bit. *But who would look at these paintings? Who would you talk to, who will take care of you when you are sick, and who would you mate with?* He chuckled at the thought. Zardan men and women always seemed their happiest after mating.

'I will stay here for a while and build up my strength,' Ghar decided out loud as he started to scan the location for a new tree-dwelling and places to hide. His eyes nearly passed over a spot, that looked unsuspicious at first, but there was something curious. Then it moved, it might have been the wind, but was a theory quickly dropped when Ghar could make out the shoulder of some creature that was big, beyond his imagination.

The river seemed too deep and swift to cross, but any attempt to take refuge in the trees would take him closer to the animal.

He held his breath and jumped into the frigid water. The water quickly reached his neck and clawed at his torso taking him with her flow. He ran—jumped—paddled towards the opposite bank and turned around to sight his assailant, to find gaping jaws bearing down on him. He grabbed hold of his spear which fortunately positioned the blunt end right into the animal's menacing palate.

The animal, dazed by the blow, managed to strike back with its enormous paw, tipping Ghar into the current. Ghar twisted back to see the animal, a wolf, a cavernous head bearing a terrifying array of menacing teeth.

The river put some distance between them, but each time Ghar glanced back, the wolf seemed to gain on that loss effortlessly. His feet could not feel the riverbed and looming ahead were rocks sticking out of the river.

He struggled to keep afloat, gulping more water than air, the banks blurring out with the rushing water occupying most of his vision. He looked back, the wolf bearing down on him, eyes given to terrible violence.

Just when he could almost feel the finger-sized teeth ripping through his body, the wolf vanished. A moment passed in the water, between life and death, hope and despair; Ghar felt a painful rap on his head, then his leg.

Ghar fought for consciousness, grabbing blindly through the water for a hold. Suddenly it felt like he was in the air in a slow freefall, the realization was quickly followed by another shattering plunge into the cold water.

As he spun in the water, not knowing which way was up, he caught a glimpse of sunlight. All of Zarda, his mothers and Dun summoned the remaining strength in his limbs to drag himself to the surface. He caught sight of a tree trunk accompanying him in the water. The fear of death was the only reason he had to clamber on. He had given his last to the forest; all he had now was exhaustion.

5

Mai

'Why do painters paint?'

Adura stopped tending the fire, 'Why do you paint, Ghar?'

'I don't know,' Ghar rolled into the warmth, basking in the yellow-red flames.

'Think about it: do you like colour and shapes? Do you like telling stories?' Adura smiled, 'Why do hunters hunt? Or why do we teach younglings the Zardan way?'

'I don't know. It is your duty to teach the young.'

'Duty,' Adura touched her fingertips in front of her mouth. 'Duty is why Zarda wants us to teach, but *why* do we teach?' She washed her face with the flames.

Ghar squirmed impatiently, 'But *why* do painters paint?'

'Your answer will only be as good as your question,' Adura turned back to tending the fire. 'Why do *you* paint?'

Ghar opened his eyes, glance by glance. There was a fire softly crackling, the bodies of small fish grilling over the flames. *How did I get here?* he thought to himself.

A shadowy figure loomed over him; Ghar instinctively reached for a spear but found his hand immobile. His whole body refused to move. He could not help feeling the hopelessness grow as the person got closer. A small, fearful yelp escaped his mouth, 'Stay back!'

The person seemed unperturbed by Ghar. Strange hands repositioned Ghar's shoulders, then his feet, straightening his back.

She seemed feminine. She had unusual elements to her face, a long nose, wide eyes, and high cheekbones. Her curious features almost distracted him from his current plight. 'What do you want with me? I do not have a lot of meat, so please don't eat me,' his whispery appeals despaired as fear led to new fears.

She moved over to the fire and replaced Ghar's fur with a freshly warmed pelt. The heat felt good, he felt a smile emerge, but he hid it, and wore a look of apprehension instead.

The girl sat on her hands and watched Ghar. Her features were so unusual that it was difficult to read her expression. Her gaze deepened, almost making Ghar look away in embarrassment. She had a resolute calm depth to her cheeks, her wide eyes grew steady in the light, the colour resting between brown and black in the sun. There was a simplicity in her features that Ghar began to like.

His mind fluctuated between his curiosity and the pain in his body.

She recovered her hands from within her furs and warmed his numb face. He was partly averse to her being there—she could still be a threat—even though it began to slowly dawn on him that she had somehow moved him from the water and had built a fire to keep him warm.

He really had a lot of questions, but the ordeal had taken a lot out of him and between her soft words, he fell asleep.

* * *

Ghar opened his eyes to the evening hues. The beautiful colours flowing through the clouds were not enough to distract him from the cold. He looked around for the girl and tried to call out for her.

The girl appeared dragging a thorny bush, but upon noticing Ghar's shivering body, she quickly changed his furs, packing in the sides to trap in his own warmth. She whispered in a strange but reassuring tongue and held him close.

Her demeanour had not changed, but Ghar could tell she was hiding something. She quietly sat on her feet, pulling the furs over

Ghar. Slowly she started to explain, in unknown words and gestures, pointing at the now receding sun, motioning towards the forest. He realized, but he did not want to admit it, that she would have to leave him for the night, maybe longer.

The thorny shrubbery made sense; she would create an obstacle for potentially dangerous animals through the night. She had dried out the furs, and prepared an assortment of berries, roots and mushrooms.

His heart sank when she pointed to the fire. It would draw undue attention, Ghar knew, but he did not care, he needed the warmth, and he tearfully pleaded with her as she quelled it with sand. With a reassuring glance, she closed the prickly circle of the shrubbery around him. He did not know this girl, but through the pain that wracked his body, she had become the tree trunk that he had latched on to in the river.

The forest continued with lively bird song and rustling leaves and insect calls. But to Ghar, there was a deafening silence, a forerunner of the impending ordeal that the night was going to be.

He reminded himself of his Zarda training, to keep calm, to be resourceful. 'Resourceful! I cannot move. By the Fathers, this is a terrible place to be.' His emotions turned on him—taunting him for being arrogant; taunting him for supporting the Gubba.

'Come on, Ghar, we've been through the cold before; just keep calm; make the cold your friend.' He let his muscles relax and closed his eyes, which further reduced his anxiety, which in turn made it easier to relax his body. Ghar was acquainted enough with the cold to know that this was an exercise he would have to repeat more through the night.

Just when he had gathered himself for the ordeal of the night, he heard a rustling. It was too late, there was no use shouting or trying to escape. The moonlight was no aid in the shrubbery, he could not see what was out there. He held his breath and stayed as still as he could. His chest tightened as the thorn walls parted.

Her silhouette caught a glimmer of light, relieving the panic that had collected in Ghar's throat. He felt his whole body relax into his

furs as she closed back the thorn wall, and gently moved towards
him. He could just about make out the uncomplicated lines of her
face as she inspected his body and his furs. All the anxiety that had
built up in the moments before, welled in his eyes.

She jumped in place for a while, Ghar thought it was because
she felt cold.

Ghar had thought about all the important moments in his life:
when he met Dun; when he first saw the painting and sculptures in
the Grand Cave; when it was decreed that he would be cast out of
Zarda. These were the moments that defined his existence. He felt
like this time with the girl was among of those moments.

The girl checked the thorn walls still jumping softly. She then
looked at Ghar. Although he could not see her eyes, he could feel
her penetrating gaze. She undid her furs, neatly placing them beside
Ghar. She panted through the cold, made an entrance into Ghar's
fur, just enough to slip in. Ghar immediately felt her warmth
rejuvenating his spirit. She arranged the rest of the furs over them
both, softly reciting instructions. Meaningless words to Ghar, but
right now they were as important as the Songs of the Zarda—he
listened eagerly.

Ghar got lost in the moment, 'Thank you. I know you don't
understand what I am saying, but without you, I think I would have
died,' he whispered hoarsely.

The girl paused, whispered some more comforting but obscure,
song-sounding reassurance. She then placed her hand on Ghar's eyes
to close them. For the first time in a long time, he did not have
doubts about keeping them closed.

* * *

Sunlight blinded Ghar as his thoughts fluttered into consciousness.
He was still hazy about what had happened the day before. He had
better mobility in his hands, but he still could not move his feet. He
brushed the furs away and lifted his torso to a sitting position. He

struggled at first, but he was determined to be strong as he pushed past the pain.

There were green, hardened marks, like what he would use for paint, all over his body, some partially covered by a leaf wrapped in strands of hide. On closer scrutiny, all the green marks were on his wounds. *The girl must have put these, she must be well versed in healing.*

He lay down again. The sun felt good as it brought warmth through the cold. There were meat scraps to his right, which he quickly gobbled up. There was a hollowed-out shell of a fruit, something he had never seen before. He propped himself up on his elbows, to examine its contents. It looked like water, he carefully brought it close to his nose, it smelled like water, he tried a bit, it tasted like water.

The thorny entrance parted; the girl was back. She knelt next to Ghar and examined his forehead. For the first time Ghar noticed her smile. Tiny, little rounded teeth demonstrated her happiness. A radiant gratefulness poured from her eyes, her mottled earth complexion rested in her cheeks, and the wind freed a tuft of hair that celebrated the moment. Her hands, small but strong, took on easy gestures, *like a deer through the forest*, Ghar thought.

'You move like a deer,' Ghar blurted out. He thought the statement was only in his head, but days of loneliness had broken the barriers of his thoughts.

She looked at him for a moment, which to Ghar was like diving into the Narun, eyes wide open to new discoveries, surrounded by the generous water, but not trapped. She said something, which he knew sounded like, 'I don't know what you just said,' but he wanted to imagine that she had said, 'I learned these movements by observing the deer in our forests.'

He dragged himself up, into a sitting position. His shins and ankles tore into his mind with pain. He grimaced, but quickly got back into the moment. Part hiding the pain, he gestured to his chest, 'Ghar.'

A look of concern crept over her face. She placed her hands on his chest, talking quickly. She slid her arm under Ghar and gently lowered him to the ground.

Ghar tried to resist, 'No, I am Ghar,' he tapped his chest again, but this time quickly motioned towards the girl, 'What is your name? You?'

She slowly stopped tending to Ghar. She looked at him for a moment and then reached over to her left shoulder, 'Mai.' She bowed her head to complete the salute.

They spent the rest of the mid-day sun describing objects—the names of trees, the river, the closest objects like Mai's spear. Then Ghar's drawings in the sand, as he drew the figures of deer, and giant wolves, and eagles. He drew a group of people in the sand, and a figure to represent Mai, and then tried to figure out the name of her tribe. It seemed to be Khamma.

As they spoke and shared food, Ghar began to think about the next few days. He was aware that Mai was going to be missed from her camp and that there could, even now, be a search party out looking for her. 'You must be thinking the same thing?' Ghar asked a confused Mai.

He was feeling much better, although still immobile, and felt he could survive the cold himself. There was a small collection of fruit, and roots built up—the roots doubled as water, and the water shell would be enough to last for a day.

* * *

The next day Ghar's anxiety was realized. Mai brought him more fruits and topped up his water shell. She left a new batch of 'leaf healer' with reminders to apply them in the morning. Then she left him with a look that was a part-smile through pursed lips, a look of reassurance.

She was gone only a few moments; he was already bored. He propped himself on his elbows and dragged himself around the confines of the thorn walls. He inspected the entrance cover; it was not as simple as he thought it would be. The thorny twigs were arranged around leafy shoots and vines which made it bigger, the girl probably did not have to obtain too many thorny twigs this way.

'She probably opens the "door" by using her spear.' Ghar reported, 'Back to talking to myself.'

The thought did remind him of his own spears, 'Maybe she hung them up in the trees.' He looked around the clearing, but his glance came to rest on a pile of furs on the ground. 'Was a good decision to wear these, otherwise I would have lost these to the river.' He realized his spears could be lost.

He found his pouch among the furs, and was relieved to find his flint knife, his fire rods—too moist to be used, and the awl that Medar had given him. He sighed with resignation that the river had taken his painting tools.

Ghar's mind rested on Mai's face. Overwhelming, scrutinizing eyes, a long equal nose and a fluid mouth gave definition to a variety of browns from her eyes to her chin.

He decided to paint her face; he looked around—he could use the green, healing paste, and the flint had an edge to draw with. He flattened out a hide.

He tried out an outline from memory, making changes to the lines, smudging out mistakes and drawing over. The green paste was not as consistent as he liked, but it did stand out on the skin, which gave depth to the painting.

The pigments took form, the strokes taking him back to Zarda, pulling him deeper into his ousting from the tribe. The shadows in the trees were making their final farewells. It took a moment, but Ghar remembered something about the shadows that he had been thinking about, that they were as important as the shape.

Mai's face in his mind, his fingers felt how the light touched her features. He filled in the outline of his painting, adding life to her cheekbones. He could have done better he felt, with the clayey textures that were available in Zarda, but this would have to do.

* * *

The thorn wall moved. Ghar noticed the shaking through a tiny gap in his covers, he quickly gained his senses and grabbed for a spear but found none to command. He looked on, helpless, as the wall parted and men entered.

A man knelt and put down his spears. Ghar trembled while the man put his hand on Ghar's shoulder. The whimpers changed to grateful tears when he finally came to realize what was happening—he was being rescued.

Mai appeared, with more men. She quickly placed her palm on his forehead and wiped the tears from his cheeks. 'I'm all right,' she said in accented Zardan.

Ghar smiled faintly through his relief. She obviously wanted to console him, but it was funny the way she used the Zardan words *I'm all right.*

'May the Fathers protect us,' Mai looked confused at the phrase, but then smiled in an answer beyond the meaning of words.

Then suddenly out of the new faces, Ghar was suddenly staring into the cold brown eyes of a beast. A beast like his attacker in the river, but smaller. He flinched, sending painful waves through his body. He called out to Mai, but when she did not answer he craned his neck to find her attending a busy conversation with the men.

He panicked as the slimy lips parted to gleaming, flesh-mincing teeth and then imparted a wet, sticky greeting across his face. A tribesman stepped in to drag away the animal. *This must be the end? I finally get eaten by a wolf, what a terrible fate.*

The tribesmen seemed unconcerned with the effect the wolves were having on their casualty. Ghar was left alone in his fears. They strapped Ghar to a frame of branches. The ride was uncomfortable, the skins twisted around his body, making it hard to breathe. And the terrain made the journey uneven, jolting his swollen legs. He hoped that the pain would fade into numbness, but it never did, each lurch releasing more agony.

He still wasn't entirely sure what Mai was doing; whether this was a rescue or a betrayal. He had heard about outsiders that eat their captives but had grown out of the tales the Elders used to deter unruly children. But now he was not so sure.

The wolf, *or other animal,* Ghar was not sure, did not seem to be around anymore. There was more pain, mostly pain, but as the group travelled through the forest, he noticed the trees changing, from the vibrant leafy giants of Zarda, to tall limber beings.

The trees are not going to save you, Ghar admonished himself. *The girl might have been good to you, but only the Fathers know what this tribe is going to do.*

He examined his could-be devourers, bearded individuals with hair left to grow to its own volition. Their frames lacked shape and, as a result, their strength was wayward. Their pelts were surprising, thick and soft, starting the thought of a sleep so good he wouldn't wake up from it.

They stopped. Ghar looked around, there was nothing out of the ordinary, probably another break for rest. They laid him down, and Mai came to his side. She inspected his legs and passed a satisfied glance at Ghar. He could hear a tone of contempt from the tribesmen; they seemed unable to grasp why Mai was treating Ghar so well; but he excused their lapse, as he wasn't sure either.

Mai knelt and tried Zardan with a mix of the Khamman language. 'Pain, your leg?'

Ghar embraced the attempt. 'A little,' he held up his forefinger and thumb to gesture something small. 'Where are we going?' he followed with his hands mimicking walking.

'Yes,' her eyebrows crimped quizzically.

'What I mean is,' Ghar thought about the futility of his question, it did not matter where he was going, he would not know where it was, 'it does not matter.' A part humoured, probably more important question was his follow up, 'Will you eat me?'

'Eat?' Mai reverted to her considerate disposition and foraged in her pouch and produced some dried meat which she offered gently.

Ghar tried to explain by holding up his hand to bite, the cold made his teeth clatter involuntarily.

Mai laughed, and mimicked Ghar's reaction to the tribesmen who all broke into a chorus of laughter.

Laughing is good hopefully? Either they were not going to eat him, or they were happy about the Zardan meal they were about to consume. Ghar strained to see the tribesmen sitting on rocks, lying on the ground and leaning on trees, in sparse discussion, the thoughts behind their faces elsewhere.

Mai clattered her teeth again. This time Ghar joined in with the rapturous combination of snorts and wheezy chuckles.

He did not know what this tribe had planned for him, but they had saved him. He was happy that they had, and he thought enjoyment was a far better way to death than worry. He was now in the hands of Mai and her tribe.

* * *

Although the journey was uneven and painful, Ghar drifted in and out of sleep. He was awoken by a build-up of chatter among the tribesmen. Ghar noticed Mai taking the lead to the rock cliff that overlooked a stream.

Ghar nearly fell out of the stretcher when the men waded in. They did not take too much care to keep Ghar dry and he could feel the icy water creeping up into the suspended fur. The sun was setting, which did not help Ghar see. It seemed like they were just walking up towards the rock face.

But then he noticed Mai clearing out a tangle of thorny vine just like she had crafted back at the river. She stepped aside to let the men through, sliding Ghar's body against the walls. Then, as quickly as he was in the crevice, he was out in the open.

He struggled to grasp what he was looking at. A sky-coloured lake which glimmered with the image of the green giant trees on the opposite shore. At the edge of his vision, Mai ran to greet some other tribespeople.

Before he could really take it all in, he was engulfed in a forest of new faces, all the same, but somehow different. Questioning tones filled Ghar's space, he could only answer with an apologetic look. The men continued to carry him, their steps more urgent, towards the lake.

He could not understand anything, he tried to pick out words and phrases that Mai had taught him, but in the end, he resigned uninformed. He imagined what they must have been saying: *What is this outsider doing here?* or *Mai should never have brought him here.* Or maybe even: *What part should we feed the wolf. Maybe we can eat too? His legs are injured, lets cook that the longest.* Ghar shuddered at the thought.

The men took him out of the frame of sticks, and placed Ghar beside a fire on the shore. Mai wrested herself free of her questioners and came to Ghar's side, 'I'm all right?' she asked.

Ghar managed a partial smile, her accent was so strong she might as well have been speaking another language. 'Yes, I'm all right.' He feebly pointed at the wolves scattered around the vicinity.

Mai smiled, 'Khamma.'

Ghar reflected that it was the same as her tribe name, *Khamma.* He listened as she explained and could vaguely understand that the Khamma held these wolves in high esteem. Ghar shivered as he began to feel the cold in his knuckles.

'Aiy,' Mai piled fire-warmed furs on Ghar, and then gently lay down beside him. Her gaze turned inquisitive. 'How say,' she moved her hands as if she was running.

The question dropped out of Ghar's focus, as he tried to understand the crowd's reaction to him, chins in hands, leaning heads to each other. *They don't look angry, that must be good.* He relaxed and remembered Mai, 'Run?'

Not convinced, she got up, and looked behind her, reacted with alarm and then motioned to run away.

'Holun,'—*scared,* Ghar guessed. 'Holun? You?' Mai asked.

She slipped back next to Ghar. He felt a security when she was close by, like he felt when he was around his Adura, or Gharra. He shook his head, 'No, I am not scared when you are here.'

The next moments saw the interest die away, including the frail conversation between Ghar and Mai. He needed her to stay, but all he could muster were questions and gestures at his new surroundings.

An older man and woman announced themselves. Mai jumped to her feet to greet them, in a very respectful bow, and lowered her tone. She quickly introduced Ghar and started to narrate a story.

The woman, who Ghar assumed was Mai's mother, knelt and gathered Ghar's hands and said something reverently in Khamman. She checked his forehead.

Mai grinned, and they continued talking. The adults left, the man headed to the rocky caves, and the woman headed down a path next to a stream behind the rocky hill. There were no tepees like in Zarda.

Some men helped Ghar back into the frame of sticks. Ghar was in the air again—they followed the woman whom Mai had spoken to. He sensed his elbow in the stream. It felt delicious, he absentmindedly leant towards the side to take a drink before Mai and the group tilted him back up.

Mai smiled as she scooped up some water and trickled it into his mouth. They clambered up a small slope and put Ghar down by a fire inside a cave. There was another person sleeping on a lush hide. The cave did not seem deep but was tall enough for the tribespeople to stand. In the corner, on a rock, there were stacks of small, wrapped hides next to an assortment of roots, flowers and leaves. It did not have the overwhelming smell of tribespeople that he remembered in the tepees of Zarda, a strong scent that filled his nose. The fire lent a slight smell of pine.

The men lifted him and put him on a fur of his own; his whole body luxuriated in it, his fingers, the backs of his knees, even the front of his hips rocked deeper into the embracing pelt.

Mai woke him from his closed-eyed enjoyment. She lifted his head and gave him some of the cool water from the stream.

The woman from before stood next to Mai. She tapped her chest, 'Manar,' with a smile that reached her eyes. Her hair was cropped short, revealing a taut neck that disappeared into a large fur that had been cut to free her shoulders. There was an unbalance in her cheeks—the left slightly higher than the other—and slight lines of the Elders graced her forehead. She felt Ghar's face and neck, then disappeared out of view. Ghar could feel she was inspecting his feet, he could hear her instructing Mai.

The cave, apart from the busy soft conversation that held Mai and Manar and the occasional cough from the other person, was silent, except for a slight crackle of the fire and the gurgle of the stream. Just the calm, sweet-smelling quiet in the cave made Ghar feel better.

Mai walked over with a soaked fur and placed it on Ghar's ankle. He yelped resistance, thinking it would hurt, but then found the cold calmed the pain.

He concentrated on his breathing, closing his eyes. It was strange that they were caring for him, but it was a good strange.

* * *

'Adura, I am safe; a camp has taken me in.' Ghar recalled their most defining characteristic, 'They have wolves!' Ghar looked at a painting over Adura's shoulder, 'I hope you are all right.'

Adura turned around with a snarly cough.

Ghar woke up. The sun's rays lit up the cave much better than the fire. The person opposite him was not there anymore. The fire was still on, and the babbling creek still gently filled his ears. But there was a new noise that he had never heard before, and the more he listened in, the more gruesome it sounded. He turned his head to the entrance of the cave and saw what looked like a giant snout of a wolf, like the beast that had attacked him. How did it find me, *maybe if I keep quiet, I won't become food.*

He watched quietly and was surprised to see Manar, patting the snout of the creature, with a tone of greeting a youngling. She turned to Ghar with a smile. *I knew it, they are making me better to feed their wolves!* Ghar cringed and pointed, crumpling his face in fear.

Manar called the creature in, its head drifted upwards, its body still out of view, tongue first, gleaming white fangs at the ready.

Ghar started to cry. Manar made sounds that seemed to be out of reassurance, but even a glance at those teeth and the hand-sized paws sent Ghar behind his eyelids. She took his hand which had lost all feeling and ran it on the animal's flank.

Ghar realized that this was the most horror he had ever felt. The fur was so comforting to the touch, but the wolf in the fur could tear him from limb to limb. *Why does she keep making me touch the wolf?*

Manar noticed Ghar's cries and stopped, leading the wolf outside. She came back, felt his forehead, her voice conveying soothing, meaningless sounds, but her eyes seemed to show regret. He reached out to her, he did not fully understand why; he felt like this new tribe had accepted him because he was injured, but by letting them help him he was accepting them.

* * *

Ghar was moved to the main camp after a woman who was coughing and vomiting blood was put in the cave. Mai made sure he had lots of furs, which seemed to be abundant. Ghar asked which animal the furs were from, but never could tell whether his questions were understood, or whether he understood their answer. The excitement of his introduction to the Khamma quickly died down. Some of the members even smiled at Ghar.

The wolves were all over the camp, playing, jumping, eating, which Ghar thought should have made them less fearsome. But he still sweated even at the slightest eye-contact with the animals.

Mai was mostly not around which did leave him open to bouts of boredom. He decided to try and walk around even though his ankles and shins were still tender and unresponsive. He grabbed hold of a long stick, looked around to make sure he was not taking away an elderly person's walking aid, and hobbled in search of something to satisfy his curiosity.

Huge, green trees stood over reddish-brown forest floors that floated over the pristine waters of the lake dotted with lazy fish breaking the surface in the shallows. The ripples in the surface seemed to travel in all directions conveying messages from shore to shore.

Ghar could see a band of youth in the distance. He was not very interested in joining them; even back at Zarda, he felt more comfortable around Dun and usually stayed away from the other children. But he noticed Mai in their midst and quickly forgot about his old ways.

He wore a smile as he softly made his way closer to them but stopped to watch when he noticed Mai with her arm around a boy. He was quite able-bodied and seemed to be making the crowd laugh. What was worse, Mai seemed to have the look of endearment that she had comforted Ghar with, only now she seemed even more endeared.

The band of laughter quietened to acknowledge Ghar's presence. Mai called out to Ghar, with a gleaming grin which brought Ghar some respite from the awkward silence, and he stepped carefully, but with more enthusiasm.

Mai started to talk happily about what Ghar guessed was his rescue. She animatedly moved her free arm about, describing how she had pulled Ghar out of the river on to the shore, and then built him a thorn wall. They quietly listened, while occasionally pausing a moment to inspect Ghar.

She ended with her arm close to her mouth, and mimicking Ghar's teeth clattering. Ghar never really got the humour in his reaction to the cold, and his vulnerable ego right now was taking a beating amongst these confident Khamman youth.

As the laughter subsided, he excused himself, gesturing he needed rest. He put on an unaffected smile and grimaced back to the caves. Just as he turned away, he glanced at Mai to find a look of concern in her eyes, even while she was smiling. It was a look he had become quite acquainted with, and over the last few days, had found sustenance in. He hid it from the group, but he was happy that Mai was concerned about him.

6

Moving Fur

Ghar sorted the tools from Medar. A bone awl, some cordage from sinew. He remembered the short time he had spent with Medar and his children, using the awl to pull the soft-ended edges of the hide together. He decided to make a simplified *moving fur*, which would wrap around his torso and shoulders, without the arms. He laid his sleeping furs out on the rock: he grimaced at losing his sleeping furs to the cause. His first problem was cutting the hide to his proportions. He wrapped some cord around his shoulders to get a feel of how much hide to use. Then he marked out his general shape with a piece of burnt wood.

Cutting through the hide along the markings was not easy. Shards of flint occasionally broke off, requiring constant knapping. His dedication drew the attention of some passing Khamma. They examined the hide as he worked on it. Ghar did not like people watching, but unsure of his status in the new tribe, he allowed them to satisfy their curiosity. *Maybe they would like to help?* He stood up, jarringly, with the soreness still present in joints. He took his own coat off to describe what he was trying to accomplish. Their surprise made him realize that they had not noticed his furs up until now.

He instinctively got them to wear the moving fur and moving their arms. Ghar was amused at their snorting delight while walking around. After a few moments of discovery, Ghar called them to attention in Zardan, 'Do you want to help me make more of these?'

He received looks of enthusiasm, which he took to be earnest positive replies.

He gestured for the admirer to return his coat, who gave it back reluctantly. 'I am Ghar.'

The already impressed tribesmen showed more excitement at the familiarity of Ghar's tongue.

'I am Tur.'

The other companion was a little more tentative, 'I am Ulan.'

Tur was more curious than Ulan. Scars and bite marks on Tur's hands were open evidence of his inquiring nature. His hair was just beginning to grow back on his scalp, which barely hid scars of a skin ailment. He started to fiddle around with Ghar's tools.

Ghar instinctively reached over to cover his belongings but eased a little so as to not to offend his host. He remembered he was still a stranger to these people.

Ulan was more reserved. He carefully watched Tur, and only inspected what Tur gave up. He was shorter than Tur, but his large chest made him look bigger. He had the sort of face that would only seem content when cutting up an animal or when overlooking the same animal being roasted over a fire.

They smelled of fresh meat and there were the streaky remnants of the kill on their arms, which was surprising considering the emphasis on cleanliness that Mai and Manar put. Maybe not all in the tribe shared the same discipline.

As Ghar prepared to show the men what he knew, the unsurety in his fingers preyed on his mind. *I don't know how to do this.* He looked over at his expectant-eyed observers and decided to shrug off his fears in view of their eagerness.

Occasional audiences built up, but it was the original group that laboured through to the evening.

They had done a few trials, and some of the initial holes had actually damaged part of the furs forcing them to cut it away.

But when they were done and the first piece was ready, Ghar examined it a last time before testing it out on Ulan, who happened to be the measure. 'You, my brother, are the first to own a Khamman moving fur,' Ghar reflected a moment on what he had just said. He was Zardan, but somehow, he found in this common moment of happiness with his new friends, a chance to be somebody else. To be Khamman.

* * *

Moving furs had taken on a popularity that Ghar had not foreseen; the tribespeople especially relished the extra warmth during cold-time. The tribe had adopted it even more than they had adopted him. The more people seen about camp in moving furs, the more people enquired with Ghar about getting their own. Ghar, Tur and Ulan were spending most of their days fitting, preparing, and attaching.

Ghar's grasp of the Khamman language was still rudimentary, but he could understand that, for the tribe, the fastened furs, were becoming a sign of status more than a practicality. The Khamma seemed to place more importance on non-essentials than the Zardan people. Collections of shells, bird feathers and other objects would be proudly shared and compared.

There were questions he asked, but the answers were unclear: *The wolves in the camp were the Spirits of Khamma. The plentiful meat and furs were provided by the Spirits. Mai had a mate, but they were not very close.*

The last answer perplexed Ghar, he was so fond of being around her; he found himself admiring how she took care of the sick; how she would stop to talk with anyone; how nice she was to him. *But her mate did not want to be around her?*

All their partially understood conversations on the topic suddenly came together while he was with Mai, collecting herbs in the forest. 'You can't have babies?' Ghar broke the silence as they searched for healing plants. 'Is that why Yan does not want to be with you?'

'I have told you this a long time ago,' Mai bristled at Ghar's delayed reaction.

'Listen, I only understand now,' Ghar softened his tone to quell her irritation. The ensuing foraging was done without many words. Ghar wanted to speak up and say something light-hearted. But he could not help thinking about how Mai felt about not being able to have a baby. The Zarda and the Khamma were similar in their views about the furthering of their tribes—new mothers were celebrated. The sign of blood in young girls was a blessed sign, and special ceremonies marked her path into womanhood.

'I know you want to know why. You always want to know why,' Mai said, giving voice to the question in Ghar's mind. 'I don't know why.'

'Have you asked Manar?' Ghar referred to Mai's mentor, the woman who helped heal him. She was another curiosity in the tribe, who spent most of her time at the cave with the sick of the tribe. The Khamma had named it the *Healing Cave*.

'Of course, I asked her, Ghar.'

Yan's wolf, Uba, inspected the thicket in front of them. He wagged his tail in appreciation of his task. Ghar had become much more comfortable with the wolves of Khamma, but he was yet to befriend any. He maintained a distance he considered healthy.

Most tribespeople that frequented the forest seemed to have a wolf as a companion, 'Why don't you have a wolf, Mai?'

'Another tale I have already explained to you,' Mai sighed, signalling Ghar into silence.

Rain started to fall, a mixture of harsh cold drops and collected cascades from the trees above. Their moving furs provided some initial protection, but the water slowly crept in through the openings.

'I need to tighten this,' Ghar pulled on the gap between the fur and his neck.

'Uba, come,' Mai called to the wolf while pulling Ghar to a slightly more canopied area. She closed her arms around him, 'Let's wait. This looks like it won't stop for a while; we can continue to look for herbs after the rain stops.'

There were moments that Ghar remembered: his mother's embraces, the first time he speared a fish, Dun saving him from falling. He felt like this would be a memory like those, his cheek finding a warmth under Mai's closed eyes, feeling her move in to fill the gaps between them,

'You would be a nice mate.'

Mai glanced at him, then went back to closed eyes to focus on keeping warm. 'What do you mean?' she whispered.

'You are so warm.'

'Isn't everybody warm?'

'Yes,' Ghar wanted to say that she made him feel warm within but was unsure about how to translate this Zardan thought into the Khamman language.

The cold rain quelled any remaining conversation.

* * *

Tur and Ulan shared the general praise for the moving furs, and their own positions in the camp rose in status as advisors to the Elders. In turn, they had befriended Ghar. They did not understand each other all the time, but there was a general goodwill and friendliness that helped them past moments of doubt.

'Today you will join us,' Tur took the base of his spear and snapped it on Ghar's flank, 'looks like you are all better.'

'Listen, you go; I might slow you down,' Ghar flinched at the new pain that Tur inflicted. He had heard of how they used the wolves to hunt; he was curious, but a bit anxious that the predators might decide he was the prey.

'Not this time, you cannot stay at home like a baby anymore.' Some bystanders fluttered into laughter.

'Don't worry about Tur,' Ulan coaxed apologetically, 'I will be right with you.'

'It's not Tur that I am worried about,' he cast an apprehensive glance at the wolves.

'The wolves are no reason to be scared,' Tur grabbed a wolf by the shoulders and walked it over. He lifted the beast to stand on its hind legs. The animal spread a grin and then flopped out its tongue happily. Tur hid behind the beast, and reasoned with Ghar, 'See, I am not so scary,' he waved the wolf's forelegs to further its appeal.

Ghar reluctantly smiled, and even more reluctantly collected his spears.

Tur stopped playing with the wolf and inspected Ghar's spears, 'This will not do. You can have some of mine.'

Ghar did not like the Khamman spear. He couldn't wield it because it was a lot heavier than his Zardan tool. 'How do you throw this?' His question started out confidently but trailed off in a milder tone so as not to upset the tribesman.

'We don't throw.'

'What?'

Ulan cut in, 'You will see.'

The group made their way through the thorny entrance. Some tribespeople, including youth like Yan, were waiting. Without much commotion the group got on its way. Ghar remembered back in Zarda there were songs and dances before the hunter's would leave, and there would be prayers to ask for the Fathers' assistance. For the Khamma, it seemed hunting was more like a chore than a sacred act.

'We have to keep the wolves close to us; they are not only the hunters, they also protect us,' Ulan explained as Ghar watched some of the tribespeople pull back some of the wolves. The wolves had a cord around their necks which the hunters occasionally held on to.

'So, you don't need to throw spears, or track the prey?'

'The wolves do most of the tracking and attacking, we just get them to the right place,' he reached down to play with the beast's tufty fur.

'But don't the wolves eat everything?'

'You will see, my brother, you will see.'

* * *

Different groups were sent to well-known buffalo grazing and drinking areas. If they found a herd, they would send a member back to this meeting location to inform the tribe, and if unsuccessful, the group would return to rejoin the rest of the tribe.

A withered yellow patch in the forest revealed another band of Khamman hunters. The vegetation in the area lay beaten down partially hiding the remnants of wolf fur scattered about. There was the acrid smell of a relief area close by. The morning mist extended a secrecy to the soft rumble of conversation that travelled through the tribe.

The wolves paced around, occasionally turning their snouts up. 'Why are they looking to the trees all the time?' Ghar had never seen the animals so excited.

'They are trying to smell their prey,' Tur replied before Ulan could. 'Careful, they might like the smell of a Zardan.'

The tribe's laughter was interrupted by the entry of another group of Khamman tribespeople. 'There's a herd of buffalo down by the Valley of the Lake,' their group leader announced. The whole group set off in the direction of the valley.

Ghar turned to Ulan, 'Is this the lake you told me about? Where there used to be a lot of buffalo.'

'Yes, there used to be a lot, but now the lake is drying out.' Ulan had a way of pausing that made it seem like he had finished talking. 'The Elders think there are less buffalo because there is less water,' he caught up with Ghar's attention, 'but I think there is enough water for the buffalo to drink.'

Ghar pieced the Khamman conversation into his Zardan understanding, 'Your answer is as good as your question,' he quietly murmured Adura's words.

'What?'

Ghar could feel the glimmer of an idea, just beyond his reach. 'Listen, my mother used to remind me to look for the right question. The buffalo are probably less because there is less water. But I think a better question would be, where are they now?' Yet another question was unleashed, 'Maybe another would be, how do you find the buffalo again?'

Ulan's eyes turned up while he tried to hold on to the thought, 'Maybe that would be a better question,' he replied after a moment of silent reflection.

* * *

After a while of walking, Ghar, out of boredom, went over to Tur. He did not particularly like Tur's type of humour—Tur mainly made people laugh at Ghar. But the trudge through the forest had drained his patience.

He dodged the inquisitive snouts of the tribe's helpers. 'It looks like the Zardan Questioner is here,' Tur announced to raucous laughter. 'And what would you like to know today?'

Ghar wanted to hold in the question out of spite, but continued, 'Listen, I don't ask that many questions.' He sighed, 'Will we get there before the sun sets?'

'See, another question. These Zardan people talk in questions,' some more laughter continued.

'But will we get there before the sun sets?'

The wolves started to get anxious. Their handlers knelt down and placed their bodies on the animals.

'We are here,' Tur whispered to Ghar.

'The lake?'

'The buffaloes.'

Tur motioned to Ghar to take the vantage. In the distance he could make out faint brown collections of fur ambling around beside a ravine. Some stopped to chomp on the grass, while others meandered back and forth from the herd.

The leader signalled his hand in different formations, the group broke up, leaving Ghar alone.

Ulan hissed, 'Come over here.' Ghar could only glance around Ulan's back, and the demeanour of the rest of the tribe kept his footsteps discreet. An arm stuck out of the group, a sweat-glistened hand clenched into a fist and then motioned downwards. The hunters crouched and crawled forward.

He could feel the fallen leaves crumble under his knuckles, the leaves rustling in anticipation. His heart beat over his thoughts, he was not sure what to expect. He realized that this was the first time he was on a hunt with men. There was no inauguration, or celebration of his move, it was simplified down to a trip into the forest.

Am I a hunter? This can't be it. Tears welled in his eyes. He felt a need to turn back to Zarda, to start all over again, to never cross Das, and to never be expelled out. *What has become of me?* He looked at the foreign faces around him. His fingers loosened around his spear.

A shriek cut through the frosty air. The wolves were released first and they quickly disappeared into the thick vegetation. The hunters split into different directions. Ghar caught sight of Ulan and tried to keep up as best as he could. But he quickly lost ground on his unsure ankles. He arrived at a scene that was nothing like depicted in the Grand Cave. The wolves nimbly dodged the beasts' horns and hooves, while nipping and biting at every chance they could get. They seemed to know how to distract the buffalo from the front while some attacked from behind. Blood already matting its thick woolly fleece, the buffalo would make a step to freedom only to have to thwart other wolves clamping on her rump. The ground heaved under the bloody dance, dust and clods of earth flew in all directions.

The men started to use the long heavy spears to jab at the lowing animal from a safe distance, again using a mix of distraction and attack. Out of sheer desperation, the beast summoned the energy to make a final leap for freedom. It broke through the barricade of wolf and man and galloped into the forest towards Ghar.

Ghar, who had been standing by as a spectator, mainly out of stupor, sweating in the thick air of the Khamma screaming and buffalo bellowing, had started to retrace his steps at the animal's advance. But an old Zardan instinct reconnected his shoulder with his spear. His feet pressed apart while his arms and torso lined up.

The fluid follow-through flowed without thought, without doubt. His arm uncoiled releasing the spear, his fingers pointing and flexing, providing direction. The Khamman spear was much heavier than his body knew and he flinched, knowing the spear was not going to land where he wanted it to.

The beast abruptly changed direction; the directionless throw suddenly found a target and lodged in the buffalo's eye. A few tottering paces spent the buffalo's remaining resolve and it buckled to its forelegs. Heavy gushes of breath filled the misty air with clouds of exhaustion. The tribespeople shrieked another cry of triumph and quickly ran around to the animal, some continuing to stab, others containing the wolves. The head of the group, a man with whom Ghar was still not acquainted, walked around with a solemn air, and gently patted the buffalo on the nose and head.

Ulan walked over to Ghar, 'That was a good throw.'

Ghar panted acknowledgement.

'But it is not the Khamman way,' he admonished. 'Your spear is connected to your body. You lose it, you die.'

Ghar nodded in further acknowledgement, but secretly hid a smile. He was not in Zarda, he had not completed the Hunter's Walk, he did not even have a Zardan spear, but somehow he still hunted like a Zardan. 'Thank you, Fathers. I might not be in the protection of my tribe, but you have protected and nurtured me even now,' Ghar whispered a prayer in Zardan.

'What was that?' Ulan asked.

'Just something we do in Zarda.'

They walked over to the kill which was being efficiently cut up. 'Here, in Khamma, we hold on to our spears,' Ulan drew out the spear from the slaughtered beast and handed it back to Ghar, who nodded in receipt.

'I thought of a better question to ask.'

'Yes?' Ghar asked, still catching his breath.

'What do the bulls want? If we know what they want, then maybe we can find them.'

Ghar smiled.

'Now, let's go see the real kill!' Ulan said.

In the excitement, Ghar had not noticed where the buffaloes, other than his kill, had disappeared to, 'Where are they?'

'Down in the ravine,' Ulan smiled.

'Why are they down there?'

Ulan stopped to consider Ghar's doubt, 'The wolves scare some of them down into the ravine.'

They walked back in the forest, tracing a path through the thick shrubbery, 'We can go down to the bottom of the ravine this way.'

'Looks like the Khamman land ends here,' Ghar said of the unending crack stretching in either direction on the forest floor.

'It surely was an end for our buffalo brethren,' Ulan had found some ponderous wit. Ghar liked the idea that the forest creatures were their brethren. He looked down and immediately stepped back to safety,

'By the Fathers, I think you are sick in the mind!'

'Come, I have been here before; stop disgracing your Zarda.'

The memory of Dun and the Zarda, and the fighting movements of Maraza spurred a courage that questioned the fear of falling to his death. He was still unconvinced but decided to follow Ulan.

Around the edge of the cliff, he could see outcrops of rock just close enough to each other to form a path to the bottom of the ravine.

Ulan expertly navigated down, his arms waving Ghar to follow. There was an unsettling echo of the hunters' proclamations celebrating the hunt mingled with the piteous bellows of the buffaloes.

Ghar stepped down on to the ravine floor, wading through the ankle-high, clear, cold stream that caressed the smoothened rocks. Ulan had already moved ahead and was out of sight. Ghar followed the voices that bounced off the ravine walls. He stopped to draw it in, the crisp browns, the greys and greens of the ravine walls adorned by the colourful rocks in the stream.

'Ghar, what are you doing? Get over here, you lazy Zardan.'

As Ghar made his way around the ravine bend, towards the Khamman voices, the whole creek turned red only parting to reveal the brown wet carcasses of the buffaloes. Some were still moving, their thick breaths of air calling out for the Spirits to save them.

The scene in front of Ghar did not make any sense. Ulan's explanation replayed in his head: 'The wolves scare some of them down the ravine.' *Those words would have never been able to paint this picture.*

Ulan thrust his spear to end the wails, 'Zardan, this is how you use a spear.'

Ghar's Zardan pride tried to find fault with the Khamman technique but, standing there, in front of all that meat and fur, he was beginning to feel a kind of pride in being Khamman too.

7

Manar

Fires busily crackled under slices of meat, uniting flavours of smoky heat with tender fat in the night air. Children played and ran around, intoxicated by the crackling firewood and the softly singing tribe, soaking in the celebratory, nose-filling flavours. The feast was the best warmth against the cold-time.

The Khamman hunters had spent the entire night at the kill, cleaning, chopping and preparing the meat and hides. Ghar was exhausted but was still excited to tell Mai about his first kill. He was disappointed to find that she was out foraging when he got back to Khamma.

He finally found Mai by the fires, 'Listen I have an amazing adventure to share.'

Yan turned up, interrupting Mai before she could speak. 'That was an amazing throw to kill a buffalo,' he slapped Ghar on the back. Yan had a likeable, trustable, strong-jawed face, that offered a kind of physical security, but did not promise emotional support. His shoulders sloped and flexed dominance even in a simple gesture. He did not have a moving fur, and most of the time at camp he would tie a fur around his waist. There was a bite mark on his left shin.

'Was that a wolf?'

'Mai's wolf,' Yan chuckled. 'No babies, and her wolf bites me.' He looked at Ghar, 'Good thing her wolf did not get a bite of you.'

Ghar crinkled his eyes in confusion. *Mai's wolf?* he turned to ask for an explanation. He had seen her angry and offended before, but now her expression was more of helpless resignation.

'Listen, she would give you a child if the Fathers wanted it,' Ghar leapt to her defence, his speech garbled in a mixture of Zardan and Khamman.

'What?' Yan retorted.

'Ghar, I don't need you to protect me,' Mai's voice trembled but strengthened with her resolve. She turned to her mate, 'Yan, I tried,' she sighed, 'but it doesn't seem to matter however much I try to explain this. I don't know what is wrong.'

'I don't need explanations, I want babies.'

Ghar could feel her, the overwhelming hollow in her chest. He wanted to strike out at Yan but held back, unsure of his position in the camp.

'I am going to go and give Manar some food,' Mai broke the awkward silence that had fallen over the group. She bowed her head and shoulders in courtesy and walked towards a fire pit.

Ghar followed her; he could hear Yan sigh gustily behind him, but it was not a sigh of disappointment, more of disgust. The smoke carried a welcome sharpness that filled their nostrils and stung their eyes. He whispered, 'That's the best smell I have smelled in a long time.'

Mai replied with a distant nod. She used a stick to prise some slices of meat and gathered her things. 'Uba, come here, let's go.'

The wolf withdrew his muzzle from his paws and stretched from tail to claw.

Ghar expected Mai to call him, but he was left standing there. 'Mai can I come with you?' he felt the need to talk to her.

'I want some time to think.'

Ghar searched for an excuse, 'Well, I would like to meet Manar.'

'You know Manar?' her widened eyes and lifted brow signalled to Ghar to be cautious about his next words. Ghar suddenly remembered why he was not keen on visiting Manar—the giant wolf.

The Khamman tribespeople treated the wolves like companions, but even they shied away from talking about the giant wolf. He had even overheard part of a story about the wolf biting a man, which was why the wolf had to live away from the tribe.

'All right, you can carry this,' Mai suddenly found a use for Ghar. She heaved the cooked buffalo flank from her arms into Ghar's. 'But no questions! You can walk behind me,' she indicated some distance, 'keep that space.'

Ghar followed her, the large chunk of meat slipping a bit from his grip with every step he took.

'Will Manar eat all of this?'

'No questions!'

Mai wore a moving fur but had had the sleeves removed. Her smooth, muscular shoulders gleamed out in the flickering light. She was a tall Khamman, her head peeked out in a crowd, but she was not awkward like some of the other tribespeople.

Ghar thought she moved like water, like the small stream that ran alongside the path to the Healing Cave, each cascade flowed with the rest of her body, 'She would have been good at Maraza.'

'I still hear talking back there.'

Uba barked into the darkness as their small group deviated from the path and started up the slope to the cave. A guttural moan came back in response. Ghar felt a shiver run up his spine. *Here comes Mu . . . why did I decide to come here?* The flame of Mai's torch revealed the soothing contours of her face, giving Ghar his answer.

Mai's torch only revealed parts of the animal as it inspected the group. Mai looked back at Ghar. 'Can you hold this?' The flame momentarily blinded his eyes, 'Don't be scared, Ghar. Mu will not hurt you; you are Khamman.'

From the corner of his eye, in the flickering flame, Ghar saw the beast grin a greeting. He inadvertently looked into its eyes, and immediately felt a threat that he had hoped he would never feel again. His legs tensed, the muscles growing both weak and strong simultaneously as he prepared to jump away.

Mu moved in closer, his nostrils agitated, excited at Ghar. And then, wholly oblivious to the terror writhing in Ghar's chest, the beast wrested the meat away from his grip. Ghar slumped to the ground, lightheaded, paralysed by the animal's boldness.

Mai laughed, she picked up the torch. 'Mu only wanted the meat, don't be scared of him.' She brought the light closer to his face. 'Don't cry!' she stuck the torch in the ground. 'Don't cry, Ghar, Mu is not going to hurt you,' she muffled the remnants of her laughter.

Ghar managed to stutter 'I'm all right,' his face stiff. It felt like all the pain that had healed from his time recouping at Khamma, rushed back into his bones. He struggled to his elbows to see Uba trotting after the enormous rump up the hill.

Mai assisted him for a bit, then noticed a figure in the shadows. Mai and Manar greeted each other with a fond embrace. She lost a bit of her habitual grace, and animatedly pointed at Ghar and chattered in a Khamman too quick for Ghar to follow. She brought Manar over, 'Ghar has now got some courage.'

He realized he was still bent at certain points in his body, so he groaned himself upright to somewhere near his full height. 'Greetings, Manar, may the Fathers protect us,' Ghar forgot he was in Khamma for a moment, 'what I mean is, may the Spirits be with us.'

Manar smiled, 'Finally we meet again. I was beginning to think the Zarda were not respectful of their healers.'

Ghar suddenly realized his misstep, 'I apologize, Hera, I mean Manar.'

Manar smiled her cheeks into her eyes. She held Ghar's hand and led him up to a fire. The light left momentary strangers on the walls of the cave.

Mu and Uba were already filling the space between the cave and the rock face, running after each other and playfully wrestling. Mu won the tussles, but Ghar could sense that Uba was thoroughly enjoying himself, nevertheless.

'Sit,' Manar pointed to a place warmed by the fire. The smoke brought a different smell than was usual—sweeter and lighter. 'I throw these in to make it fragrant,' Manar answered Ghar's deep breaths, handing him a collection of bark and dried flowers.

'Manar, can I talk to you alone?' Mai interrupted the demonstration.

Although mentor and mentee moved to the far side of the cave, Ghar could still make out some of the angry words being exchanged. *She wants to have a baby*, Ghar thought.

Manar's tone pacified Mai, and to some extent comforted Ghar as well. They walked back to Ghar and sat down beside him. For a while they watched the wolves, whose wrestling gradually subsided to pushing which eventually gave way to lying caught up in each other and then lying down exhausted.

Manar looked at him, like she had almost forgotten he was there. 'It's nice to have people here other than Mai,' she tempered her statement glancing at Mai. 'Mai is like my own daughter, but still, it's nice to have somebody else here.' She tore off slices of the meat and extended it to Ghar and Mai, 'please eat.'

'Manar, this is for you,' Mai admonished her mentor, 'you don't eat enough!'

'I am old, you are young, eat and grow strong.'

Ghar smiled, 'Yes, we will eat when we go back down.'

'I think I will stay here with Manar. Ghar, you can stay too.'

The succulent, tangy, bloody meat was not too far behind in Ghar's memory and Mu's cavernous torso heaving in the moonlight also made going back attractive, but then he caught a look in Mai's eyes, 'All right, I will stay here.'

After sharing the meat, Mai quickly curled up by the fire and beckoned Ghar to come closer and nestle. The night air nipped through the pulsing heat. Manar lay down beside Mai as well.

They talked late into the night, Ghar liked being where he was, studying her closed eyes in the rhythmic firelight. Mai seemed to be a light sleeper, like it was in her nature to be awake. Her eyelids occasionally fluttered, slightly open, as her body somehow rolled in on itself.

During the day, she's like a graceful deer, in the night she is like a pile of deer bones, Ghar smiled as he fell asleep.

* * *

The morning was pre-empted by Mu and Uba wrestling in front of the cave. Ghar's eyes opened to his first real look at Mu and almost choked on his own tongue at the sight. He had had an idea of the beast's enormity the night before, but here in daylight, Mu looked like he could swallow a child whole.

Manar emerged from the cave, 'Some dried fruit I have been saving for a special occasion.'

Ghar thought Manar was a much better sight for his eyes, than the gruesome bulk of Mu. He sat up and took the fruit gratefully but waited for Mai to eat.

Mai, who was already up, standing, stretching in the sun, turned around to the announcement of fruit. 'Aiy, these taste so good. How come you never give me these when I come alone?'

Manar laughed, 'We must encourage the Zardan to come and visit.'

Ghar figured he was queasy from watching Mu, but his gut bravely accepted the challenge of eating. He chomped down, the dry texture exuded a sweet, tangy flavour that made his face squash his eyebrows into his chin.

Mai had Uba by her side before he could think of anything else, 'I will go get some of the leftover meat,' and left without any chance of a reply from either Ghar or Manar.

Ghar watched them disappear around the rocky face. Manar looked at him expectantly and he realized that he had nothing to say.

'So, what do you find different about Khamma?'

Ghar smiled, it was rare that somebody else asked the first question. He glanced at Mu, who was licking his paws in the shade, 'The wolves are definitely different.'

Manar laughed. 'Yes, every other tribesperson that I have met has run away before I could tell them Mu was not a danger.' She chuckled, offering Ghar more fruit.

'You have met other tribes? Have you met a boy named Dun? He was from Zarda too,' Ghar's mind raced through the possibilities.

'No. Who was Dun?'

'He was my friend,' Ghar sighed. 'Sorry, Manar, I interrupted you, may the Fathers, I mean, the Spirits forgive me.' He quelled the sadness with the face-twisting fruit that Manar still held out.

'No, it's all right to have questions. And don't apologize about these "Fathers"; you are from a different tribe,' Manar reassured Ghar.

'That's also different—you are able to accept me as a member of the Khamma,' Ghar reflected.

'When Lu attacked you, I was quite surprised to hear about it.'

'Who is Lu? Lu attacked me?'

Manar's eyes curled inquiringly, 'Mai's wolf, you know, the wolf that attacked you.' She pressed on, 'a giant wolf like Mu.'

The events and the past conversations started to connect, to make sense. Ghar had heard about a wolf, but the wolf that attacked him surely was not like the wolves of Khamma.

'Lu chased you into a river, and then both of you fell through a waterfall.'

'I fell through a *waterfall*? What is a waterfall?' Ghar wanted to make sure he fully understood the tale.

'Yes waterfall, the river—falls—down.'

'A waterfall!' Ghar's eyes grew big.

'Yes, Mai chased after you and Lu, but could only find you,' Manar looked at the sky. 'You call them the "Fathers"? They were looking out for you that day.'

'Lu was her wolf?'

'Yes, he was even bigger than Mu.'

Ghar felt a revelation when he looked at Mu, 'Did Mai lose Lu because of me?'

'No, I don't think she blames you, I never thought of it like that,' Manar placed her hand on Ghar's shoulder. 'I remember she came back, she looked exhausted, but she had real strength in her voice. She wanted to rescue you.'

'She lost Lu because of me.'

Ghar watched Mai emerge from the rocky outcrops below that hid most of the thin faint worn path to the main camp.

'Mai, I am sorry,' Ghar quickly got to his feet and bowed, 'I didn't now know you lost Lu because of me.'

Mai shrugged with a chuckle, 'You only understand this now?' Her amusement quickly gave way to introspection, 'You did not cause his loss, he was just difficult to control.' She laid the meat from the camp on a hide. 'Even Mu sometimes just does what he wants to do.'

Ghar's guilt eased where it had lodged deep in his chest, 'But Ulan told me that losing your wolf is like losing yourself.'

Mai looked at Ghar, almost as if she were journeying somewhere and had just returned, 'I lost a Lu, but I gained a Ghar.'

8

Water Powder

Ulan had recently been shaved, angry-red welts criss-crossed his scalp, new hair budding out of the remaining red patches.

'What happened to your hair?' Ghar asked, sleepily, still catching up with the morning sunshine. He had just come back from the lake after performing his morning ablutions. He rolled out some of the paintings he had been working on.

'Little insects, nasty biters. All they do is hide in the hair and bite,' Ulan felt the top of his scalp with a gleam of gratitude in his eyes. 'Any more and I would have happily peeled off my skin.'

Ghar winced, shoulders bunching up, at the thought of the insects and then at the vision of Ulan's scalped head.

'Looks like I have a new brother.' Ghar and Ulan turned to the new voice.

'Ah, Nara. Well, I wish I were as fortunate as you; you never have to shave your head,' Ulan declared at Nara's smooth head, with a touch of humour in his voice. Ghar found it amusing, but politely declined to laugh. 'This is Ghar, he is from Zarda, from beyond the falls,' Ulan introduced Ghar.

'From beyond the falls? Those men are not friendly; basically chased me until nightfall.'

Ghar recognized the vehemence. 'Have you seen them?' He was suddenly struck by a thought, they might actually have been the outcast Gubba, 'Were they brown, or fair-skinned?'

'They looked like you,' Nara confirmed that they were Sanaa. Ghar felt his limbs go numb, as he sat back on his haunches. Memories of Adura and Gharra rushed through his mind.

Nara squatted in front of Ghar's paintings, a delighted thin, long finger traced out the landscapes.

Ulan patted both Nara and Ghar on their backs, 'I've had my fill of Nara's stories; I need to get to the lake, a cool crisp bath might soothe my head.'

The sweat on Nara's scalp glistened in the sunlight. His tightly wrapped furs could not hide the bony appendages that swung animatedly to assist his tale. His gaunt face was equal to his bony limbs, which spoke of uncomfortable hunger. Ghar had become unacquainted with starvation, being with the Khamma. Unlike the Zarda, the Khamma in general, had a lot to eat.

'I noticed these, so I came over to talk to you. You know something? I have seen this mountain.'

Ghar stirred at the remark, 'Seen it? Have you been there?'

'Yes, I think so.'

'I've never been there; this is a picture that I remember in the Grand Cave.'

'What is that?'

'Sorry, Grand Cave—those are Zardan words. It is like the cave here, but where Zardan people pay tribute to the Fathers.' Ghar sifted through the fur scraps he had painted on, 'Here, this is the Grand Cave.'

Nara knelt, further revealing his scant limbs. Ghar flinched at the sight, but gathered his resolve to continue, 'Our tribal Elders would meet in the Cave,' Ghar smiled at the memory of the lush furs that surrounded the central hearth, and the beautiful paintings. 'The walls were covered in paintings and they were much bigger paintings than this portrayal.' His eyes came to rest on Nara's knobby knees, forcing another awkward silence.

Nara wiped some sweat that had accumulated on his bare scalp. 'I have not seen the cave, but I have seen the mountain.' He squatted in a cross-legged position, but immediately leant in, tugging out a painting that was in the pile. 'Now, this symbol, I have seen.'

Ghar had drawn the shape from memory, 'It was the last mark I saw when leaving Zarda. I don't know what it means; it was on a large rock in a yellow field.'

Nara perked up, 'Yes! That symbol was painted all over the rocks.'

Ghar smiled and sighed, happy to meet somebody that had shared his Zarda, 'Do you remember how you got there?'

'I think so . . . it's a long journey.'

'Maybe we will go to Zarda, when I am stronger. I will go home,' Ghar mused.

Nara was serious though, 'When you are ready, we can go to this Zarda.' Nara's confident tone lifted Ghar's spirits. Every day as a Khamma took him further away from Zarda, but Nara was a way back. *Maybe the Fathers will find a way back for me.*

* * *

The wind whistled through the trees, swirling the fallen leaves in a dance that livened up an otherwise uneventful narrow valley. Small uneven hills, part rock, part earth, part tree, flanked the forest floor that looked ordinary, but upon a closer look, yielded Ear Mushrooms, that Ghar initially thought would be beneficial for hearing, but was quickly informed that they formed part of a mixture that was good for curing fevers. A steady, whirring sound of insects, that ebbed with the strengthening wind, accompanied the young Zardan and Khamman. A grey, overcast sky swaddled them in cold. Out in the forest, away from the tribe, Ghar comfortably switched back to his old ways. He mimicked the actions of the Zardan martial art—Maraza—much to the amusement of Mai.

Ghar smiled quizzically at Mai, 'Do you think this is funny?'

Mai's face flattened to apologize, but then she continued laughing. Ghar mock punched her, which she deftly sidestepped.

Mai stopped giggling to call out over the wind, 'I think it's getting really rough; we should head back . . .' her voice trailed off with the rushing air.

'It doesn't seem so bad; maybe we could stay a little longer,' Ghar relished being out alone with Mai.

The air suddenly turned white; a cold, white dust flew about in the strengthening wind. Ghar found himself leaning into the wind and losing his step as he tried to work out which way to go, but the white dust surprised him off his feet. Its cold claws bit into Ghar's skin, causing him to flail about madly.

'Get it off me,' the words escaped his breath.

He felt Mai grab him by the shoulders, urging him to get up. The white wind was now shrouding everything they said to each other and Ghar could not even see his own hands in front of him. All he felt was the tug of her hand leading him into the cold.

Ghar's visibility cleared as they approach a crevice opening. He watched Mai push Uba in. She turned to Ghar, but the wind still overpowered her voice. She stepped aside and pushed Ghar, following him in. It was more a crack than a cave, which only gave them space to stand sideways.

'What was that?' Ghar cried out over the howling gale.

'I have never seen anything like this,' Mai opened her hand to reveal the white powder, which was only slightly visible in the dim light. She took it up to her nose.

'That might be poisonous,' Ghar latched on to her wrist.

'It's water,' she tilted her hand into Ghar's. It was cold, but it did feel like water. Ghar leaned back and made as much room as he could to sit. Mai easily twisted her body to fit beside him, enough to squeeze in Uba as well. 'What do we do now?'

'I think we just have to wait,' Ghar looked out of the entrance, at the rushing white powder, whirling and whipping about maniacally.

As they watched and listened to the blizzard outside the crevice, they adjusted themselves in different positions to get comfortable. Finally, Mai pulled Ghar to lie down. She flexed to occupy the tiny space that was left over, moving Uba into position at their feet, 'It's good your moving furs don't come off so easily.'

The storm that was bellowing outside, angrily taunted Uba, who whimpered in submission. 'Well, I did make them, so they must be pretty good,' Ghar tried to smile through the cold.

'Such humility. Especially from somebody stuck in this place.'

As she nuzzled closer into his face, her warm moist breath soothing his cheeks, a feeling escaped his deferential self, *I like being stuck here with you.* His eyes popped open, at his blunder, as his mind frantically searched for a way out. But then he realized that although he had thought it, his mouth had not betrayed him. He closed his eyes, relieved, but his curiosity stayed awake at this new idea of being alone with Mai. *Being stuck here isn't all bad.*

* * *

A soft light did not do much to break the cold. Ghar had been through freezing cold nights which would force the tribe to huddle together in a pile by the fire to keep warm, but the night before was a story that would perplex any Zardan.

'Are you awake?' Ghar noticed that even graceful Mai could only stagger to her feet as she woke him up.

'Yes,' he was weary, but had so many questions. 'Have you ever seen a storm like that before?' He watched Mai slide through to the cave's entrance.

'You should look outside.'

Ghar crawled, grabbing at the damp rock for a partially firm hold. His shoulders felt uneven, and his feet unsure. He wiped the slimy residue from his eyes that had built up with the cold. His mouth felt shards of dryness despite the cold—he inspected the damage with this tongue. 'Do you have any water?'

'I think there's a bit left, but you should really come out and see this,' her arms gingerly flexed backwards both to offer water and beckon him to the new sight.

As Ghar reached for the water skin, he looked over Mai's shoulder. The white patches on the forest floor at first stunned his vision. He blinked and rubbed his eyes, it was hard to understand what was outside.

Uba was already outside, sniffing and whimpering at the powder. He pawed at it tentatively to confront the new substance. Ghar reached past Mai to the forest floor and inspected the cold, white powder between his fingertips, feeling it crunch softly into water as he ground it.

Mai touched the water in Ghar's fingers and examined it herself, 'Water?'

'It's just water, it's water powder,' Ghar held it closer. 'Why is it so cold?'

'What about the camp? I hope they are all right?' Mai's tone grew urgent.

Ghar looked at Mai, the unfamiliar lines of her face did not lead him to Khamma, instead it pulled him back through the unforgiving mountains and all the way back to Zarda. 'What about Zarda? what about Adura? and what about Dun?' The worries flooded in, overwhelming him and shrouding his thought.

Mai glanced back at him, the browns in her eyes refocusing him on Khamma.

'We should head back,' Ghar reluctantly deprioritized his fear for his former tribe. Uba seemed to acknowledge the order and quickly set off in the direction of the camp. Droplets of water softly dropped from the trees. 'I hope they're all right.'

* * *

They arrived at the entrance of the Khamman rock to find blood stains. Distant wailing of men, women and children filled the air. Mai ran ahead with Uba in tow. Ghar stood there in disbelief. He tracked the blood into the forest. *Somebody must have been injured.*

The usual thorny entrance had been cast aside; spots of blood led to the water. Ghar waded through the frigid water, everything was colder—the stream, the wind and even the rocks seemed colder.

He clambered up the banks to an unrecognizable Khamma—men and women huddled over fallen tribesmen, people trying to heal the sick. Ghar rushed to a group to help. He pushed through a gap, to see a lifeless body. He reached down to give aid but found a coldness that pervaded everything that the water powder touched—he withdrew his hand in alarm.

Mai stepped past him carrying steamy water skins, 'I'll give him some water to drink, can somebody warm his body with furs?' She supported the tribesman's head with her arm and coaxed him to drink.

'Come on, warm him up, don't just stand around!' she barked at some of the tribespeople. They sat close to him, rubbing fur on his skin. 'Stop it, those furs are wet and cold,' she pulled at them prompting her helpers to do the same. 'Go to the caves and bring back dry furs.' She glanced at Ghar, 'Ghar come over here and take these to the fires.'

Ghar stood there stock-still, not able to figure out what was going on.

'Come on, don't just stand there!'

Ghar obeyed the command, panic clouding his ability to act, to help the injured tribesmen. He positioned the furs next to the fire, propping them to stand as much as they would. He decided this was how he would help. He ran over to the next victim and brought back the furs to warm and dry.

He found Manar close to the water's edge, bloodied, binding the gashes of a whimpering hunter, his eyes clenched shut displaying the silent pain. Ghar tried to stay focused, 'Give me his furs.'

Manar glared at him incredulously, 'Can't you see I am trying to tie his wounds?' Her mild manner returned when Ghar's face furrowed into an even deeper fear. 'Just be careful. Here, slip it off.'

Ghar's fingers uncomfortably prised between the matted fur and blood-sticky skin. He put the furs to the side, but stopped to inspect the rest of the hunter's body. 'That's a big gash, but the other wounds are small,' he reported back to Manar.

'This is more than he can take,' Manar wiped the blood off her hands. 'It's too deep, he is still bleeding.' The hunter had gone quiet during their conversation.

'Let him sleep,' she took a deep breath, 'his body needs all his strength to heal.'

Manar quickly washed the blood off her hands in the lake, which usually was never allowed. She put in a final check and instructed some tribe members, 'Keep Tuya warm, and don't let him move about.'

Ghar watched Manar rush over to another victim. Part of him felt like they were trying to catch a river in their fingers, but knowing that Manar knew what she was doing, gave him the strength to persevere through the night.

* * *

There were souls who had passed, marked by the urgent calls of their immediate families that slowly morphed into prayers. The injured, for now, were asleep mostly. Ghar prayed to the Fathers to aid the Khamma, to save his new family as they had saved him. To give solace to those grieving, and to heal those who were hurt.

The burials had finished quicker than Ghar had expected. He found a place to rest near a fire, picking at the soil accumulated under his nails. Digging the graves had given him a place to bury some of his anxiety. The sounds of the injured accompanied the weak flames. He was alone. Mai, he thought, was with Manar. The wind still had a stinging touch that reminded him of the cold water powder. He warmed his hands with his breath, the night sky reminding him that he had not slept last night.

Yan sat beside him, 'I was with them when they fell.'

Ghar turned towards him. The whole day had gone by without an explanation, without a moment to think about what had befallen the tribesmen, 'They fell?'

'The cold dust, it blinded all of us. We were out hunting, and we could not see what was left or right, or even up or down.' Yan's face turned more furtive with each word. 'We really could not see anything. I could not even see who was in front of me. I could not even open my eyes even if I wanted to see anything.'

Ghar found Yan's exaggerated speech tiring and misplaced in the current moment, 'Yan, slow down. The men . . . where did they fall? What happened to them?'

Yan glanced back, annoyed, but continued, 'At first we could not do anything, I could hear somebody screaming, but I could not figure out from where. Then, out in the distance, I hear Tur shout, "Follow me," and I did. He guided us to the bottom of the ravine.' He half rose to demonstrate how he walked while crouched. 'I kept low to the ground to feel my way forward. We found them, some not speaking, and Tuya screaming.'

Tuya, the man with the gash, Ghar reminded himself.

'We could not carry all of them, so we decided to put them close to the rock face, and each of us huddled against the other for warmth. When the water powder weakened, we started to carry back people, I tried to be as fast as I could.'

Ghar noticed a guilty glance that was wholly out of character with the Khamman hunter. 'Listen, you shouldn't feel bad that you could not save all of them.'

Yan wrapped his moving fur tighter, 'I am strong, Ghar. My friends come to me for help.'

'You can't be strong always; the Fathers will test you sometimes with strength and weakness.' Ghar remembered an adage that Gharra used to tell him and Dun, especially during the days without food: 'Weakness will teach you to be strong and remind you to be strong for the weak.'

Yan drew in a deep breath, 'I don't ever want to be in that position again. We must prepare for the next white powder.'

Ghar looked at his companion. Even in the face of this calamity, Yan found a way to firm his resolve and lead. This both impressed Ghar and also made him feel his own ineptitude. He was always behind Yan's lead, especially when Mai was around.

'Listen, I agree. Let's prepare. That would be a proper remembrance of the fallen,' Ghar sat back proud that he was able to accept Yan's lead even though he did not like it. The cries of the injured quickly cut him down from his perch.

Ghar looked out across the lake which seemed to be swaying softly in the moonlight. The shimmers rocked his eyes slowly, back and forth, as he accepted the rest he felt he did not deserve.

* * *

'Tuya's wound is not healing,' Ghar announced.

Manar was barely visible in the tall pungent shrubbery. She turned away from her labour just enough to convey her concern, but her continued diligence in collecting herbs spoke a confidence that he would be all right. 'We will have to wrap Tuya again, he is moving too much. Come, come in here and help me take back some of these leaves.'

Ghar fought through the itchy shrubs that left slightly burning abrasions, small enough to not take seriously, but big enough to still be a nuisance. His moccasins saved his feet from the tiny white hairs that unapologetically scratched through the thin skin on his shin.

'Listen, I could have waited for you outside the fire grass,' Ghar thought the name of the grass was apt.

Manar glanced back, this time her eyes crinkled in amusement, 'If you did, I would have missed out on your wincing.'

'That's playing with your prey.'

A chuckle escaped her stoic demeanour. She was a very practical being; she had hacked away most of her black hair, so she didn't have to tie it back. Even her smile seemed more of a way of healing people. She had also been fitted with a moving fur but, like Mai, Manar had

had it made without the sleeves to facilitate movements. Her skin had lost its youthful bounce in some parts of her exposed limbs, but her movements mimicked the calm movements of a deer. Manar's hands had more bruises than her peers, which alluded to her work with the mysterious plants. Ghar thought, *a useful curiosity.*

Then in a response to what Ghar thought was the weight of the events of the storm, she broke down, 'Youth is so easily wasted.'

Ghar caught her at her elbows and rested her on his chest. He was not used to this proximity with an Elder; it was not usual in Zardan culture, and even in Khamman culture there was usually a barrier of respectful discomfort. The soft cool tears that he wiped from her cheeks whispered what was in her thoughts. As they stood, leaning on each other in the grass he could feel beyond her apprehension about the next days, the fallen, the need to help the injured and the new tumultuous future the water powder foretold. She feared that she herself was slowly dying. Ghar knew because he had heard Adura express the same fear.

Her forehead softly brushed against his lips, which he curiously accepted, and responded to gently. A weakness started to grow through him as he started to explore with his mouth, the ridge of her eyebrows, the soft skin that varied in depth from her cheekbone to her chin, the wetness of her mouth, the sharp hardness of her teeth. She began to claim his mind, he could see nothing, or hear nothing, except her. And then she pushed him away. A slight airy chuckle came through the tears.

Ghar, still weak in the knees, tried to stand up straight. He looked down, he felt like a part of him was trying to tear through his moving furs.

Manar looked down and started to laugh, the red in her eyes still peering through ambivalently. 'I am too old for you,' she smiled. 'And even if I were not too old, you must ask the permission of the Elders first,' she added mockingly.

Ghar was not sure what had happened. In Zarda he was not of an age to have a mate. He did not even know what it meant.

And until he met Mai, he did not understand the attraction that the adults talked about. And now he was in Khamma, where none of the customs came easily. He quickly became aware that he might have made a mistake with Manar. Tears escaped his eyes, hiding his face.

'No, no, don't cry, you'll make me cry more,' Manar took a step forwards and cradled Ghar. 'We should leave this place, or we'll create a lake,' Manar prodded Ghar out of his melancholy. Ghar gathered his emotions and rubbed out his cheeks.

The walk back to Khamma was filled with Manar mainly describing healing herbs and roots, stopping on the way at different plants to compliment their healing properties. Ghar could only think of going back to that moment in the fire grass and undoing the embarrassment that harassed his heart. *Why would you do that, Ghar? That was so awkward,* he chided himself, his eyes staring blankly at the ground. *No good can come from the fire grass,* he concluded.

'When I was young like Mai,' Manar interrupted Ghar's plunge into remorse and sorrow, 'I had a partner too,' the corners of her lips livened the words that glided through. It vexed Ghar that she did not seem concerned at what had happened. She seemed happier than usual. 'He was a beautiful man, tall and fast. He would tie his hair much like you do. His name was Aran.'

Ghar wanted to interrupt her, to try and make her feel the way he felt, but inquired a more acceptable, 'What happened to him?'

'He died,' her cheeks sank, but a smile cultured by frequent fond reflections prompted, 'he tamed wild pups, but he himself could not be tamed.' Her eyes scanned the forest floor as if looking for some memory of her mate. 'He jumped in the river after a fish that escaped, still holding his spear. He was never a good swimmer. The more he gained on the fish, the more the river gained on him.'

Ghar noticed there was a fondness to her speech about her mate, even in his demise. Her words had taken on a greenness, like plants slowly and gracefully emerging from the dead ground.

'He went through the rapids at Karad rocks.'

Ghar remembered the name, 'That was where I went through, after being attacked by Lu.' The jagged rocks of Karad shook him from Manar's story for a moment.

'He was not as fortunate as you. The rocks left a painful, blue mark on his chest. He still somehow held on to his speared fish. It was really big enough to feed a whole family, maybe big enough to even eat a whole family.'

Ghar reflected that her poetry had begun to reach its limits.

'The blue mark did not go away, and then he started coughing, then coughing out blood. He tried to live, he wanted to live, but he just coughed too much, and even with all the medicinal herbs we gave him, his fever continued unabated until the end.'

'That's really sad,' said Ghar. 'What did his name mean?'

'It didn't mean anything.' Ghar's gaze questioned her. 'Does your name mean something?'

'It means "river".'

'Why would they call you a river?'

'Adura and Gharra, changed our names so that, even though we were switched, Dun and I would still be a part of our birth mothers.'

'Gharra and Ghar, that's beautiful,' said Manar.

'Maybe they thought I resembled a babbling brook,' Ghar quipped.

'More like a tumultuous, wild river,' Manar chuckled.

Ghar connected the sudden humour from his companion as a way to deflect the earlier awkwardness. She was reacting differently not only to Ghar but also to herself. He felt comforted by the realization—that his embarrassment was shared.

* * *

The lake, which the forest greens majestically oversaw was still a sight that cooled his eyes, but there was a grief in the air, a certain unshakeable solemnness about the tribespeople. Even the wolves had lost the wagging in their tails.

Ghar followed Manar back through the camp, he still felt an awkwardness with Manar, but she seemed to turn her focus back to the wounded. She knelt beside Tuya, taking off his furs, and instructing his mate, who was sitting beside Tuya, to warm the furs.

Manar checked for a fever, before looking at the wound. 'He is moving around too much. He needs to stay still,' her hands came up with blood as she inspected the hide which she had used to hold the wound together.

'Can I have a look at the wound?' Ghar felt an idea coming to life.

'There is nothing much to see; these wounds require lots of rest and to remain still,' Manar sternly rejected Ghar's request, glancing admonishment at Tuya's mate.

'Listen, let me look at it,' Ghar started to undo the strips of hide, to looks of consternation and then anger from Manar and Tuya's mate.

Manar finally relented, 'Ghar, you better not hurt Tuya unnecessarily.'

The wound opened up, a sticky fluid the only resistance. He examined the deep cut, 'The skin around the edges is a bit frayed; we will need to remove that.' Tuya, who was still asleep, trembled as Ghar's fingers grazed the bare flesh, 'I think I can attach this, like a moving fur.'

'I think you have lost your mind to the forest animals,' Manar looked bemused.

'No, Manar, look at the moving fur, this is skin. The buffalo live in this.' Tuya's mate started to sob at the discussion. 'Listen, I can do it,' he thought for a moment, 'actually Ulan is better at this.' He shouted across the camp, 'Ulan! Come over here quickly!'

Ulan trotted over but skidded to a stop at the sight of the wound, 'Why is that open? Wrap it up, Manar!'

'Another learned healer,' Manar scoffed.

'Ulan, we can attach this up.'

Ulan's eyes seemed to scream out in terror, 'You want to attach a man? Like a buffalo skin? Alive?'

'Why is this so difficult to understand? Look, this is moving fur, this was the skin of a buffalo and we attached it, does it open?'

Ulan stood there, slowly breaking into a smile, 'We can attach him up!'

Ghar would have given him a look of amusement, but he was already running towards their collection of tools. Ulan joined him at the crevice where Ghar kept the tools for attaching furs, 'Let's use the thinnest fibres, really thin.'

'Good idea. How much do you think we will need?'

'Let's just take it all.'

They ran back to Tuya, Ghar trying to stomp out his doubts with each step, *this has to work.*

Ghar and Ulan broke through the small group that had collected around the spectacle; some voices raising concerns in Ghar's ears were drowned out. He knew this was the right thing to do.

'We might need to hold him down, this is probably going to hurt,' Ulan warned.

'You hold his arms and you, hold his other leg. Yes, sit on it,' Ghar instructed some of the onlookers, who seemed keen to be a part of the new action.

'Listen, let's start. Ulan, you go first.'

'No, you go first,' the look of terror returned to Ulan's face.

'I think you said you wanted to remove the damaged skin. You should cut it off with a flint,' Manar reminded Ghar. It was Ghar's turn to look terrified. 'All right . . . I will do it,' Manar dismissed their concerns. 'You only have ideas, no courage.'

Ghar gratefully accepted the judgement of cowardice, *at least I don't have to cut Tuya's skin.*

Manar sliced away the thin strips of severed skin that was already drying up.

'I think the rest of the skin is thick enough to hold,' Ghar readied himself. 'I will start. We should keep it thin, not too deep, because that will cause a lot of pain.' He positioned the flaps together gesturing to Ulan to hold it closed with his hands.

The thin awl punctured the skin uncomfortably easily. It did not feel like hide, it felt alive. Using the curve of the awl, he estimated the point where it would emerge. The shaft twisted menacingly as it bore a way through Tuya's flesh. Then, when the needle was nearly out, Tuya screamed himself awake, but upon seeing the answerless faces of Ghar, Ulan and Manar, he fainted again.

'I think it is better that he is unconscious,' Manar voiced out.

They scanned each other's faces. The doubt, which had been put aside before they had started, now sat in between them, grinning, mocking their effort.

'Let's continue. We will only know if it works when we are finished. For now, treat it like a moving fur, keep the stiches close and tight,' Ghar took his chance to lead.

Ghar had finished a small part of the cut, when Ulan found some nerve, 'I would like to try.'

Ghar accepted the assistance; his limbs had grown heavy, being so still, and his feet were close to falling asleep. He got up to walk around, to see Mai's radiant face beaming at him from among the crowd.

He felt the need to explain the procedure, 'So far, the attaching has gone well. We plan to attach the wound up so it will not open, like how we attach the moving furs.' An approving murmur rippled through the crowd. Ghar exchanged a nod with Mai and turned back to complete the task.

Ghar was surprised to find Ulan had already finished. He turned back to his audience, slightly embarrassed but recovered to proclaim, 'The wound has been sealed!'

The crowd cheered, in a show of appreciation that had been forgotten since the water powder onslaught. They pushed in to have a look. Ghar himself wanted to further examine the fibres holding the sides of the wound together, especially as he was surprised at how quickly Ulan had finished. He managed a glance before being jostled away.

'Good work, Ulan, that was really fast,' Ghar put his arm around the burly tribesman, who had made way for the crowd. Ulan smiled in appreciation. Manar and Mai joined them away from the attention. They all sat down in the relative quiet; Ghar mostly basked in his new method.

Manar said smiling, 'I am not sure whether it will work, but I think, if it does, you will become a healer.'

'A healer—like you and Mai?'

Manar looked blank, she usually had an answer, but now her thoughts seemed lost in her deep-set eyes; she did not know, but a calmness in the lines of her face reassured the group, 'Not just like Mai and me, maybe better than us. Healer of Khamma.'

The high praise left Ghar bereft of words, 'Thank you, Hera.' The Zardan phrase for Elder slipped out, but he felt that it was apt. This Zardan had found a place in Khamma; maybe a part of Zarda could find a place in Khamma.

* * *

The wound-healing had restored some modicum of confidence to the camp. They had taken out the wolves for a hunt, and mouth-watering aromas of fresh meat being grilled wafted through the camp. There were also more people tending to themselves, bathing, cleaning out latrines and arranging the food rations and the skins in their proper places. Ghar recalled that they were not as fastidious as the Zarda were, but this new Khamma that had emerged from the tragedy, now known as the 'Water Powder Storm', was becoming more organized. It was as if the Khamma had cast off their canine advantage as a mere complacency and had set about building a more resilient Khamma.

The more Tuya's wounds healed, the more the tribesmen looked to Ghar for his thoughts. Manar had pulled him away to teach him about the suitability of the furry leaves for indigestion and explain whether sky berries helped cure a fever or were only to be used on external wounds. He enjoyed the talk; her seriousness came out in excited eyebrows and a twitching nose. It was his chance to gaze to his fill.

'The meat is in my eyes, my eyes want to eat,' Manar said as the promise of a good meal floated flirtatiously in the air. Generous cuts of succulent, melting meat changed hands ending with the hungriest or greediest receiver. Some of the more sought-after parts of the buffalo, such as the heart and liver, were savoured before being passed on.

Ghar's entry to the campfire grill was greeted by a meat-muffled cheer. As an Elder emerged and led him to a grilling spit, Ghar turned to Manar, whose knowing smile led him to believe that something good was in the offing. Ghar was handed a full heart. The slightly charred skin generously supported a softer interior and felt victorious to his fingertips. Ghar had never taken the first bite. *It's just a heart, just eat it,* he tried to convince himself, but then he realized the tribe was watching him with bated breath. Maybe he would choke, maybe it would fall to the ground while handing it to the next person.

Ghar closed his eyes and bit in. Thick blood-rich liquid accompanied the soft inner flesh, all of it wrapped in a smoky pine. He broke into a smile of joy he had never known before, not back in Zarda in either of his mothers' arms, not back when Mai first found him, not when he now thought about Manar.

He raised the heart triumphantly and roared, releasing what he had supressed for so long, a rush of memories—losing Dun, his disdain for Das, his survival against the rocks of Karad. He was taking the first bite.

Ghar had handed over the precious delicacy to an excited member, the soft meat still being relished in different parts of his mouth, when he suddenly remembered Adura who, even though regularly commended for her part in maintaining the Grand Cave, always seemed to shy away from the limelight, which made her even more admirable. Ghar bowed his head, as Adura would do, and made his way through the crowd back to Manar.

'Let's go,' he said contentedly.

'Wait. I have not had a turn at that heart.' Ghar liked moments like these, when Manar would lose her serious demeanour to take on a childish need for entertainment, when her eyes would widen and her cheeks would fill up.

'Manar, you really delight me!' Manar glanced back, partly welcoming; but a reserved smile returned the compliment.

Ghar sensed her discomfort, 'I will go and collect some meat for us.' He walked over to a fire where the cooked pieces of meat were beginning to pile up. He looked for the charred pieces with the soft redness inside; he remembered that Manar seemed to enjoy those the most.

His mind returned to Zarda, imagining how a meal like this would be an event that would be portrayed up in the Grand Cave. His train of thought was interrupted by Manar taking the meat out of his hand.

Manar bit in, a soft whimper of contentment escaping her mouth, 'This is the way to live.'

Ghar secretly took pleasure in Manar's voluptuous reaction. He was studying her, discovering what made her happy, or what comforted her when sad. The effort to please her usually ended with some interesting return, a glimpse behind her more planned and pragmatic self, or a new facial expression, or just physical proximity which Ghar was beginning to relish more and more every day.

The idea of a mate would frequent his mind, *am I ready for a mate? When would I be ready for a mate? Would Manar be my mate?* The thought would jolt him back to reality, *of course she wouldn't: she says she is too old for me.* He felt like his chest would implode at the thought, but inevitably a grin at the idea would linger.

Her short, unusual hair gave his mind different forms to play with—a friendly, wise chin held up soft cheekbones and riverside swirly ears. The descriptions excited Ghar.

'Manar, your cheekbones are like smooth rocks.'

'What does that mean?' Manar looked up from her meat, confused.

'I mean like the smooth rocks under the water,' Ghar suddenly felt that he ought to have spent more effort on what to say and not just what to think. Manar felt her cheekbones, her eyes straining towards them.

'Listen, what I want to say is that your hair is like wolf fur.'

'Are you making fun of me?'

Ghar breathed in slowly, hiding his nerves, 'Listen, what I mean is, you remind me of nature, the calm rocks under the water, the safe security of the wolves, the brown beauty of your eyes like the generous earth giving life to the green trees.' Another silence fell between them. Manar smiled at Ghar. But even though she gazed at him, he could feel her looking past this moment, glancing through her life. The lines on her forehead relaxed, reminding Ghar of her recollection of Aran. He felt that she was only happy because of something Aran had told her, and that his own refrain had only triggered Aran's memory, nevertheless he was happy; happy that he could make her smile.

'Ghar, that was very poetic, what you said, and it created in me a feeling I have not felt since Aran,' her eyes studied the ground, as if she was unsure where she could step, but there was a resoluteness in her voice. 'I do not want to become your mate. You must stop. I will keep mentoring you, but you cannot pursue me as a mate.'

Ghar was taken aback, but he understood. *She sees Aran in every good thing I do for her.* She could experience the pain that must have been following all his kind acts. He lifted his eyes to see Manar's face, resolute and tense. *It does not matter what her reason is,* he realized. *She does not want to be my mate, that is reason enough for me to stop. I should not need a reason.*

'I am sorry, Hera, please forgive this shortcoming.'

Manar nodded, a clenched smile accepted his apology. She turned back to her meat, while Ghar stood there, too awkward to leave, but too hurt to stay in the moment. He took a step back in his mind and changed the subject, 'So furry leaves are meant to cure indigestion?'

9

Tan

'Son, don't worry, we are safe, Dun is safe,' the young sun shone through his fluttering eyelids.

He awoke abruptly, *what about his Dun, what about his family, what about Adura, what about Zarda?* He had nearly forgotten his past completely, partially distracted by his new position in Khamman and partially, by his infatuation with Manar. He suddenly felt alone, separated from the figures of his youth. And all his accomplishments loomed over him, mocking his insecurity.

I think Dun would be all right, he pictured his muscular friend, shouldering his way through the water powder storm, saving his brethren.

A new-born had cried most of the night driving most of the camp towards the lake. They lay lazily strewn around, desultorily talking to each other, trying to enjoy the heat of warm-time, after what seemed like a longer cold-time, and not as warm. The more motivated members were bringing more firewood to drive up the heat.

The occasional, fiery embers would drift around looking for a thought to break or a conversation to interrupt.

Ghar got up to wash up in the lake, and spotted Nara on the lake shore, his body seemed entangled as usual, 'Nara, may the Spirits accept us.'

Nara looked back without moving the rest of his body, which further emphasized the lack of connection between his limbs,

'May the Spirits accept us indeed, my Zardan friend.' His exposed shoulders had streaks of red swelling.

'How did you escape the water powder?'

'I did not witness it.'

'The water powder, the white dust that turned to water after a while?'

'Yes, I know, some of the tribesmen told me about it. I did not encounter it.'

Ghar was surprised. It had not occurred to him that the water powder did not cover every land. Nara's wolf, Uru, limped over.

'What happened to Uru?' Ghar examined the blood-matted fur on his forepaw.

'We were attacked by a bear.'

Ghar was surprised at Nara's nonchalance, 'Attacked by a bear!?'

'Yes. Uru was so brave, ran right up to the bear, and dodged most of the blows. After enough barking, the bear ran away. I think bears are scared of loud noises.'

'What did you do when the bear attacked?'

'The same as always, I climbed up into a tree. I would never be able to match a bear. I wouldn't be much of a match to any wild animal while I am alone.' He paused for a moment; his chin dipped in a moment of remorse. 'I lost a wolf, Uyun, to a bear; I ran up the tree, but the bear just followed me and would have made me his meal, if not for Uyun, who attacked the bear from behind. But she got too close. I can remember the terrible crunch of bear on wolf. My only hope was that her death was quick. The bear then ate part of Uyun right there in front of me and then carried off her remains.'

'That's an amazing story; that should be a tale to tell around every campfire,' Ghar was staring directly at Nara's shiny forehead, but now the shimmer was respectable. He suddenly remembered the Zardan symbols that Nara had seen, 'Have you seen any more Zardan markings?'

Nara's eyebrows squashed together while his eyes stayed on Ghar, 'Do you mean the markings I found in the yellow field.'

Uru looked up at Ghar with big eyes, his red paw raised. Ghar looked around for Manar, then quickly helped the wolf to the water's edge, washed out the blood, and inspected the wound. *Looks like it's healing.*

Nara had closed his eyes to recollect his memories, 'Other than the bear, there was nothing interesting during this trip.'

Yan walked over, his large shoulders imposing as always, lending him authority, 'By the way of the Wolf.'

Ghar and Nara were both surprised by the formality of his greeting. Nara replied, 'What have I done now?' Nara replied.

Yan smiled continuing with a superiority, 'The same as always, losing pups to bears while you go on wild expeditions.'

'I have the Elders' blessing,' Nara replied.

Uru barked with what seemed like agreement, bringing a smile to Ghar's face. Yan's tone grew annoyed, 'This will not be for long; the water powder has brought us new challenges; we should maintain our resources, instead of sending wolves into the stomachs of bears. Wolves are a gift from the Spirits.'

Nara turned away, dismissively. A low whistle in the wind blended into the animosity between the clansmen, adding a cold end to their argument.

Ghar spoke up on seeing Yan's back, 'Who are these Elders who support your trips out into the forest?'

Nara, turned back, a hint of annoyance in his eyes, 'These aren't "trips". I am not just going for a stroll in the forest. I am getting information about the forest, and the other tribes, like your Zarda.'

'I did not mean to offend you, Khamman brother. I only wanted to ask who the Elder who supported your—' Ghar paused to look for a less adversarial word, 'who supports your missions.'

'Important missions.'

'Yes, I agree, important missions,' Ghar's curiosity compelled agreement.

Nara's eyes suddenly glistened with the acknowledgment, 'Really important missions!'

Ghar nodded in acknowledgement.

'Tan is the Elder who leads these missions.'

Ghar remembered Tan, he was the Elder who had given him the first bite of the heart at the tribal feast, 'Are you the only man who goes out on these missions?'

'I am the only Khamman who is brave enough to go,' Nara smiled with pride. 'The journeys take many days and there are many threats to overcome and survive.'

'But wouldn't you rather stay within the security of the tribe?' Ghar thought about his life back at Zarda. 'It is actually easier here, with the assistance of the wolves, than back in Zarda.' A glance up the bank revealed a group of mothers playing with their children. 'Do you not want that?' he motioned Nara's attention with a quick gesture of his chin.

'I am not interested in a mate,' Nara took a pensive moment. 'I mean I understand why, the urges, it is the way of nature. But my urges are different.'

Mai had told Ghar about Nara's penchant for boys rather than girls. There were similarly rumoured tribespeople back in Zarda. 'Is that why you spend long times away from the camp?'

'No, I told you, I have important missions!' Nara retorted, lowering his tone. 'It is easier to be away than having to answer all these questions, but my main reason to be out there is to protect Khamma.'

'Listen, I understand. I have an uncommon inclination as well: I like Manar.'

'You like older women?' a raised corner in Nara's lips accompanied the gibe. Ghar's eyes widened in surprise at the accusation, but then realized Nara was only being humorous. 'I guess everybody has their story.'

They gazed out at the forest of various colours standing guard over the lake. Ghar looked across at his friend, the expression on Nara's face as deep as the water that cooled them. 'Out there, is a place for all our stories,' said Nara. Uru pushed in between them, making sure he was included.

'No reason why that place can't be right here,' Ghar smiled.

* * *

'I want to talk to Tan,' Ghar declared while walking into the Healing Cave.

Manar glanced a moment upwards but quickly looked away as the sun shone brightly through Ghar's long unkempt hair. 'You should cut your hair.'

Ghar pulled out something sticky from his strands but avoided studying it so Manar would not notice the action.

But Manar shrieked, 'I saw that!' She took a deep breath, her eyes scanned the wide array of herbs before her as if in the hope of some permanent solutions to Ghar's cleanliness. 'Come, sit here.' Manar took up position behind him in the sunlight, Ghar facing the interior of the cave. She pulled out a piece of flint and proceeded to slice away the hair. Every clump that had a foreign body was equally scrutinised and denounced. 'It's amazing you don't have fleas.'

Her dwelling hosted a miscellany of scents—dried butterfly-leaves, furry rain-collectors, shade-loving 'bitter-to-the-taste'. But what really gripped Ghar's attention were the gradients of green-red and the brown-yellow, and the cascade the arrangements made on the cave walls.

'Wait, listen, I want to talk to Tan.'

'Why do you want to talk to him?' Her flint hit something solid, which invoked another groan.

Ghar was struck by the fleeting inquiry, 'I don't have a big reason; I was just curious about Nara's expeditions.'

'Tan loves feeding bears.'

'That's what Yan said!' Ghar was surprised at Manar's common stance with Yan on this issue.

'It's true.'

'Is that what Tan says?'

'I'm playing with you, Ghar,' Manar smiled to hear her sarcasm hit home.

A path sliced through his hair uncomfortably close to his ear. He looked up, 'Maybe you could be a little more careful with that.'

Another clump came off in response. Manar drew in a long sigh, 'You can go talk to Tan, but be warned that sometimes he can be overbearing.'

'But I was thinking perhaps you could introduce me; I don't know any of the Elders except you.'

'I am not an Elder,' Manar turned insulted, the easy contour down her cheekbone to Ghar quelled her hurt pout, 'not yet.' Ghar remembered her aversion to being older. He turned to gauge her reaction but was surprised to find her scanning the herbs neatly arranged in a row, awaiting the needs of the next visitor to the Healing Cave. 'All right . . . let's go now.'

'Now?' Ghar missed a breath, and anxiety welled tears in his eyes. 'I don't have everything I wanted to say right now.'

'The wolf pup is not trained to cry; he is only punished when he asks why.'

Ghar accepted the decree. He knew he could argue, but even in success he would still follow her.

* * *

'Tan,' Manar's tone turned unusually deferential, 'I would like to introduce you to Ghar.'

From the rocky perch that overlooked the Khamman camp, Tan proclaimed, 'Ah, the boy who attaches men.' He had a long, satisfied face. Strong, vibrant, white hair sprouted from his temples, culminating in a knot on top of his head. His frame told a story of a man who used to be at the helm of the hunt. His calm observant eyes stood guarded by strong bones that sloped down into a chin with white and black bristles that marked wisdom in his face. He was an unusually large man, with wide-boned shoulders that would win both physical fights and verbal arguments.

'Yes, the boy who attaches men,' she smiled, 'and questions everything.' She held up her hand to stop Ghar from talking, 'Before you talk, Tan, I have not been able reach out to Nara.' She rummaged through her knapsack and brought out a stalk of fragrant but visibly decaying leaves. 'Could you ask Nara to gather these?'

Ghar fought the look of amused disbelief at realizing Manar's true intentions for meeting Tan.

Manar brushed his nose with the sprig with a gentle, acknowledging gleam in her eyes, then handed it to Tan, 'Tell Nara to pick these on his way back, or they will get old.'

Ghar raised a hand to stop Manar from leaving, but his gaze was already caught up in Tan's inspection.

'So, what do you want to talk about?' Tan shifted on his perch, sliding a foot underneath him while the other dangled in the air. His left hand trembled slightly but enough to catch Ghar's eye. 'This may shake,' Tan grabbed hold of his spear, 'but, like my wolf, it stands to attention when called.' Tan's demeanour lowered Ghar's gaze. He paused, an Elder's pause that was meant to give younglings a chance to catch up, 'but do not let my elderly foibles distract you; what do you seek, boy who attaches men?'

'Tan, I would like to know why you send Nara out on his expeditions?'

A slight, betrayed look crossed Tan's face, but as with the spear, he seemed able to quickly regain composure, 'The bears need something to eat,' Tan smiled.

It was Ghar's turn to be caught off balance. He lowered his voice to sound more reverent, 'I know that is a story repeated in the camp,' Ghar tried to look like he was not guilty of indulging in that quip, 'but I don't take rumours seriously.'

'You may be as intelligent as I thought you were,' Tan got off his perch and walked to the entrance of his cave which had a tall but narrow opening, that only allowed them to sidle through sideways.

He looked out on the camp, people busily tending to firewood, or carrying away smoked meat to be stored. 'Not many ask me why I send Nara to explore,' Tan straightened to his full height and traced the extent of the camp with his finger, 'I cherish the Khamma, and I do this for them.'

Ghar nodded, silent, aware of the disparity of their positions in the camp.

'The Spirits have blessed us with the wolves,' Tan closed his eyes in prayer, his face smoothened towards the ground in reverence, 'but we must be vigilant. There are new challenges that come from places that we do not know; new threats like the water powder.' There was a sternness in his voice that Ghar recognized, a sternness that had built up through the repeated explanations of Nara's trips into the forest. The spate of words did not abate, did not present a space for questioning, as Tan continued, 'that's why Nara goes out there. I would go myself, but I am not physically able to.'

Ghar could see Tan hide his quivering hand in his fur, 'I suppose that is not a reasoning easily accepted by the Khamma?'

'Full bellies birth complacence.'

'In Zarda we were going hungry every day because our hunters would come back empty from most expeditions.' Ghar's thoughts drifted back to Dun, 'But some situations are far worse than hunger.'

Tan gazed silently at Ghar for several moments, ending with a satisfied nod. His attention turned back to the camp, 'Young Zardan who attaches men, let's prepare ourselves for hunger, and whatever is worse than hunger.'

Ghar bowed out of respect. 'Hunger and whatever is worse.'

10

The People of the Tall Grass

The warm-time seemed to visit Khamma, only as a guest; the dawn of a new day revealing the cold again.

'I have never felt nature be so unsure of herself,' there was always a ponderance in Tan's statements that had Ghar stuck in thought, while Tan moved on to the next sentence. Tan grasped the opening edges of his moving fur, pulling them in closer as a chilly wind interrupted their conversation, 'these are proving very useful in this time.' His fingers seemed to never end as they drew out from the fur, and even when out, they seemed more like small trees than hands.

'Tan, Hera, what did you want to talk about?' Ghar was caught off guard by Tan's visit down to the lake. Ghar had been repairing a moving fur seam that had come undone, he had quickly concealed his activity while accepting Tan's praises.

'Nara and Manar will join us here by that campfire. I told him to wash himself first before coming to see you. Being out there, he sometimes forgets about being presentable.' A smile began to emerge in the corner of his lips, and a dreamy glaze built up in his eyes, 'Nara saw a tribe close to where Mai found you.'

Ghar remembered that Nara had told him about seeing Zardan signs, 'Wait, let me get my paintings.' He bowed as he walked past Tan, tucked the moving fur he was working on under his arm, and then started to run towards the outcrop where he kept his belongings. The thoughts sprinted with him. *Could this be Sanaa or Gubba? What if Dun was with them.* Thinking about Dun always left him feeling an anxious hollow in his chest, but it was a feeling he wanted to feel, this was the only way he could experience his friend.

He dropped the damaged moving fur in the cave, reached into the rock crevice and retrieved the rolled-up hides, and quickly ran back. *I used the paintings to find you Dun,* Ghar imagined the triumphant conversation he would have with Dun if he found the Gubba.

'I am back,' Ghar announced to the questioning faces of the Khamma who were deep in discussion around the fire.

'Yes, Ghar, we can see you,' Manar's voice emerged from around the vast girth of Tan.

'Hera,' Ghar greeted her, while listening in on Nara's discourse.

Nara paused, acknowledging Ghar's arrival, and then continued, upon receiving an approving glance from Tan. His hands then crawled characteristically into the air to colour his story, 'There was a small group of them, not carrying much, they might have had a camp nearby.'

'Did they bear any of these marks?' Ghar's paintings fell to the ground as he unfurled a hide with symbols of the Zarda.

Nara's eyes gleamed with recognition, 'Yes that was their symbol, they had that marked on their arms.' Ghar suddenly felt like he was being propelled back through the forests, up the ravines, through the valleys, back to Zarda. Nara seemed to relish the moment, he flexed his tired-looking toes and fingers to reveal experience-teeming scars, and his face raised in the sun even seemed good to look at.

'This may seem like a good story, here, safe by the hearths of Khamma,' Nara narrated, 'but these were dangerous hunters, with spears at the ready on their arms.'

Yan's voice spoke up from somewhere behind Ghar, 'Nara, you endless brook, can you get to the important part?' He broke through the group and stood next to Tan.

'And what is the "important" part?' Nara asked crossly, his words bruised.

'What were they doing? why were they so close to Khamma?'

Ghar mumbled to himself, 'Those are important questions.'

'It looked like they were hunting,' Nara turned to Ghar. 'You told me that "an answer is only as good as its question."'

The sage advice resonated in Adura's voice inside Ghar's head, 'Yes, I believe that is true.'

Nara grinned, a smile hiding a secret, '"Who?" is my question . . . who are these new tribesmen?'

Ghar glanced at Yan, a quick raise of the brow to accede that Yan's questions were better. He turned back to Nara, 'Who are they?'

'They were fair skins,' his wrists and elbows waved in excitement, 'I think you called them "Gubba"?'

The realization hung in the air for a moment, as Ghar's heartbeat caught up with the rest of his body. A relieved breath of the morning air quickly broke into a sorrowful shudder, 'What am I doing here?' he exclaimed, 'Dun is out there, my friend, my beautiful brother.'

The leaves gathered in the wind, heralding Yan's rebuttal, 'These savages are on our hunting grounds and we should go greet them?' His breath frosted the cold air maniacally, as he closed in on the group.

Tan stuck a gargantuan arm out to deter Yan's impetuosity, 'Calm your temper.'

Ghar's tears started afresh, nipping at his skin, as he looked at Yan in disbelief, 'Savages? These are the Gubba.'

Yan squeezed past Tan, and glowered at Ghar, standing so close that he could see the brown of Yan's eyes, 'This is the faeces of Zarda, the part they cast out.'

Ghar's glanced down, initially backing away, but a familiar rush in his body spurred a glare directly into the eyes of his aggressor, 'These are my brethren, like the Khamma are my brethren. If you have a problem with them, you have a problem with me.' His knees felt weak, the same feeling he had felt standing up to Das.

Yan turned away muttering, 'I don't know why I waste my life talking to you. This is our forest, these outsiders are not welcome.'

Ghar slumped down to his haunches upon Yan's retreat. He was exhausted, the weight of Dun now sat on his chest, every breath was a struggle up from the water's depth. Ghar looked up at Tan, 'I can go alone. I just want to make sure they are all right.'

Tan's furrowed expression turned characteristically satisfied, a slight hint of a smile, eyes narrowed as if in enjoyment of the moment, 'A little excitement might just wake up our tribe, and besides, if these Gubba pose any threat, we will set the wolves on them.'

Ghar shuddered at the thought, but he hoped he had heard sarcasm in Tan's declaration, so he nodded meekly.

'I will set up a party of hunters; let's see what these Gubba are doing on our hunting grounds,' Tan set off towards the caves.

Nara opened an uncomfortable thought, 'If there was a fight, would you side with the Khamma or with the Zarda?'

'You are Khamman, and you are Zardan. If you need to choose a side, then choose the side of what is best for both,' Manar replied for Ghar.

Choose the side of what is best for both, Ghar sealed his troubled thoughts with Manar's advice.

* * *

With the sun still early in its journey across the sky, Tan assigned a group of hunters along with Nara, Yan, Ghar and Mai.

'We should take Mu for protection,' Yan argued with conviction.

Ghar heard too much malice in Yan's conviction, 'We are trying to meet the Zarda, not eat the Zarda.'

Snorts and muffled laughs followed Ghar's poetry. Yan turned away, his jaw protruding even more than it usually did.

Nara led the way, and for the most part, was alone. His gait was a combination of steps, hops and quick trots that matched the terrain. Ghar thought that out in the forest he looked graceful, not the usual mess of gangly limbs that he was at the camp.

Ghar walked with Mai for reassurance, he wanted to find the Gubba, but there was also a part of him that did not want to discover that something bad had happened.

The cool morning slowly gave way to an uncomfortable warmth; the sun at its highest point, the heat worsened by the punishing pace that Nara was setting.

'Nara, we need to stop for a break,' Yan surprisingly called out to a collective groan of approval.

Nara stopped and turned around, with his usual alarming dexterity, relaxed and calm like he had just woken up. 'Already a break?' a respectful tinge of mockery. 'I think the Elders are more fit than you weaklings.'

'I still can't keep up with you,' Yan took a deep breath, breaking his panting, 'you move like a deer through the forest.'

Ghar looked over at Mai, remembering how her graceful movements reminded him of a deer.

'I nearly outran a deer some time ago.' Nara tempered his statement when he saw the sceptical head tilts and questioning squints. 'Not by being faster, but I outran him as he got tired and I think he was sick. I had just lost my wolf, and the hunger started to control me.'

Yan interrupted, 'Which wolf?' with a tired smile.

The joke missed Nara completely, 'Una, got attacked by a giant wolf. She thought the giant wolf was a friend and trotted right into those gnarly fangs.' Nara was standing over the troop narrating the story, hands mimicking the cavernous jaws ripping the Khamman canine apart.

The group settled into silence, some to comprehend Nara's tales, but mostly to let their calves loosen. Ghar spent the silence trying to imagine what Dun looked like now, how warm Gharra's hug would be, what it would be like to play with Ra. Mai leaned on him travelling with him in his mind.

Ghar felt his sweat dry. He, along with some of the group, had taken off their top moving fur to cool down. He took a swig from his water-skin and passed it to Mai who had climbed into a short tree.

'All right, let's get moving again,' Yan got up, motioning to the group to get ready. The group grudgingly gathered their belongings and rose.

'What happened after Una got eaten, Nara?' Mai was still curious about the story.

'I stood there, like a rock, I could not move.'

'Didn't the wolf attack you?' Mai asked.

'The wolf fell asleep,' Nara had turned around, talking as he walked backwards, 'and I just crept away. After I was safely far enough, I just started to run.'

'Probably saw your meatless bones and thought it better to take a nap,' Yan mused to the laughter from the rest.

'I think you spend far too much time in the forest, Nara,' Ghar broke through the laughter, 'if I were there, I would have probably died of fright.'

Nara was gauging his flesh, 'I do have meat.'

'I am sure you would been a very tasty meal, but are we even going the right way? You are walking backwards,' Mai admonished Nara.

Nara smiled, 'I know this forest forwards and backwards.'

'Listen, Nara, this is important. My tribe is out there, if we can find them, we can join their strength with the Khamma,' Ghar reminded.

Nara glanced over at Yan and furrowed his brow, as if to request approval for Ghar's declaration. Ghar ground his teeth, deciding to stay out of their gesturing and silent conversations. He had seen Tan talk privately to Nara and Yan and felt that there had to have been some reason for having been excluded from their discussion.

Nara led the group further through the forests and hills, successfully beating daylight's end, so that they could rest through the night, and see if they could find the Gubba in the morning. He guided the group up the crest of a small hill that commanded a view of the territory. Long, yellow grass swayed gently in the breeze, creating lake-like ripples. The crisp rustle of the leaves lulled a song that reminded Ghar of Zardan chants.

'I saw the tribe on the other side of that mountain,' Nara's voice trailed off as he placed his knapsack and spears on the ground. 'Now it is time for a nice warm fire.'

The evening breeze had ushered in a chill that signalled the group to get ready for the night.

* * *

Ghar was in a tepee, pine-scented smoke flirted with his nostrils, reminding him of the Zardan roasts after a successful hunt. The hides of the tent were a collection of deer and other animals, but they were actual animals, legs kicking, mouths agape and shut.

Adura and Gharra sat on the other side of the flames, barely visible. 'My son,' Adura's voice glided through the tent, sending a wave of relief through Ghar's body, 'it was not easy to give away Dun and then adopt you,' Adura glanced at Gharra, 'but part of it was surely not me adopting you, but you adopting me.'

'Remember who you are from,' Gharra cut in, 'and to the Fathers you will return.'

Ghar grimaced at the new sun. He had not slept at all the whole night. He had managed to stay awake during his lookout shift, mainly because some animal had been attacked and then proceeded to wail. But even after a hunter took over as lookout, he still found it hard to sleep.

'Did you hear that animal?' Mai sat beside Ghar, who was still lying down.

Ghar glanced around. *No Yan.* That brought a smile to his face, 'Yes I did, annoyed me to the hairs on my head.'

'Then why are you smiling?'

'I am just happy to see you,' Ghar grinned even wider.

A smile crept over her face, but she quickly admonished, 'You Zardan and your outlandish ways,' she tossed a handful of leaves at Ghar.

'No, don't do that. I want to sleep some more.'

The morning hues blended away into blue, while wisps of clouds stoically watched over the group. Mai got to her feet and pulled up Ghar by the arm.

Mai's touch felt different, there was a raw feeling that flowed, a feeling that reminded him of the thrill of the tempestuous wind on top of a mountain.

The rest of the group had assembled out by the field of tall grass.

Nara took the helm, gripping Uru's collar, 'We have to cross the Tall Grass. Keep your eyes open and watch what you step on. There are snakes and scorpions in here and the occasional big-tooth cat, and I don't want to carry any of you back to camp, either in pieces or whole.' The wolves started to bark. 'See, they already sense the danger.'

Ghar noticed movement in the grass, 'Nara, there is something out there.'

'Yes, young Zardan, you must be watchful.'

A group of men broke through the grass, a mere spear-throw away. They looked scared, spears in their hands.

'Who are you and why have you come here?' Yan shouted. 'Khamma, get ready to release the wolves.'

Ghar noticed the look of weariness on the strangers' faces. He felt that he must have had that same lost look when he was exiled from Zarda. He remembered Medar had that same bow in his shoulders and the same stony stance.

The air took on a frenzy and the sun suddenly seemed to blaze, tearing their eyes with sweat.

'Khamma, relea—'

'No stop!' a desperate cry from Ghar curtailed Yan's battle-cry. He could feel the pressure of his tribe's questioning glare even though they were transfixed on the tribe in front of them. Ghar stepped forward placing his spear on the ground, gently walking past the snarling wolves. He unfastened the moving fur from his torso and placed it in front of the outsiders. He took a step back and knelt on his knee, gesturing to them to receive his gift.

A startled look mixed in with the apprehension that was on the men's faces. The stranger, who seemed to be the most senior among them, moved forward reciprocating Ghar's moves, unfastening his own fur, a more conventional wrap around the shoulder. He placed it next to Ghar's moving fur. He picked up Ghar's offering and then examined it, a look of confusion at first was followed by a slight smile, entertained by the new object.

Ghar got up and slowly walked over to the stranger. He could hear Yan's stern reprimand, but it seemed distant, like Yan was far away in the mountains. All he could focus on was getting this man into his moving fur. The man seemed to enjoy the sleeve, taking his arm out, and slipping it back in, and then feeling the sleeve over his arm. He turned back to his tribe to say something, Ghar imagined he was telling them: *This is an amazing creation.*

Ghar helped the man into the other sleeve and completed the action by fastening the fur in the front. The man stepped back, waving his hands in every direction. By now the only people not giggling were the Khamma.

Ghar stood back from the man, 'I am Ghar.' He motioned to his chest, 'Ghar.' He waved his hand to the Khamma standing soundless behind him, 'These are the Khamma.'

The man smiled and yelled something out, with his arm held high in the air. Suddenly Ghar could see people appearing out of the top of the grass, men, women, and even children. Without another word the man and his tribesmen started to walk back into the grass and head away. Ghar turned back to his tribe, to see faces drained of their colour, and the wolves seated like nothing had happened. Ghar jumped up, the excitement he had held in all this time, talking to the new tribe, released itself in height. He started to yelp, in the traditional Khamman celebration.

'What are you celebrating for?' Yan asked sourly. Ghar was about to explain, but Yan cut him off, 'We should have attacked those invaders!'

Nara interrupted, 'Yan, we would have all been killed; there were so many of them.'

'Then we would have died honourable deaths.'

'Maybe it's better to live an honourable life,' Ghar muttered.

Yan jabbed his spear aggressively, 'What's that, Zardan? Is it a Zardan custom to speak without being heard?'

Ghar decided to step back, 'Listen, I did not mean to interrupt your honourable death, but let's forget this and continue looking for Dun, I mean the Gubba.'

'I don't care about your tribe. I want to report you immediately to Tan.'

Nara spoke up, 'Maybe it's better we go back; we should warn our tribe of the new strangers.' Ghar heard Nara's voice shift from his usual deep, confident tones, to a tone that urged caution.

Yan shook his head and started to head back the way they came, 'Nara, please lead us home from this ill place.'

Ghar turned back to the tall grass, he felt a void in his chest that urged him to run through the field to find the Gubba. Mai called out behind him, asking him to return. He looked over his shoulder, to see the Khamma slowly leaving. *Remember who you are from.* His mother's words haunted him. He heard Mai call again. Ghar realized that as much as he was from Zarda, he was also from Khamma.

I'll come back for you Dun, Ghar thought into the forest.

* * *

Arriving in Khamma was not as rewarding as usual. It was a quiet trek back to Khamma, the tribespeople silent, unsure about what to think of the events that just taken place. Ghar himself was trapped between thinking about how his actions might have prevented the Khamman group from being killed and that they had not even tried to look for Dun.

The group followed Yan to Tan's cave, to where Tan was seated, perched on the rock face just outside the entrance, 'I did not expect you back so early?'

Yan quickly broke into the details of what had happened.

Ghar was still mostly focused on planning the next trip to find Dun, when he heard his name mentioned in Yan's report.

'Ghar stopped us from attacking the intruders.'

Ghar spoke up in his own defence, 'If we had attacked them, we would have been killed. This looked like a whole tribe, not just hunters.'

Tan's eyes peered away in thought, 'So you failed to defend Khamma?'

Ghar realized he was already on the blameworthy side of this argument, 'No. I saw that they were not aggressive.'

'What are you saying? Can you read minds?' Yan was now shouting, his sharpness creating space between himself and the other youth.

'I could see from their behaviour,' Ghar contended.

Mai spoke up, 'We could have all been killed; we did not know for sure what they wanted, but they just walked away after Ghar gave him his moving fur.'

Yan looked at Mai with a contempt that Ghar had never seen before, 'You killed your mother, you lost Lu, and you won't give me progeny.' He stepped up to Mai menacingly, 'and now you won't defend Khamma.'

Killed her mother? Mai's mother died during childbirth. Ghar stepped in between them, cringing, knowing he was going to take a blow. He felt an arm drag him to the side from behind.

Mai slammed her spear into the ground, 'Don't you dare accuse me of not defending Khamma. I have spent my life learning the healing ways.'

Yan seemed surprised at Mai's vehemence, and shrank back to Tan, 'I tried my best, Tan.'

Tan's face had not changed at all, somehow in the din, his face had turned even more stoic, 'You should all have listened to Yan. I put him in charge.'

Yan turned back to the group with a pouted smirk, vindicating himself.

Tan continued, 'Yan and Nara, come talk to me in the cave. The rest of you leave.'

11

Gubba Zarda

Ghar felt the new buds of grass through his moccasins as he marched towards the Elders' caves. The familiar smell of pine burning in the fire pits was not what greeted him; instead, happy, sunlight-inspired Elders lay basking on the rocks mostly without their furs. 'What are they doing?' Ghar whispered to Mai.

'It feels good,' Mai glowed from behind Ghar. 'The sun is nice and warm, but the air is cool enough to make sure it isn't too hot. It's a good way to spend warm-time.'

'It reminds me of snakes sun-bathing on the rocks during a sunny day.'

'Yes, it does.'

Manar cautioned, 'Be careful; if they look like snakes, they may bite like snakes.'

'Agreed,' Ghar chuckled. 'I hope Tan is here.' He had asked Mai and Manar to help ask Tan for permission to go look for the Gubba.

'It looks like he is,' Mai lengthened her gait past Ghar.

Tan was perched on a different rock, but not in view of the camp. However, he had the usual look of closed-eyed contentment.

'Tan, we need your advice,' Ghar announced. He remembered Manar telling him it was easier to ask for knapped advice than approval.

'You can go into the forest, to search for your brethren, but only you, Nara and Uru.'

'But I wanted your advice,' Ghar got a sharp elbow in his back, 'although I think your proposal is fine.'

Tan continued, his eyes still closed, 'I want you to remember their position and if they get too close to the Khamma, I want you to come back immediately.'

'But I want to find Dun, my brother,' Ghar felt like Tan's instructions were closing him out of meeting with Dun, 'and I would want to talk to him.'

Tan opened his eyes, staring directly into Ghar's, 'This is not why you are going there. You are to find them and remember their position,' he closed his eyes to signify the end of the conversation.

* * *

The forest trail had gathered a thin coat of soft grass. Some of the less-used trails were being gobbled up by the forest, adding to her collection of secrets. Uru led the group, occasionally sniffing at the tufts of grass as if stalking some unknowing prey. They had started out at the top of the sun's path; Ghar had agreed to take a shorter, more difficult, route with the aim of making camp in the late evening.

Ghar felt the sharp bite in his calves as Nara increased his pace, the forest shadows growing long, 'We don't have to go this fast; my muscles will fall off my bones if we keep going like this.'

'We need to get there quickly, so we can return to warn Tan of any imminent attack.'

'Attack? Who is going to attack us?'

'Your Zardan friends.'

'Why would they attack us? Why would any tribe attack us?'

'I don't know, but this is a very important mission.'

'Listen, I know it is a very important mission,' Ghar knew the trail to Nara's confidence was a layer of assurance that the risks that Nara took on these quests were worth it.

Nara turned around; his neck participated little in the exercise. Then, without any discernible change in direction, his whole body spun to face Ghar, his head again seemed to float on his neck.

Ghar held back a gasp, the constraint in his chest forced the bones in his back to shudder.

Nara proudly accepted Ghar's approval with another double-jointed nod of his chin.

'How do you do that?' Ghar felt another involuntary flinch.

'Do what?' Nara was surprised at Ghar's question. 'Didn't you want to know why your friends would want to attack us?'

Ghar nodded his head, trying to mimic Nara's movements.

'What was that?' Nara rolled his head again.

'I was trying to show you how you move your head.'

'You Zarda are strange.'

Ghar found his eyes trying to figure out how Nara's knees were participating in walking backwards. *Surely they are not bending backwards?* Ghar shook himself out of his own imagination. 'All right, why would the Zarda attack us?'

'Because they want the wolves.' Ghar looked at Uru. It was an entirely valid proposition. The Zardan Hunters, despite their prowess, were returning to the camp empty handed. The way the wolves could be used to herd the buffalo into the ravine was something Ghar could have never imagined.

Nara turned away again, body part by body part, and upped the pace. He patted Uru's flank who ran on ahead.

Ghar's muscles soon felt like they were on fire, his body questioning each step. Nara had taken up a position, short of Uru, in the distance. Out in front, in solitude, seemed to be where he wanted to be. Almost free of the responsibilities that marshalled the tribespeople—this freedom was not an unintended consequence; Nara had built this role for himself, in which he could indulge in adventures and discoveries, and not have any burdens of Khamman life weighing him down. For a moment, Ghar felt a twinge of envy; he could focus on painting, or sculpting, or on thinking about the curiosities around him, instead of improving moving furs or learning the properties of new herbs or cleaning hides.

'Didn't we take the path down through that field last time?' Ghar called out to Nara who had started to ascend what seemed like a vertical ravine face.

'Not so loud,' Nara hissed, turning around, his limbs remaining in confusing directions. He whistled to recall Uru. He turned back to Ghar, 'Let's go up into the mountains and see if we can get a vantage point.'

Ghar could almost hear his legs cry out in agony, 'Why not just make a path through the thicket?'

'That would take too long, and besides it will get dark soon. Some creature of the forest will make a warm meal out of us.'

'Up the mountain sounds better,' Ghar followed Nara up the slope, step by step, on small outcrops and protruding tree roots. 'I need to stop for a bit,' Ghar felt like there wasn't enough air to breathe.

Nara climbed back down with Uru, 'Fine, there is only a little more to the ridge above, from where we should be able to see the tall yellow grass. You come join me up there, I will wait for you.'

Uru started to growl at a spinney of trees further down on the same mountain slope, his shoulders clenched, hackles rising, spearing him from head to tail. Nara grabbed at Uru's collar, intercepting the attack.

Ghar watched the trees, through his wind-watered eyes. Uru sensed something was out there, and the wolves were never wrong. *There must be something,* or 'Somebody?'

'What do you mean "somebody"?' Nara asked

Ghar did not want to scare Nara by suggesting that they were being watched. He did not want to turn back on Dun again, 'Some animal, I meant.'

Uru continued to growl, interspersed with melancholy whimpers of excitement. He urged Nara to investigate, pawing at the dirt that separated the group and the trees.

'You rest here,' said Nara cautiously, the browns of his eyes still investigating the mysterious woods that held Uru's fascination.

'Do you think there is something out there?'

'No, you will be fine.'

Ghar thought for a moment, *why wouldn't I be fine?* But he was tired, and Nara would only be up the slope, so Ghar could surely run to Uru's protection if needed. He recounted to himself how tired he was, not just in his muscles, but his head felt exhausted, running back and forth between Dun and Mai, to his struggle with Yan, to Tan's abstruse intentions. He took a deep breath to let go of all the pain and then sat down on a rock that barely peeked out of the ground. He looked back to see Nara already hopping up the mountain side. Ghar focused on getting his breath back to a less discordant rhythm, something like the Zardan songs; there was always a calming, strengthening effect in the recital of the songs.

By the lake of knees depth,
His spirit is given to the forest,
Watched over by the Fathers,
The journey he must take,
To the Fathers,
Who will renew them as Hunters.

He stopped to think, in a way he owed the water powder for the new, albeit sceptical, trust that the Khamma had in him.

Who will renew them as Hunters? Dun would just mumble that last part, Ghar recalled, as he tried to identify anything out of place, before continuing. They were climbing the mountain under the cover of a narrow stretch of trees. To his right, the slope steepened and hid behind a ridge. To his left, a wide field of rocky grass spread out to touch the next barrier of trees. He glanced up and down the thicket edge, there was still this feeling, an uncomfortable thought, like the shadows of the late evening sun were playing a trick on him, that there was movement between the grey-brown tree trunks.

The forest had given up a secret, a fur-draped figure appeared in front of the trees at the end of the grass field, in a familiar posture with an exploratory knee perched upon a rock, a stance that owned the territory. Ghar, for a moment, could not move, trepidation overtook his body, but as his eyes slowly peeled away the identity of the stranger, his fear gave way to a sobbing realization, *Dun*. He tried to say it, but his mouth could only release unformed air.

'Dun!' Ghar screamed finally, after an everlasting moment, the sound clawing at the insides of his throat; the forest and sky bowed converging a path to his lost friend, aiding his moccasins through the grass.

'Ghar!' Dun's call felt like the Zarda was calling him back, welcoming him back into their ranks. Ghar fell into Dun's arms, a long unending tumble, as if he had started to fall the moment Dun was taken away from him. It was only Dun who could catch him. Through his tear-flooded eyes he was surprised to see Dun crying too.

'What are you doing out here?' Dun asked both crying and laughing.

'Das expelled me from the tribe,' Ghar tried to think of a starting to the story. 'It doesn't really matter; I have found you.'

'That slimy toad marked you,' Dun examined the scorch scar on Ghar's hand.

Ghar could not stop looking at Dun's eyes, 'This is not true? You are not true?'

'What are you talking about?' Dun athletically let them both down into the soft comfort of the grass. 'These arms are as true as you will ever need them to be,' he flexed.

'Only the forest is here to be impressed with your arms.'

Dun hopped up to his feet, turned back towards the forest and nodded, 'Well the forest and your friend,' Dun looked up towards the top of the mountain. 'And what about the wolf? Are you friends with wolves now?'

Ghar smiled, it was so easy to reminisce on his hardship in Khamma now, adapting to the new tribe, overcoming the fear of the gnarly fanged wolves. But worst was the feeling that he was all alone. 'How is Gharra? And Ra?' Ghar couldn't believe he had not thought about his birth mother until now.

'They are well. Listen, let's call your friend and his wolf and go back to camp. It's too dangerous to be out here in the night.'

'Nara,' Ghar stood up and called out, 'Nara come down; this is Dun.'

Ghar turned back to a further collection of familiar Gubba. Their furs seemed even more tattered than they were in Zarda. Their high cheekbones and strong brows flew him over the forest and valleys back into the Grand Cave. His fingers rehearsed the silhouette of the portraits, taking joy in the undulating forms of their faces, in discovering some hidden meaning that he had lost.

Ghar was suddenly ambushed by embraces, from the other Gubba. 'I really can't believe that any of this is real,' he repeated to Dun and the rest of the Gubba.

He continued to embrace each of the other tribesmen, whispering prayers. Nara's head tentatively led the rest of his body into sight, with Uru, almost unable to contain the mix of aggression in his gnarly teeth and the apprehension in his soft whimpers, with his tail between his legs.

The Gubba took a step back at the approach of Uru. Ghar walked towards Nara, to introduce him to the rest of the tribe, and to grab hold of Uru's collar, to show the rest of the tribe there was nothing to be afraid of.

Uru's leash eased under Ghar's soothing words. He knelt in the grass, losing his body in Uru's thick, soft mane. Uru's heavy breathing would only let up, for the beginnings of a menacing grin. Ghar beckoned the tribesmen again, Dun being the only Gubba to walk over. 'Dun, this is Nara,' he gestured towards Nara with his elbow as he tried to keep Uru in a calming wrap.

'Nara, by the Fathers,' Dun took a path around Uru to embrace Nara, whose face arched like a bird that was about to take flight.

Ghar chuckled at the introduction. Nara was not as close to him as Dun was, but he felt there was this common trait that they all shared, they were not really accepted in their tribes. 'He doesn't understand Zardan, Dun,' he looked over to the rest of the Zardan hunters to see that their eyes were more filled by the wolf.

Dun raised his hand in acknowledgement, and then called out to the entire group, 'Night is coming soon, let's get back to camp.'

Be sure his tracks will be different, Dun started to sing.

But his path will always lead back to Zarda, Ghar joined in with the refrain. He looked at Dun, his eyes tearing, pausing to catch his breath.

Always back to Zarda.

* * *

'I know where they are taking us,' Nara whispered to Ghar, Uru still excited, firmly between them as they trekked with the Gubba.

'You don't have to whisper, these are friends to us, we can trust them,' Ghar reassured him, 'and they can't understand you.'

'All right,' Nara continued to whisper, 'they are taking us to a cliff, full of caves.' He turned his head just enough to keep sight of all the Gubba. 'The caves are not so accessible but have a good vantage from a height; I am pretty sure some of those caves are inhabited by bears.'

'Well, you live with wolves, maybe they live with bears.'

'This is no occasion for jokes, we could get eaten.'

'Listen, this is my old tribe, there is no way they would live with bears,' Ghar stopped to console Nara, but found his companion's face in much want of good news, 'let me ask Dun.'

'Dun,' Ghar called out, 'do you live with bears?'

'Not anymore; funny story, actually.'

Ghar walked over and grabbed Dun by the arm, Uru jumped with the momentary ease on his collar. 'Please tell me there are no bears in your caves.'

'How do you know about the caves?'

'The caves in the cliff?'

'How do you know about the caves in the cliff?' Dun's voice dripped with concern.

'I don't know; Nara told me.'

Dun grabbed Ghar's arm now, 'How does he know about the caves?'

'He's our scout.'

'He watches your enemies?'

Ghar glanced out at Nara, who in turn was carefully studying his surroundings. There was the nervousness of a deer on his face, like he was looking for ways to make a hasty escape. 'I think he watches everything.'

'So, is that why you are out here, to watch us?'

The abruptness of the question halted Ghar's direction of thought. 'Of course not,' his eyes scanned the rocky outcrops resting patiently among the tall pines, for an answer to Dun's query. 'Mostly not. Nara told us of a tribe out here, fair skins, with Zardan symbols. I immediately thought it was you and the Gubba. I wanted to find you, but yes, Nara is here to see what you are doing.'

'But then if we show you our camp, aren't we in danger?'

Ghar thought for a moment. He could not really answer that truthfully, because he still did not understand Tan's intentions, 'Honestly, I do not know. But I know the Khamma, and they have adopted me as their own. And anyway, even if you did not take us to the camp, eventually the tribes will meet. I think it is better for us to meet like this, and get to know each other, present ourselves as friendly.' Ghar called out to Nara, 'Come here and talk to Dun.'

Nara sceptically walked over, dragging Uru by the collar, who by now had become more accustomed to the Zarda, offering up a friendly tongue or a long sniff. The tribesmen however still stumbled, trying to maintain more than a bite's distance away.

'So, you were right; we are going to a cliff with caves.'

'I know that,' Nara shrugged nonchalantly.

'And Dun says he is not to be feared at all.'

Nara took another turn inspecting the tribesman, 'That sounds good.'

Dun interrupted, in a more sombre tone, 'Listen, Ghar, since we are divulging truths,' Dun kept the browns of his eyes out of contact with Ghar.

'Yes, what do you want to tell me?'

'The truth, and I could not tell you, because I do not know this truth myself,' Dun revealed.

Ghar could suddenly sense his companion's secret. He knew it when he first saw Dun alone in front of the forest. 'Where did you bury her?' The tears started to fill his eyes.

'We use a cave for those who passed.'

'We must go there before anything else, please.'

'What's wrong?' Nara asked politely in Khamman. 'Why are you crying?'

Ghar answered in Zardan, 'I have just learned that my birth mother is dead.' He looked at Nara's uncomprehending demeanour. He repeated it in Khamman.

'I am sorry, my brother.' Ghar had never heard a dejected quality in Nara's voice before. It was a sincerity that broke through his lofty notions of himself, 'We will go and see her grave.'

* * *

The group was greeted by a mix of celebration at the presence of Ghar and fear at their sight of Uru.

'This is Gubba Zarda,' Dun introduced the new camp.

'We are still Zardan,' Ghar liked the name. *They can't stop us from being Zardan, not Das, not any other Elder.*

'Is that a wolf? By the Fathers, who brings a wolf into the camp?'

Ghar heard different versions of the same refrain and was surprised at the lack of reaction to Nara. But he could not stop to address them. All he could think of was that Gharra was gone.

'Listen, Dun, I have been dreaming about them, about Gharra, so much since I was expelled.'

'I do too,' Dun neatened his furs and pulled his hair tighter into a knot, before gesturing to Ghar to do the same. The warm-time days seemed to keep the sun in the sky longer than usual, giving tribespeople time for singing and storytelling. This was how Ghar wanted to remember the Zarda, these moments when the tribespeople were excused from their daily tasks, life would become about each other.

The cave opening was marked with Zardan symbols, which surprised Ghar, as he knew no Gubba who was versed in the symbols. There were even the beginnings of a painting on the outer walls although the colours had run due to rain. There was a slight pungent smell, of decay, *am I imagining the smell of rotting bodies?*

'Gharra was buried there,' Dun pointed to a mound in the cave, it was barely discernible, but it seemed quiet, and undisturbed.

'I do not know who is buried in there, Dun.' Ghar felt like he wanted to cry, but there was a hope in him that stopped him from grieving. 'I deny this, I deny Gharra is in there,' he turned around and walked away towards a stream that supported the camp. He did not feel thirsty, he needed to drink to fill the growing emptiness in him.

Dun followed Ghar to the stream.

Some children had gathered around Uru, they seemed to be the bravest of the tribe, even Dun had not ventured so close. He looked back at Dun, 'How can you all be so happy, with Gharra gone?'

Dun's whole face seemed to slink towards the ground, 'You are right, Ghar,' he whimpered. 'Everyday it hurts less, and sometimes it hurts more.' He put his hand on Ghar's shoulder.

'I don't accept it,' Ghar offered an answer without a real question. 'None of the tribe's members should accept it.' His mind frantically searched around Adura's advice to ask the right questions, but all he wanted to do was deny that this was happening. He put his face in his hands. It slowly became clear that he could not find a question because he did not want an answer. He only wanted Gharra, which was a situation no thought could reverse. He could hear Dun's voice attempt consolation, but the words did not give rise to any meaning. The only place he could see Gharra was in his sleep, 'Dun, I need to sleep.'

Dun, who was still halfway through a sentence, gave him a look of alarm, 'Yes, brother, you sleep. I will go make sure your Khamman brother is all right.' They walked towards the campfire where Nara and Uru seemed to be enjoying the children's attention.

Ghar did not even spread a fur on the ground. He just lay down and closed his eyes, while the sounds of the camp and the forest slowly receded into the night.

* * *

Dun's voice called out of the fog in Ghar's mind, 'Ghar, are you awake?' He could feel Dun's hands on his shoulders. 'Ghar, are you awake?'

Ghar groaned out a response, 'Yes I am. I need some water.' He got up, pulling off a fur that had been placed on him, standing up awkwardly, his limbs not up to the task, he brushed past Dun. He hobbled down to the stream, where he scooped some water on to his face, he drank part of it and part, he pushed into his bristled skin, relieving some of the weight on his mind.

Dun opened up a small, folded skin, to reveal an assortment of dried meat. The smoky aroma filled Ghar's mouth with a trembled longing. He walked over and sank down beside Dun. He was hungry, especially since he had not eaten anything the previous day.

'I usually save the nicest strips for when I am really down,' Dun smiled at Ghar, 'Take what you want.'

Ghar took the fattiest strip he could find. He bit in, the harder, smoky crust gave way to a soft, fatty centre, 'By the Fathers, this is the best meat I have ever tasted!'

'It's mountain goat; amazing story how we caught it. We were up on a ledge trying to get a view of the terrain. Gharra looked down, this goat appeared from under the rock. She looked at the goat and the goat looked at her. She speared the goat right in the hip and it fell down into the ravine.' He ran his fingers on some charred marks on his spear, 'After finding the dead creature, we roasted part of him on the mountain.'

Ghar reflected that the piece of meat in his fingers was a part of what Gharra had left for them. He saved the meat in his own collection of dried meat that he retrieved from his pouch. 'You won't believe how they catch buffalo in the Khamma camp.'

Dun propped forward in curiosity, 'What do they do? Do they use that wolf that Nara has?'

Ghar felt happy to surprise Dun, 'They have a pack of wolves, and even a giant wolf.'

'What? By the Fathers!'

'And the beasts don't just catch an animal, the Khamma use the wolves to scare all the buffalo off a cliff. So much meat . . . so much meat we cannot even take it home,' Ghar had never said it aloud, but that did sound wasteful, *why not try to kill only the animals they needed?*

'But if you have so much why is Nara so thin?'

'He spends long periods away from camp, watching for dangers to the Khamma. I think usually he does not eat for days,' Ghar ended more unsure than he had started, 'but I think also that he is not comfortable in a camp. Like right now, all the children around him; I have never seen that in Khamma.'

'All right.'

'He looks happy for now; I think we can leave him like that.'

Dun hesitantly brought up Gharra again, 'You need to visit Gharra, brother.'

'I know,' Ghar had decided sometime in the night that he had to make peace with the idea that he could not make peace with what happened to Gharra. Not accepting her death did not mean that he would have to stop living as well.

* * *

Ghar and Dun walked over to Nara, 'How are you, my brother?'
Nara, sat cross-legged on the ground, filling in the few Zardan words
he knew with gestures and sounds, playing with the enthralled Gubba
children and Uru. The group kept close to the remaining warmth of
a smouldering fire.

Nara beamed, 'I am good; these little Gubba really love Uru, they
might steal him,' a busy sound of giggles accompanied the group.

'That's funny, Nara. They actually might,' Ghar laughed. 'I am
going to visit my mother's grave, would it be all right to leave you
here?'

'Yes, of course. When you are done, we need to talk about when
we are going back to Khamma.'

'Yes, brother.'

Ghar motioned to Dun who was trying to get closer to Uru,
'Let's go, Dun, we can play with Uru when the younglings are done.'

Dun trailed close with a slight look of embarrassment, 'I can't
believe that wolf doesn't want to make a meal of us.'

'He would, if we wanted him to,' Ghar could not help letting go
of a joke even in the circumstances. The laughter they shared slowed
down to happy eyes, as they approached the burial cave. Ghar looked
at his companion and realized there was so much of Gharra right there.
Maybe his instinct to deny Gharra's passing was because it was not true.
She had not gone anywhere; she was right there with her sons.

They entered the cave, and Ghar knelt close to Gharra and Ra's
grave.

'How did she pass, Dun?' It was a question that had been on
Ghar's mind, but it felt like an inappropriate inquiry. Although it
still felt wrong, he needed to know.

'The clouds started to fall on us,' Dun stopped and looked up at
the sky. 'It was terrible, the force, the cold, the sound.'

Ghar quickly interrupted, 'Water powder?'

'What's that?'

Ghar was speaking in Khamman, he switched to Zardan, 'What
I meant was *water powder.*'

'Yes! It did turn into water,' Dun's eyes grew unusually large. 'The only way we escaped it was by hiding in the caves. The tepees were blown over.'

Ghar remembered that night, he was with Mai, stuck in their own cave, 'I escaped like that too; Mai and I found a cave.'

'Who is Mai?'

'Another really long story,' Ghar said with a long breath, 'but if you escaped, then how come Gharra did not get to the caves?'

'We found them downstream in the cloud water powder. I think they did the right thing by looking for the stream,' Dun suddenly stopped, as if he had lost something, and had only now realized it was lost. 'They were all together, Gharra, Ra, Sar, Mul, and Tun. Just all huddled together,' Dun wiped the tears from his cheeks, but they kept getting replaced by new sorrow.

Ghar wrapped Dun in his arms, 'Whatever happens, whether we live, or we die, we do it together.'

* * *

Ghar and Dun sat beside Nara and Uru who still had a following of adoring younglings. The sun had moved to its hottest point in the sky, which surprised Ghar because he felt like he had been at Gharra's grave a lot longer.

'We should leave at least by midday tomorrow,' Nara placed a hand on Ghar's shoulder.

Ghar turned from Nara to Dun, 'Nara is saying we should leave tomorrow.'

'What? You have only been here for such a short time,' Dun shuffled around the burning brands. 'You must stay here for a while. We can go hunting.'

Ghar thought about the Khamma, especially Tan, 'Tan allowed us to come out here so that we could keep track of the new tribes. If they were to send out a search party for us, they would be a lot more aggressive. It's better that we return to camp and tell them there is nothing to fear.'

'Let them be aggressive, we have seen worse.'

Ghar looked at him incredulously, 'The Gubba are not warriors. And besides they have wolves. You cannot even get yourself to approach Uru.'

'I will get my courage soon.'

Ghar could hear in Dun's voice that this argument was more about Ghar leaving, than about martial prowess, 'Why don't you come with us?'

Dun turned his face then his whole body, questioning Ghar's question.

'We can show the Khamma that you are not to be feared.' There was a feeling that Yan being the angry bear he usually was, might end up fighting Dun. He smiled, imagining the beating that Dun would impart on Yan.

'What are you smiling at?'

'Nothing, but you will come with us,' Ghar turned to Nara, 'Dun is coming with us!'

'What?' Nara asked, his eyebrows snapped together.

'It would be good for Dun to come, to talk to Tan, to show the Khamma that the Gubba are not of harm.'

'I don't think that's a good idea,' Nara advised, his chin moved into the tips of his fingers.

A youngling who had been idling around in the sun, crawled over and leaned on Nara. Nara looked over at Ghar, with eyes mellowed and fulfilled cheeks. He looked down again at the infant. 'All right, maybe Dun should come. I think we should tell Tan the Gubba are not a danger to us.'

12

New Beginnings

Ghar could imagine the excitement Dun would feel as they waded through the shin-deep brook that guarded the entrance to the Khamman camp. Dun marvelled at the tall rock faces that looked over the travellers, hiding the possibilities of what could be on the other side. A lazy Khamman sky made a final push of sunlight for the day.

The green of the giants on the far bank broke through the opening and Ghar looked over at Dun, 'We are in Khamma, my brother.'

A front of wolves were their greeters, tongues lolling and limbs splashing. Ghar felt Dun take a step back. 'It is all right. Let them get near you; when they know that you are no threat they will be fine.' A growl accompanied his advice. 'All right, Usa is a growler; he may look angry but he's really friendly inside, especially if you do this.' Ghar went around the white, frenzied teeth and scratched the beast behind the ears, causing Usa's grin to temper down into close-eyed relief. 'You like a good scratch, don't you?'

Dun extended his fingers, only for Usa to return to a growl.

'Don't worry, we can try again later. The other wolves are friendlier.'

Nara started to head in the direction of Tan's cave, 'We should go see Tan before any other,' he talked while walking, craning effortlessly to address Dun. 'Follow what I do, be respectful and we will tell Tan that you are not a threat.' Nara talked in Khamman forgetting that Dun did not know any.

Ghar interrupted him, speaking in Zardan, 'Listen, you do not have to talk, just be quiet and respectful.' He nodded at Nara who proceeded to Tan's cave.

'Tan is the leader?' Dun asked.

Ghar had never thought about that. 'He is the most respected Elder; the Elders decide on issues.'

'But what if they disagree?'

Ghar looked around at the Khamman camp, tribespeople sitting around mostly not doing anything, 'I guess when you have so much meat people don't have to decide anything.'

'Do you think we wouldn't have been expelled from Zarda if we'd had enough food?'

'That's a good question,' Ghar closed his eyes, he could hear Nara calling to them from Tan's cave above. He smiled at Dun with a glance towards Nara, 'Let's go before we get expelled from this camp.'

A laugh escaped Dun's quick clasp over his mouth.

'I think when the tribe is happy, tough decisions don't have to be made, so let's keep the tribe happy.'

* * *

'So . . . this is a Gubba,' Tan came down from his perch, and stood an arm's length away from Dun, who had a visible nervousness in his hands. Tan touched Dun on the cheek, a deep probe as if to find the true nature of his colour. Tan returned his finger to his own cheek for comparison. A smile broke out on his face, like a sudden curiosity was opened and instantly satisfied. He made another uncharacteristic sigh, seemingly of relief, 'You say these Gubba people are not a danger to us,' he turned to Nara.

'Yes, they are not a big tribe, and they don't seem like they can fight. I don't think they can hunt very well either,' Nara said.

It's good Dun does not understand this, Ghar thought as he tried to gauge Tan's face. Emotions almost did not suit the long ridges that resembled the Khamman caves. Tan's demeanour seemed better suited to his customary deadpan expression. It was as if Tan, like the rock face, had weathered every storm possible—*new tribes or water powder is not going to change this Elder.*

'All right, I accept your judgement. How about the bigger tribe you found, did you encounter them again?'

'No, Elder, we were interrupted when we met the Gubba.'

'Then you must go out again.'

Ghar voiced out, 'I will go with him, Dun can help.'

'No, I want you to stay here. And help create more moving furs.'

Since when did Tan care about moving furs? Ghar thought; part of him felt pride that Tan was aware of his achievements, but part of him was alert, suspicious of Tan's motives. 'Right now, Ulan is making the furs.'

'Look out there,' Tan climbed his rock to his seat of vantage, 'Ulan is not there, neither is Tur, this has been the status since you left,' He aimed his stony demeanour at Ghar, 'I want the Khamma to have moving fur, I want us to be ready for the next water powder storm.'

Ghar's mind proffered a tiny seed of a thought, barely able, like an infant, but it held promise: *what if I train the Gubba? The Khamma don't want to do this.* He looked over at Dun, who looked hungry, especially since there was a crisp joy of smoky fat lingering in the air, calling those hungry tribesmen. *The Khamma can give the Gubba the remaining meat from the hunts.* He looked over at the resolute hollowed cheeks on Tan's face and decided to come back later to discuss his plan. 'Yes, Hera.'

'Then go, I can see that the meats have caught the attention of your Gubba brother.'

Ghar looked at Dun and held in a laugh. The solemnness on Dun's face did not match Tan's joke.

'What?'

'Nothing, my brother,' there was a real happiness with Dun around, something he only nearly felt with Mai. 'You must meet Mai.' He bowed to Tan and accidentally to Nara, and then grabbed Dun by the hand and made his way down the rock slope taking care not to pull Dun into a fall especially with the waning light.

'Can we eat first?'

Ghar looked over, maybe Mai was hidden in the crowd. Along with Dun he walked over to a campfire where a long, thin stick threaded with slabs of meat was being passed around, which Ghar intercepted. He sheared off a piece and handed it to Dun.

Dun looked like he could not believe what he had in his hands, 'By the Fathers, this is a portion enough for a whole family!'

'Buffaloes, they eat like buffaloes,' Ghar smiled both at his own joke and also at being able to share a secret joke.

* * *

Ghar caught a glimpse of Mai with Manar, standing just beyond the firelight's reach. He grabbed Dun by the hand and walked quickly towards them. As he got closer, he noticed that Mai did not look happy. He could see her lips wobble while she bravely strived for composure to present a more welcoming face to Ghar.

'This is Dun, from Zarda, my brother, whom I have told you about.'

'Dun,' she said, 'welcome to Khamma,' she greeted in Khamman. Her voice quavered slightly from the remnants of hurt.

Ghar instinctively walked over and embraced her, 'What happened?' he looked over at Manar, who paced in place, arms akimbo, her brow uncharacteristically furrowed with a scowl.

'Yan again, tormenting her about the baby . . . again.'

Mai spoke out from Ghar's shoulder, 'I'm all right. I want to meet Dun.'

Ghar heard the hurt pride in her voice; she did not want to be in this forlorn position in front of other people. He thought it was better to start over with Dun's introduction. 'This is Dun,' he turned around to a clearly lost Dun, whose spear had accidentally leaned towards Mai. Ghar pushed the tip back up. He repeated in Zardan, 'This is Dun.'

Dun nodded a greeting.

'Dun, pretend you are hungry and motion you want to go and eat.'

'But I am hungry.'

Ghar felt his head hurt at Dun's unawareness. He mouthed a 'just do it' and gestured towards the campfires with his eyes. He turned back to Mai, making sure with his peripheral vision that Dun had left.

'You didn't have to send him away,' Mai turned to a spot between Ghar and Manar.

Uncharacteristically, Manar became visibly angry—her eyebrows turned alive, while the campfire flickered in her eyes lending them a dangerous sparkle, 'That blundering buffalo accused Mai of deliberately not giving him a child. He thinks that instead of becoming a mother, Mai would rather focus on being a Healer.'

'That's crazy,' Ghar was not entirely sure why Yan's accusation was not believable, but Manar's intensity prompted an endorsement. 'Are you all right?' he turned his attention to Mai.

'I don't know . . . I feel like I've become numb to these small wounds that he inflicts on me,' her hands cascaded towards the sky, 'but those small wounds become a large wound. A wound that even attaching cannot help.'

Ghar understood that analogy, he remembered something Adura used to tell him, *a few raindrops will leave you wet, but a storm can anger the Narun*: 'So what do we do? Should we ask a tribesperson like Tan to intervene?'

Mai and Manar broke out laughing, a sound that still held sadness.

'Wouldn't he talk to Yan? Reason with him?'

'He would probably feed Mai to the bears?' Manar concluded with even more raucous laughter. Ghar retreated; he realized the situation did not actually need a solution, but more a chance for Mai to discuss what she was going through. He had been here before. 'Let's paint?' Ghar could feel colour come through the pain he was feeling, like the upsetting blues of yearning for the sky while underwater, or the happy greens that greeted the tribes during warm-time.

Mai looked at Manar.

Manar turned to Ghar, her wise eyes sat atop her cheekbones, ceding Mai's emotions to him, to take care of her, 'Go with him, maybe looking at something different will help keep the pain small, but your ambition tall.'

'Oh Manar, your poetry truly is abysmal,' Mai, even with a scarred voice, was strong enough to deliver the truth.

'Why don't you come with us as well?' Ghar asked Manar.

'I am hungry; maybe I'll join in later.'

'We can take some meat with us,' Ghar could tell Mai was about to say she was hungry too.

'Yes,' she suddenly smiled, 'I like painting, even though I'm not good at it.'

Ghar scanned the campfire to see where Dun was and found him gesturing his way through a wordless conversation with a Khamman tribeswoman. He remembered Dun had always seemed to enjoy whatever he was doing, which prompted a saying that Adura would tell him when he started to paint: 'Enjoying something is the path to getting good at it. That's what Adura used to tell me.'

'Well then I enjoy being a healer,' Mai said on a deep breath of resolve.

Ghar met her eyes, with his acknowledgement of the impediments to her resolve, 'Then you will be a great healer.'

* * *

The flavours of the meat clouded up in the dim, fire-lit air as Ghar, Mai, Manar and Dun, the feast's remaining contenders, took turns breaking through the hot slabs that they had laid out on a bare hide.

After joining Dun and the other tribespeople at the campfire, they had eaten their fill—Ghar, Mai and Manar to quell their emotions, and Dun to bury memories of every time he had ever gone hungry.

'By the Fathers, if I eat any more of this, I might start to look like a buffalo,' Dun faced the sky, breathing in not just the aroma of the grilling meat, but the security of the camp, and the plenitude of food as well.

'That's such an interesting thought. Becoming a buffalo by eating them,' Ghar raised his eyebrows at Mai, 'maybe we could become wolves by eating them.'

Mai yelped in sympathy for the wolves but soon saw the humour, 'I can already howl like wolf,' Mai continued in a subdued rendition of a smooth, but ear-piercing, wail that set off some of the wolves in the camp as well but was quickly shushed by the tribespeople who were trying to sleep.

'The wolves have spoken,' Manar said. 'I left Mu with his meal, he should be finished by now. Come to the Healing Cave if you want to talk more.' Mai bowed while seated. Manar turned to Dun, 'Nice to finally meet Ghar's brother.'

Ghar interpreted, 'Manar says, it's good to meet you.' Dun smiled and waved as much as his full belly would let him.

As Manar proceeded to the Healing Cave, Ghar got up and walked over to the lake to wash his hands. He then walked over to the crevice where he hid his belongings and brought back his painting tools and colours.

'Let's paint,' he mixed powders in water and fat, checking the consistency, and then ground the pigment with more fat.

'Can I do my own?' Mai asked.

Ghar remembered his lessons with Adura, where he would help fill in the shapes that she would draw out, 'This is the best way to learn.'

'All right,' Mai said, but with obvious disappointment.

Ghar shrugged, 'Here, take this hide,' he pulled out a smaller piece, 'I'll move so you can sit closer to the fire.'

Meanwhile Dun had crouched lower and lower still, until he was reclining on his side, 'I think you can go ahead and paint, I am going to enjoy my sleep.' He adjusted his head to be closer to the fire, but just far enough to avoid the crackling embers.

Mai immediately started to paint, mostly with her fingers. Ghar could not make out what she was painting, but he did become acutely aware that she was using up a lot of his favourite red, which was a colour that was very difficult extract from the petals of flowers. But she was clearly enjoying herself, 'Mai?'

She emitted a quiet murmur for a response, her attention mostly on her painting.

'Are you all right? Do you need any help?'

Mai murmured again. Ghar chuckled, it was interesting to disturb her when she was concentrating on something. He focused on his own painting, a depiction of the Sanaa, expelled from Zarda, but finding Zarda again through the Gubba. He thought a river could be the appropriate symbol to connect all of them together. 'A river flowing into itself, and then into itself, and on and on.' He turned to Mai and Dun, expecting a reply, but they were both asleep. He looked at Dun again. Now that they were back together, maybe Ghar would find Zarda again someday.

* * *

Ghar and Dun had spent the day meeting the other tribespeople, exploring the caves, eating the leftovers, and bathing in the lake. They lay bare on the bare rock taking in the cool evening sun.

'I have to talk to Tan about something, but I have to do it alone,' Ghar told Dun. Gubba Zarda's predicament was not born from being expelled, but had started even before that; when the Gubba were prevented from becoming hunters and barred from the knowledge that the Zardan Sanaa men were taught.

But maybe the Gubba did not need to hunt. He had been thinking about the wasted meat that lay rotting in the ravines around

Khamma. Teach the Gubba to make moving furs for the Khamman tribe and in exchange, take the superfluous meat from the hunts.

Dun seemed largely distracted with the new sharp smells of cooking meat. He looked over at Ghar, 'Should we swap places? You go to Gubba Zarda.'

'So, you did not hear me—I want to meet Tan.'

'You go, just find me there later?' he pointed to an assortment of roasting buffalo. Dun got up hastily, putting his furs back on.

'I did mean alone,' Ghar's words drifted behind Dun as he walked quickly towards the roasting spits.

His thoughts accompanied his footsteps all the way to Tan's cave. 'Tan, Holder of Wisdom,' Ghar used praise to prepare Tan for his request.

Tan was on his rocky perch, observing the tribe as usual. 'Yes, Zardan who attaches men,' Tan replied, a hue of amusement in his voice, 'how is your Zardan brother taking to our camp? I see he is quite occupied with filling his belly,' Tan stretched out a long finger towards the fires by the lake.

'He is happy that we are together,' Ghar said, 'I am happy that we are together.'

Tan gazed at Ghar, a long, slow contemplation that to Ghar seemed more like a question than a look. He then turned his attention back to the camp. Tan's long jaw seemed relaxed, almost not interested in maintaining his face's shape.

'Tan, I have something to ask you,' Ghar found his attempts to build up a conversation like wading through sluggish water; it seemed better to just ask what he wanted to.

'Say what you think,' Tan still faced out into the camp.

'I agree that all the Khamman people should have a moving fur,' although Ghar wholeheartedly believed in what he was saying, it still felt a bit insincere, considering that he was only saying it to support his request.

Tan turned his ear slightly towards Ghar, revealing a tinge of interest, but staying fixated on the camp.

'Why do you look out on the camp?' Ghar indulged his curiosity for a moment.

A trace of a smile crept up on Tan's cheeks. 'Because I enjoy it,' Tan turned to Ghar, his face returning to its long, well-traversed state, 'although I think that answer would not be enough for you.'

Ghar felt like he had made a mistake in asking Tan.

'I think that's a good virtue to have,' Tan reassured Ghar, 'to look for what's not plain to the eye.'

Ghar's muscles unclenched.

'So, you said you had something you wanted to ask.'

'Yes, Tan. Well, as I said before, I agree that all the Khamman tribespeople need moving fur. We don't know when the next water powder storm will strike, but I think it's best to be prepared.'

Tan turned, showing some interest, 'Will you make the moving furs? I have not seen any progress from Tur or Ulan.'

'I have a plan,' Ghar softened his voice giving Tan the space to command the discussion. 'Have you ever noticed the amount of meat that we cannot consume after a kill.'

A look of disappointment crossed Tan's face and he turned back to the camp with a sigh, 'Yes.'

It was not the reaction Ghar really wanted, but he had to try, 'We could give the Gubba this meat.'

'And why would we do that?' there was now a rough annoyance building in Tan's words. Again, it was not the reaction Ghar wanted, but he did want Tan to feel like he was controlling the discussion.

'I can train the Gubba to make moving furs, for Khamma, and in exchange we give them the extra meat.'

Tan sighed, he did not look entirely happy to think about it, but his furrowed eyebrows indicated that he was thinking about it. 'I want the Gubba to also harvest the meat for Khamma.'

Ghar thought that was a lot of work, that was a lot of meat, but it was something he could convince the Gubba to do. He bowed in deference, and stepped back, 'I will get it done, Tan.'

'Do not tell the tribe about this; I will announce it to them later.'

Ghar nodded; it had not occurred to him that this decision would be significant enough to merit an announcement. He walked back into the evening air; the warm smell of sizzling meat accompanied the green giants who took refuge in the coming night sky.

Dun was seated at a fire with Mai and some of the other Khamma, biting and munching through the fresh roast, exchanging the events of the day. 'Is the meat good?' Ghar sat down beside Dun.

'Is it ever not good?' Dun slobbered out a response, the juicy fibres still too hot to hold, let alone, eat, but he greedily moved it between his fingers, hastily blowing on it before tearing bite-sized shreds with his teeth. His eyes gleefully watered while chomping down, the heat escaping his mouth with every bite. 'This is so good, Ghar, I think this is too good for any tribesman, I think it could kill you.'

'Too good to kill you?' Ghar smiled.

'By the Fathers, let them protect us,' Dun prayed.

'I talked to Tan,' Ghar was happy about the way his discussion with Tan had panned out. 'He agrees with my proposal to share the meat with the Gubba.' Dun mumbled something incoherent through the meat. 'You might want to swallow first,' Ghar advised and then continued, 'and in exchange, the Gubba will help make moving furs for the Khamma.'

Dun put his hand up, 'You mean we will help hunt for the buffalo?' He finished the remaining piece in his hand.

'No. I mean you will make moving furs, and in exchange you can take the extra meat, which is a lot.'

'This sounds like Zarda, the Sanaa hunt, while the Gubba clean the hides, or bring firewood.'

Ghar interrupted, 'But Dun, you need food, and right now the Gubba can't hunt because you are not trained in the ways of the hunter.'

'And whose fault is that?' Dun's face had lost some of the meat-inspired vigour, his fingers played, not with the hot meat, but with the hurtful proposal.

Ghar understood Dun's view of the arrangement, but still thought it was eminently better than hunger. 'What if you did this for some time, gain some strength and health, and then we relook at this solution again?'

'I don't want to take this to our Elders; it will be like going back to Zarda, but only the bad part.'

Ghar felt uneasy, his chest was running, almost tripping over its own beat. He could see Tan take up a prominent position by the fires.

'I have an announcement to make,' Tan called out. Ghar cringed as he looked for support from Dun, who was now staring emotionlessly at Tan. 'The boy who attaches will get his people to make moving furs for us.'

The cheerful rumblings through the camp were replaced by a more confused drone, with heads turning to each other.

Tan continued, 'They will also help carry out the preparation of the meat and hides.' Ghar's cringe continued down his spine, he had not even told Dun about preparing the buffalo. 'In exchange the boy's people will take the remaining meat for their camp.'

'So, we will give them meat?' a voice cried out from the crowd.

'Yes, and we will get moving furs in exchange, for every Khamma.'

'What's going on?' Dun whispered, his face still crumpled in annoyance.

'Tan just told the tribe you will make moving furs for the Khamma.'

Dun frowned, 'What have you done, Ghar?'

Ghar thought the better question would be, *what will the Gubba do?* But considering Dun's reddening demeanour he decided to keep it to himself.

* * *

Ghar still did not know how the Gubba Zarda would take to his plan, 'Would the Elders even consider our arrangement with the

Khamma?' The furs, like the impending proposal with the Gubba Zarda, weighed down on his shoulders.

'It's too late for that,' Dun replied curtly. 'They will listen to us, otherwise you will have to find a new place to live.'

Ghar's eyes widened. He reached out to slap Dun on the back, but missed, 'Can't I live with you?'

Dun smirked, 'You Sanaa are not pure enough to live with the Gubba.'

'By the Fathers, Dun, your jokes will drown me someday.'

Bena, a Gubba Elder approached the travellers, 'By the Fathers, good to hear from the young hunters. What have you brought back to us?'

Ghar liked most of the Zardan Elders, but Bena had peculiar quirks that were hard to tolerate. He was neither physically imposing nor overly wise. However, he was quick to impose on any discussion or decision, and even if he happened to be wrong, would stubbornly stick to his position even when corrected. He had a way of criticizing, but also being complimentary just enough to not warrant a retort. *Your painting is nice to look at but lacks the stories that I have seen in the Grand Cave.* Ghar remembered that encounter because he had just been critiqued by Adura that same morning about a lack of form in his strokes. 'Hera, we have indeed brought some furs. Sorry I missed you when I last visited.'

'By the Fathers, that's quite a story you have: standing up to Das and then getting banished from Zarda. I admire your resolve, but I have always thought your inability to listen would get you into trouble.'

Dun quickly walked over and put a hand on Ghar's retort, 'Hera, as Ghar said, we have brought hides, and an arrangement with the Khamma. It would be best to call a meeting with the Elders and the tribe to discuss this.'

Bena tugged out a hide from the roll in Ghar's arms and felt through the fleece a smile forming under his beaky nose, 'It has been a long time since I felt a new fur. What is this? Is it buffalo?'

'Yes, Hera,' replied Ghar.

A fire had been kindled in a higher cave, and in the waning sunlight, provided a flickering light to the tribe below. Some of the Gubba were already accepting the sun's invitation to rest and had taken refuge under the rocky outcrops. A small group had started singing the Songs of the Fathers, which took Ghar back to Zarda. Another group appeared with spikes laden with fish parts and the sweet smell of flesh that relayed a fresh kill. Quickly a tribesman climbed up the rock face to the fire to take a burning brand to start the meal below.

Bena walked past the activity and instructed a tribesman to gather the Elders. He then knelt and tried to warm his hands in the newly lit fire and sat down.

Ghar noticed Bena's moccasins were damaged; a gaping hole revealed an old, tired set of toes. The rest of Bena's furs were growing old, *much like their owner*, Ghar thought. The Zardan tribal marks had long worn out on his hides, but the style of fastening was still reminiscent of the Zarda. His hair had a mix of white, and the hair on his face had not been shaven off in some time. Although his brown eyes had the steadiness of a man with focus, somehow he was never really listening to what the other tribesmen were saying.

A stream of Elders gradually took up the remaining space around the fire. In the meantime, Bena told the men and women tending to the fish to cook at another fireplace.

'So, Zardan younglings, what news do you bring to us?' The group slowly sat down.

Dun took the lead, 'We have come back from Khamma with hides,' he threw a quick glance at Ghar to confirm that he was on the right track. He took the hides and placed it in view of the Elders, 'All of them new. The Khamma have the aid of wolves in their hunts, and they eat buffalo even when they are not hungry.'

'Why do the Khamma give us this gift? What do they want from us?' Bena asked. Ghar was surprised, he did not expect a question on the actual topic.

Dun replied, 'Hera, this is not a gift, they are a part of a plan. The Gubba are to make moving furs in exchange for meat and hides from the Khamma's hunts.'

A small murmur hummed across the listeners. The Elders turned to each other in consultation.

Bena spoke up, 'Why should we make moving furs? Why can't they just give us the extra?'

Ghar looked at Dun, *this sounds more like the Bena we know,* he tried to say with his eyes. Dun was about to reply, but Ghar stepped in, he realized that his original request to Tan was the extra meat for the moving furs, not just to take the extra meat as Bena suggested. But, in retrospect, the Khamma would not have agreed to this, 'Even if they had said yes, they could decide—at any time and for any reason—to stop sharing,' Ghar remembered his own acceptance in Khamma, the murmurs of disapproval of an outsider. 'But, if they need you, then they have to give you the meat and hides.' He looked for some sense of agreement in Bena's face, but there was nothing behind his eyes.

'But then ask them if they will give it to us for free,' Bena repeated.

'I just explained—they will not do that.'

'Did you ask them?'

Ghar's fists clenched, which surprised him. There was a whole host of annoying tribesmen in Khamma, but somehow Bena was getting to him.

Dun put his hand on Ghar's, 'Hera, what Ghar is saying is that the Khamma will not give the extra without something in return; we don't need to ask, we know them.'

Ghar continued, 'And the Gubba need food to eat; this is a way towards meeting that need.'

'We can eat fish,' Bena replied, visibly annoyed, pointing at the tribesmen cooking the fish.

'And when the water powder comes again will you wear fish skin?' Ghar knew he was now on a path to insolence but he was tired of restraint; he had held back for so long in Khamma. 'You are not even considering what I am saying, Bena. Surely the best way is to think about it and convey your decision after some discussion.'

Bena looked cautiously at the other Elders, and then nodded, 'I don't want to make something for another tribe; sounds like what used to happen at Zarda with your Sanaa brethren.'

Ghar stopped, this was something he had not thought about. The Zarda had needed the Gubba but had still cast them out. *Wouldn't that make life harder for the remaining Sanaa?* 'Hera, that was what Das wanted, not the Sanaa, and not the Zarda. And if you remember the Songs and look at the cave paintings, there was no call from the Fathers to cast anyone out.' Ghar noticed the intent eyes that had joined them by the fire, the group had seemed to stop what they were doing. 'I studied the paintings in the Grand Cave, and it showed the Sanaa and the Gubba living together,' a rumble of discussion quickly ensued. Ghar moved closer to Dun and whispered, 'Why are they surprised at this?'

'Why wouldn't they be surprised? I am surprised too. You never told me that this was Das's doing.'

'I thought we discussed this—at the Grand Cave, the paintings, the songs.'

'What does that have to do with Das? In the camp we still blame Kuna.'

Despite Dun's low tone, the tribe collectively called out, 'By the Fathers, curse Kuna!'

Ghar remembered his conversation with Adura about what had actually happened. 'By the Fathers, Dun, I have not told you about what happened to Kuna,' Ghar got up before Dun could reply and waved to get the tribes attention. 'My Gubba brethren, there is something you should know about Kuna.'

The crowd resonated with the same refrain as before, 'By the Fathers, curse Kuna!'

'Kuna killed a small deer and was bringing it back to Zarda. If you remember, it was a hard time, the Gubba were not given

any rations, so Kuna might have thought he had to do it himself.'
Ghar took a deep breath—he had learned, while listening to Tan,
that when talking to crowds it was important to take pauses, to lure
listeners to the argument, 'Gorsa told Adura that Das attacked Kuna
first, killing him,' Ghar paused again because of the murmur that
had built up. 'Das lied to the other hunters and claimed that Kuna
had attacked him, and that Kuna's defeat was a sign from the Fathers
that the Gubba were against the Zarda and needed to be killed.'

'Kuna caught a deer?' Bena asked.

'Hera, surely that is not what you're taking away from my story.'

'It's not easy to catch a deer in the forest; I just want to know
how.'

A voice from the group of Elders interrupted, 'Bena, I think you
should focus on the treachery of Das.'

Ghar could feel the incredulous eyes on Bena. Bena skulked back
within the Elders' group and turned his attention to the food.

Ghar continued his revelation about Kuna, 'Thankfully some of
the Elders, in their wisdom, forced Das to only expel the Gubba, and
not kill them.'

'They were going to kill us?' Dun asked.

'Das wanted to. Not the Zarda. And not the Fathers,' Ghar
looked around the tribe. A silence had fallen over them, their faces
full of fear, but also relief.

'Listen, my brethren, the way forward is to create a need with
Khamma. It might seem like we are making the moving furs for
them, but we will get both meat and furs from them,' Ghar felt the
anxiety in his chest release as he ended his appeal; he had wanted to
talk about how the meat and furs from Khamma could benefit the
Gubba as they rebuilt their tribe, but the story about Das being the
true reason for the expulsion of the Gubba, seemed to capture their
attention better. He sat down, exhausted.

A Gubba stood up, her voice echoed off the rocky surfaces, 'I
want to make the moving furs.'

The rest of the tribe slowly followed, with only a few still seated.

Ghar stood up again to honour their decision. 'We start learning tomorrow,' he smiled at Dun, while collecting the approving nods and optimistic gestures from the tribe.

Zardan songs started up again, but this time it seemed like the whole tribe participated.

* * *

'Isn't it interesting that the whole tribe made the decision last night?' Ghar glanced at Dun momentarily and then refocused on arranging the hides and awls.

Dun was carefully copying Ghar's arrangements of hides and tools as he helped set up the display for the tribe, 'I usually don't find your interests interesting.'

Ghar mock scowled. The bright sun aided in squinting his eyes, 'Your humour is a waste of your voice.'

'Your voice is a waste of your voice.'

'Listen, enough jokes. Usually, the decisions are usually made by the Elders; but yesterday, everybody made the decision starting with Kara,' Ghar had talked to Kara after the meal. 'I asked her why she stood up. It makes so much sense that each Gubba has a say in the decision-making. I think if we had done this in Zarda, we would still be there; we could complete the Hunter's Walk.'

'The Hunter's Walk is not for the Gubba,' Dun reminded Ghar.

Ghar remembered the persistent edict that repeated through Zarda, 'That's what Das and maybe some Elders believe. But we know that our tribespeople don't believe that; we know that our mothers don't believe that. We don't believe that.'

Dun looked back at Ghar, taking a deep breath, 'What are we going to do then?'

'We are going to stand up.'

13

Khazagu

The last of the sun's glow faded out over the horizon. The usual cooking fires were broken out for the last remaining fresh meat from the last kill. There was an assortment of smoked meats, organs and a collection of warm-time fruits like red squash face berries, black cough berries and sweet plums. Usually, the fruits were eaten upon plucking, but during warm-time, there was enough to bring back to the camp. Ghar, Mai and Dun took up places near enough to a fire for warmth but far enough to indulge in a conversation that might not have been considered proper in the tribe.

'So, in Zarda, the tribesman doesn't choose a mate,' Dun compared the tribes. Ghar translated but tried to signal with a lowered hand that he did not like the conversation.

'That's so strange,' Mai's large eyes and tilted head were visible signs of surprise. 'How do you know who your father is?'

Ghar reluctantly translated again, and Dun answered, 'We don't know; I guess all the Zardan men are our fathers,' he told Mai.

Ghar decided not to translate for Dun again. He looked at Mai and changed topic, 'It doesn't really matter, let's look at the painting of what I think the moon, sun and stars are.' He turned to Dun, 'Mai wants to look at my painting.'

Ghar had brought it with the intention of displaying it at some time during the night. He thought the painting looked interesting—

it told the story of day and night for both the Khamma and the Zarda. He rolled out the hide and held it up to the firelight.

'So that's the sun?' Dun pointed to the yellow round shape. 'And this, the moon?'

Ghar nodded, repositioning the painting to get a better light from the fire.

'What's the round, with people on it.'

'That's us.'

'We are on a round?'

Mai wanted to be a part of the conversation, 'Why does Dun look so confused?'

'I am telling him about how the Khamma and the Zarda are on a round,' Ghar pointed to the people in the picture, 'That's us.'

'Now I'm confused.'

Dun countered, 'Listen, if we were on a round wouldn't we be rolling?'

Ghar drew a deep breath, he had hoped Mai and Dun would understand his drawing faster. 'If you draw a really large round, a small part of it looks flat.' Ghar placed the painting on the ground where it was still illuminated by the firelight and pulled out his clay round, and picked a small pebble from the ground, 'This pebble is a tribesman; if the round turns, with the tribesman, you can see how the night becomes day.'

Mai asked, 'What are you saying now? . . . in Khamman, please?'

'When the round turns, with a tribesman on it,' he turned the clay round, 'night turns into day.'

'What? This is getting more confusing.'

'Look up at the moon, its shape. Now come to my shoulder and look at the clay moon.'

Mai moved closer, 'What am I looking at?'

'Really? You don't see it?' Ghar felt a bit uneasy that Mai and Dun looked at him with worry.

'See the shape of the moon, doesn't it look like the light on the clay moon?'

'Yes?'

'That's how it gets that form.'

'I thought the Spirits feed the Giant Wolf with a piece of the moon?'

'What?' Ghar's eyes opened wide.

'What "what"?'

Ghar felt like they were deviating from the journey he wanted to make. 'Listen, I don't know anything about a Giant Wolf. I'm saying that when the moon is over here, and we are over here, then this moon shape will occur.'

Dun had been studying the painting, 'I think you have a fever, Ghar.'

'Listen, I'll try showing you again,' he stood up and took Mai by the hand, 'now stand here.'

Ghar told Dun, 'Watch us. I am Khamma Zarda, and Mai is the moon. And the fire is the sun. See how Mai goes around me?' He led Mai around him in a circle.

'What is Khamma Zarda?'

Ghar stopped to glare. 'It's us, Dun; it's all of us . . . on this place!'

'Shouldn't it be Khamma Zarda Gubba?'

'All right, it doesn't matter, but all right. And you are completely missing the essence of what this painting is about.' Ghar started to turn slowly. 'And Khazagu, turns, when I face the sun, it is day time, when I slowly turn away it becomes evening and then when I am fully turned away with my back to the sun, it's night time.'

'Khazagu, is easier to say,' Dun agreed.

'What is Khazagu?' asked Mai, still moving from toe to toe.

'An easier way of saying Khamma Zarda Gubba.'

'Yes, it is,' she did not seem overly interested in the answer. She started to move quicker, 'This is amusing; maybe you should go around the sun.'

'That's actually interesting,' Ghar switched back to Zardan, 'Mai says Khazagu should go around the sun. I never thought of that.'

'Why can't the sun go around the Khazagu?'

Ghar could tell that Dun was mocking him, but it was curious question, 'That's also interesting, it's just more difficult to move that campfire around me.' Ghar started to spin gently while moving around the campfire, although he felt his feet were not keeping up with his own body, and Mai, graceful as she was, made Ghar feel even less coordinated. 'Listen, I will say turn and then I will do a spin, while I am doing a spin you walk around me fast enough to return to the same position.'

A group of tribespeople, already curious when Ghar and Mai started spinning near the fire, now seemed captivated, 'Mai, what is that?'

'It's Khazagu,' she gave a Ghar a quick starry glance. 'We spin and move round the fire.'

'I also want to do it; can we join in?'

Ghar was a bit sceptical, he whispered to Mai, 'How can there be multiple Khazagus?' He looked up at the stars, and then at the tribespeople, 'why not?'

He arranged each Khazagu and moon around the campfire, some closer to the fire and some further, and explained what they had to do. He turned to Dun, and asked, 'Can you say "*turn*" to get them to spin and walk around?'

'What's "*turn*"?' Dun did not understand the Khamman word.

'Just clap,' Ghar wanted to get to the actual movements. 'You lead us, every time you want us to make the movement, you clap.'

Ghar explained to the tribe what Dun would do, and then signalled to start. 'Let's see if this will work,' he smiled at Mai.

'This is so enjoyable, Ghar,' Mai's face lit up as she glided across Ghar as he waited for the next clap.

He had lost their focus on his painting, but watching Mai enjoy herself was more than he could have wanted.

After a night long of attempts, and further changes to the steps and signals, the group seemed to get coordinated. Ghar called out to Dun, 'I think we are getting good at this!' To his surprise Dun was right beside him. 'What are you doing here?'

'It was going so well, so I decided to join in!' he called out in accented Khamman. 'No moon, I can be crazy,' which prompted laughter around the fire.

'Are those moves from Maraza?' Ghar laughed as Dun started to get the tribe to clap while moving.

Dun laughed, 'We aren't in Zarda, but we can bring Zarda here.'

Ghar yelled in approval; he looked around at the happy faces, but in the distance, just within the reach of the fires' light, he could see Yan, eyes squinted and nostrils flaring. He knew Yan had to be contended with sooner or later. He could feel his courage and resolve flowing into his clenched fist, and then Mai's cool, delicate touch gently allayed it.

'Don't let him drag you into this, Ghar; save those hands for painting, and bringing colour into our lives,' Mai drew closer and buried her face in his neck.

* * *

Ghar and Dun would occasionally stay back at Khamma to adjust some of the moving furs and measure the moccasin sizes for the tribespeople, especially the children, who sometimes outgrew their initial estimations even before attaching. Some of the trees had a touch of red-brown, heralding cold-time. The colder it got, the more the Khamma would try to heat themselves up in the warm midday sun.

'It seems to be getting colder quicker. The forest is not even brown yet, and I feel like sleeping in a pack,' Ghar said. They rested near the crevice where Ghar stored the moving fur tools.

'I agree. I think it's going to be hard this cold-time,' Dun looked worried. He took the chance to lie down and examine his bruise-dotted fingers.

'I hope we don't see another water powder storm,' Ghar tucked his fingers into his furs to warm up, before he resumed his work on the moving fur.

Mai came from the direction of the Healing Cave, 'How are our Zardan friends doing today?'

'We are good; we did not see you when we woke up?'

'Aiy, a youngling has a cough; Manar asked me to watch her while she takes some rest,' she tucked her hands in her moving fur. 'It is a bit cold today. I hope we are not going to get another water powder storm.'

'That's what I said!' Ghar relished the occasional shared thought.

'I should learn more Khamman, so I can talk to you both,' said Dun.

'Give it time, Dun,' Ghar reassured his Zardan friend. 'Actually, why can't the Khamma learn some Zardan?'

'Why do you keep saying Khamman?' Mai asked.

'We were thinking the Khamma should learn Zardan, and some the other way.'

'I want to learn,' Mai sounded eager.

'Does Mai want to learn?' Dun asked, 'Would she be willing to teach the Gubba about healing?'

Ghar relayed Dun's question.

'Of course, I would. I think Manar would be really interested as well,' Mai shook her weariness off.

Yan's voice unexpectedly bellowed from beyond the group, 'Mai, you ungrateful mother killer!' and then he rushed towards Mai.

Ghar stepped out in front of Mai, his fists clenched, 'You had better go back the same way you came, otherwise I will—'

'Otherwise, you will do what? Zardan faeces!' He was toe to toe with Ghar, his hot breath and sputum an unwelcome accompaniment to the shouting. Yan turned to Mai, 'Did you tell the Elders you want to stop being my mate? You don't give me children, and now you want to stop being my mate?'

'Yan, I have warned you,' although Ghar's fury was still holding up his knees, Yan's physical advantage over him had started to unsettle his gut. Ghar was about to unleash a fist he had little confidence of landing, when Mai stepped in front, going at Yan's face with outstretched hands. Yan stumbled backwards, his fall was prompted by Mai's foot behind Yan's ankle. Her hands still on his face, she pushed her knee into his chest.

Dun nonchalantly walked over and stepped on Yan's hand, disabling him further.

'Let this be the last time you call me a "mother killer"!' Mai shouted, her left hand moving to Yan's neck. 'If you ever do that again, I am going to be known as the "Yan killer"!'

Yan tried to push Mai off, 'If you don't let me go, I am going to—'

'Say you will stop calling me a "mother killer",' Mai interrupted Yan.

'I will call you whatever—'

Mai moved forward putting her weight on Yan's neck.

'Let me go, let me go,' Yan choked hoarsely. 'All right I won't call you that.'

'Call me what?'

The sounds coming from Yan's mouth were mostly unformed, airy croaks, '"Mother killer" . . . I won't call you a "mother killer".'

Mai released his neck, planting a final knee on Yan's abdomen as she rose. She staggered slightly, her limbs trembling momentarily, but stood tall, 'Now get away from here, unless you want to be killed.'

Yan scrambled up, his furs partially unfastened, his face coloured by his usual anger, but with a new tinge of embarrassment. He glared at Ghar and Dun, his eyes scowling beneath flickering eyebrows that promised punishment. He limped off towards the caves.

Ghar suddenly felt exposed. Yan was well respected in the camp, while Ghar, although acknowledged for his creations, was not. 'I hope this doesn't become stealing honeynest from the bees without smoke.'

'I would love some honeynest right now,' Dun smiled, a jovial glow in his eyes.

Ghar mouthed incredulously, 'Are you crazy?' at Dun. He turned his attention back to Mai and reached over to her shoulder, 'Where did you learn that move? it looked a lot like Maraza.'

Mai turned back to Ghar, a soft chuckle behind her sunken eyes and hollow cheeks, 'Dun taught me that.'

Dun asked what the argument had been about. Ghar smiled gratefully at Dun; even though he hadn't had a clue about what this fight was about, Dun had helped out Mai. 'I think Mai and Yan are not mates anymore.' Ghar turned to Mai to confirm this, 'You and Yan . . . not mates anymore?' There was relief in his chest that she would not have to go through the daily tirades, but at the same time he knew how much her commitments meant to her. Being Yan's mate was not only a commitment to Yan, but also a commitment to the Khamma.

'Yes, I told the Elders yesterday.'

'How do you feel?'

'Like when I was a child, learning to swim, that feeling of reaching the surface of the water. I feel safe, for now.' She pressed her forehead and ran her fingers down her temples, ending on her chin. The morning air still had a lingering coldness which revealed Mai's sigh.

Ghar held Mai, reassuring her, with his chest pressed close to hers. Although he could feel her body, he could sense her mind was not there, her long arms stayed limp by her sides, and her cheek did not approach Ghar's. Ghar held her shoulders, 'Mai, you had to do this; nobody should have to endure Yan's rage.' He did think that Yan had some cause to be sad, but Yan's anger betrayed Mai's efforts. 'Not having a baby is not your fault, you have already told him this, you can't control it.'

'I know that,' Mai replied. She straightened up and then rested her chin on Ghar's shoulder, 'But what happens now?'

'We should talk to Manar, and then take her with us to Tan.'

'I have already talked to Tan and the Elders, Ghar.'

'Yes, but there is still opportunity for Yan to say this has something to do with me and Dun, which could change the Elders' views,' said Ghar. Mai did not seem keen, Ghar felt her lean on him further. He tried to bolster her as best as he could, 'We need to take control,' he had had the same feeling when the Gubba were sent out of Zarda, the feeling that the Elders were making decisions without talking to the tribe.

'All right,' said Mai, losing further conviction. 'I feel alone.'

'Listen, I am here with you,' he could feel Dun thinking the same thing. '*We* are here with you.' He recalled Mai rescuing him from the river and bringing him to Khamma. 'Listen, you saved me, now it is my turn to save you.'

* * *

'Why didn't you tell me you were going to the Elders?' Manar stopped tending to the sick child in front of her.

'You would have told me to hold on.'

'Because that is the right thing to do.'

Ghar interrupted, 'Mai needed to get away from the abuse.'

'Ghar you are a Zardan, you don't understand how this will look to the Elders,' Manar gave the child to Mai and motioned to her to keep her warm. 'The tribe will see this—Mai did not give Yan a baby, and now she is trying to abandon him.'

There was a collective silence after Manar's prediction. Ghar had not thought about that, and he was not sure whether Mai knew either. *Surely she knew?* If they had felt like they were trapped by wolves on the left, now it seemed that more wolves were coming in from the right.

'There is yet another way that the Elders could go. I think Yan will try to say that Mai is following the ways of outsiders, and that she should be punished.'

'He could do that as well,' Manar agreed.

'I think the best way is to describe the daily torment that Yan imposes on Mai and support our argument with tribespeople who saw the same,' Ghar urged.

Manar sat down on a large tree root that sprung out from between the rocks, 'Mai, would you reconsider? Because, if we go through with this, there could be further retaliation from Yan and his friends.'

'How can I reconsider, Manar? You say I should have patience, eat more beetle berries and try harder to make a baby with Yan, but you don't live this. I do.' Mai gazed at the baby cradled in her arms, her face turned soft, 'Sorry you have to hear this, baby.'

More silent contemplation ensued. Ghar decided there was no benefit to this argument. 'Listen, this has already happened, it has flowed away like water under our feet,' Ghar knelt before Manar and rested on his haunches. 'We need your help, Manar, we need you to talk to the Elders and make sure they hear our side of it.'

Manar looked at Mai, 'Is this what you want?'

'Yes, Manar,' Mai's eyes glimmered with intent, but then she bowed her head to study the grainy, rocky floor. Ghar felt that she could have shown more interest to keep Manar on plan. He didn't want Manar to go to the Elders and make weak excuses on Mai's behalf or plead for leniency. He wanted Manar to emphatically maintain that Yan was the wrong-doer.

'Manar,' said Ghar earnestly, 'we have to make the Elders understand that this is Yan's fault. I don't want them to be blind to this truth.'

Manar shook her head, 'I don't want to, but I will,' she walked over to Mai and compared the infant's warmth under the moving fur, to her own. 'These Zardan inventions make things harder for me,' she gently stroked the child's hair back from its brow. The child sighed a peaceful smile. 'But you also make things easier.' Manar revealed the scar of a stitched wound on the infant's leg.

'Thank you, Manar. It is an honour to help.'

'Whatever happens, it's going to be interesting.'

* * *

'We have Kasa and Bayu, who will speak for you, Mai,' Manar smiled brightly as the evening grew long. 'Most of them admit that

Yan was unnecessarily aggressive towards Mai, but they are not willing to say anything against Yan.' Manar who had been talking with tribespeople had just sat down with Mai and Ghar, who were enjoying the warmth of a soft crackling fire on a large flat rock that overlooked the lake.

'I don't understand why people stand by him. He's so aggressive and foul tempered,' Ghar remarked, slightly annoyed.

'He's likeable,' said Mai. 'He is aggressive, I know.' Mai scratched her head struggling to explain. 'I think he is simple. He doesn't think or know so much, but he can tell a story about some adventure like no other person can.' Mai smiled reminiscing, 'Like the other day, he jumped off Green Rock Waterfall. To feel like a bird.'

Ghar who was concentrating on keeping Mai safe from Yan and the Elders felt conflicted. There was a part of him that wanted her to be his mate, not Yan's, and his own actions seemed to be furthering that cause. It felt deceitful, but he knew he needed to put that guilt away. *This is about Mai's safety; this is not about you.* 'Then let's use that against him. If he will tell a simple story, then we should make our story complicated like falling into the white waters.'

'How do you want to do that?'

'I think we need to collect all the parts of this story. Mai, tell us the story of you and Yan.'

'What? Right now?'

'Yes, let's hear from the beginning until today.'

Mai sat down and took a deep breath, 'Do I really have to? How is this going to help us?'

'Just do it, when was the first time you wanted to be Yan's mate?' Ghar knew this was going to hurt him, *but maybe it will blunt this stinging guilt in my chest.*

Mai looked around, checking to make sure they were out of earshot of the others. She reached for her knee, her fingers moving gently across revealed a scar. 'I was just a youngling, and we were playing, just over there,' Mai pointed to the rocky bank on the lake. 'I think I was chasing another boy, and I fell, and I looked down, and there was a big wound. Yan came over and carried me gently to the water's edge and washed my wound.'

Manar gave a hum of approval.

Mai responded with a sad sigh, 'We would spend a lot of time together, talking, eating, sometimes just lying around in the sun.'

'Go on,' Ghar felt his insides writhe and turn over.

'He asked me about being his mate when we had just seen Alun and Ana take their pledge with the Elders. I thought he was joking, but then he got all serious, and said we were the best-looking people in the tribe, and that we would have good-looking children. That sounded good to me.'

Ghar continued the uncomfortable questions, 'When you started to try for babies, did you try everything? Manar being a healer might have had advice for you?'

'We did, we tried in the morning and in the evening, we tried before and after eating, we tried in the camp and out in the forest.'

Ghar interrupted, 'I think that would be enough ways. What about any herbs or potions?'

'I tried the rough berry with prickly mint mixture in water to increase my strength, I tried the mashed honeynest with stinging root,' Mai glanced at Manar, 'I also ate buffalo unborn baby, big-nose deer unborn baby, but those were not from Manar, Yan brought them for me.'

'You really did try,' Manar said with tears in her eyes. 'I am sorry, my child, I saw past the pain you were going through.'

'Manar, you don't need to apologize, I would still follow anything you advised,' Mai reached around Manar, embracing her. 'So Ghar, is this enough for a story?'

'I think this is good. Let's make something the Elders will listen to.'

* * *

'My brethren, by the way of the Wolf, we are here to hear the pleas of Yan and Mai,' Tan stood up to make an introduction to the group that had congregated around the Elders' Fire. Most of the camp huddled towards the fire, for warmth and to hear what Tan was saying. There was a slight thrum that travelled back and forth in the group, with frequent eyes cast in the direction of Mai, Manar, Ghar and Dun.

That doesn't bode well for us, Ghar thought as he tried to deflect the stares towards Yan.

'They made a sacred pledge to Khamma when they chose each other as mates. Now Mai wants to break that pledge. There are usually punishments for such behaviour, but we have heard our sister, Manar's pleas to hear Mai's story and circumstances. However, in fairness we will also hear Yan's story.'

Yan stood up, 'By the way of the Wolf, Elders, it is by your wisdom that we will be guided to the stars.'

I think I am about to vomit, Ghar thought to himself. That Yan's tone was so subservient was both nauseating and impressive at the same time.

Yan teared up and the murmurs floated away with the embers of the fire. He gestured towards Ulan's child, 'We want those, we need those, that's why we take the pledge with the Spirits, the Spirits who have blessed us with the wolves.' A rumble of agreement grew through the tribe. 'And when we do have those children, we pledge them to the Spirits, to learn the Khamman ways and help maintain our tribe, so that our children may join the Spirits as stars.'

The rumble of agreement had grown into a steady stream of praise.

Ghar quietly caught Mai's attention and tried to keep her calm with a nod and a confident half- smile.

Yan continued, 'Mai, I thought, would make fine children, especially with the combination of our looks, a part hunter, a part healer.'

Some more agreement flitted excitedly between the members.

Ghar felt a twinge of anxiety pass through his torso; the camp seemed to accept Yan's story so easily.

'And you know our Mai, her life was not pleasing to the Spirits, she killed her own mother.'

The tribe fell silent, which to Ghar was a good sign, the tribe seemed to reject Yan's allegation. This was a slander that he would overhear in ungracious conversation, but never in Mai's presence.

'But,' Yan continued, 'I was still willing to take her, teach her courtesy and respect for the Elders and the Spirits.'

Ghar thought there was something off about what Yan was saying. *Surely it was Manar who had taught Mai to respect the Elders and the Spirits. But even though he was lying, it was hard to deny it. What if he did teach Mai something?*

'I got nothing in return for my generosity,' Yan looked around the tribe. 'I cannot offer the Spirits my child as gratitude for the wolves. She would not give me a child!' Yan had avoided looking directly at Mai all this while, but now he seemed to glare at her with the sharpness of a spear.

Ghar placed a hand on Mai's arm to quell her clenched fist.

'And now, after that humiliation, Mai wants to break the pledge we made to the Spirits and the Elders. I think the Spirits will not accept us among the stars.' This elicited a collective gasp. Ghar noticed that even Tan looked worried. 'I ask of you Elders, Holders of Wisdom, that we do not let this kind of shameful betrayal go unchastised.'

The group, including the Elders, broke into smaller conversations. Ghar could hear agreement with what Yan said.

'Mai, remember all the parts to your story,' Ghar remembered confronting Das in Zarda during the expulsion of the Gubba. 'Make sure you remember to respect the Elders; and even if you might not like what they say, be gracious.'

Mai looked at Ghar with eyes that were reluctant to see what was next.

'Don't worry, be yourself,' Ghar confirmed with Manar and then looked over at Tan to indicate that Mai was ready. Manar whispered in Mai's ear, as Mai stood up.

'My brethren, we will hear now from Mai?'

A lone voice from the crowd cried out, 'Mother killer!' which elicited hisses of disapproval.

Mai looked back at Manar and then Ghar. Ghar gave her the most confident smile he could rustle up until his face hurt. He clenched his fists with unease.

'I hurt myself when I was younger; there, at that rocky bank.'

'Louder, my child,' an Elder prompted.

'I hurt myself when I was younger, over there at that rocky bank. This handsome boy gathered me into his arms and then healed me; Yan healed a healer. After that, he was kind to me, teaching me to hunt, helping me collect herbs and mushrooms and special healing plants,' Mai remembered Ghar's advice to look at the female Elder, 'and he was exciting, always doing something crazy that made my chest pound.' She looked at the Elders with full eyes and with a deferential hunch to her shoulders, 'So, when he asked me to be his mate, I said yes.' Mai took a pause, the whole camp doing their best to listen to her voice.

Ghar breathed a little easier, his neck felt flexible again.

'And then we tried for a child. We tried in the morning, we tried in the night, we tried in the camp, we tried in the forest, we tried before food and we tried after eating,' Mai's hands took her words and threw them into the sky and towards the forest. Ghar smiled when some of the tribe looked at the sky and the forest.

'And then I ate rough berries and stinging root.'

A disgusted voice emanated from the crowd: 'I hate rough berries!'

'Yes, I had those in the morning and in the evening and in the night. I even ate an unborn baby buffalo.'

The crowd groaned at the revelation.

'I did all those things because I wanted to respect the Spirits and the Elders, and I wanted to respect Yan,' she looked over at Yan with outpouring eyes, 'but it did not work. I am a healer, and Manar is a healer, but sometimes our healing does not work. But, in spite of all this, I still wanted to keep trying, respecting our Spirits and our Elders. The only reason I come here to ask for your relief, Holders of Wisdom, is that my thoughts are being broken by Yan's scoldings; I find it hard to carry out my duties as a healer. I might accidentally give rough berries for a bad stomach, or a round mushroom to treat a bad throat, either of which will make it worse,' she looked over at Tur with his baby, 'Tur would want me to give the best care to his child, right?'

Tur was surprised to be called upon, he put his hand up in agreement.

'And Kasa and Bayu will also tell you of the berating that I have got from Yan, and truthfully most of the Khamma have experienced it. It is not out disrespect to Yan, but out of my need to do my duties. Finally, as Yan has said, our duties are to pledge our children and maintain the Khamma. I cannot produce children, but I can help Khamma prosper if I can concentrate on healing. Please let me be a healer so I can continue to heal you,' Mai looked around at all the Elders, 'please consider my plea.' She returned to sit with Ghar and Manar.

There was another silence that broke into concerned dialogues, with some voices whispering punishments and others calling for the healer to be freed. Ghar was happy that Mai had completed the story with nearly all the details that they had discussed, but he was still unsure of how the Elders would consider her plea. Especially after Yan's strong reasoning that he would not be admitted amongst the stars.

Tan indicated that the Elders had reached a decision. He took a long look around the tribe, 'We have agreed that not giving the Spirits a child is a transgression, but we also believe that Mai is not able to produce a baby, which is akin to not being able to walk, or not being able to breathe properly. We ask that Manar continue to provide healing to Mai so that she may fulfil this beautiful act of gratitude.'

Tan gestured towards Mai, 'On Mai's request to be relieved of her pledge, we agree. We think the current aggression between them is not conducive to the life of a leading hunter or a healer,' the female Elder caught Tan's attention, 'or to the life of any tribe member,' Tan continued.

Ghar could tell that Tan was not entirely committed to what he was saying next, 'We have to treat each other, especially the people who are in trouble, with care and respect.'

Yan stared at Tan, his deference had gone with this decision by the Elders. He stormed away from the campfire without further words, his friends followed.

'You are free, Mai,' Manar whispered, her happiness almost too shrill for a whisper, 'I am sorry I ever pushed you into something bad for you,' tears rolled down her cheeks leaving a flickering trail and ending in her wide smile.

Ghar joined in the embrace, pulling in Dun. 'Dun, Mai is free,' he whispered.

'I could guess.'

'Thank you, Ghar,' Mai turned around while still in his embrace. 'I had accepted that I was to be punished.'

'We should never give up, Mai,' he placed the side of his forehead on her cheek. His right wrist rested on Manar's shoulder, exposed enough to reveal the burn scar which Das had given him as a parting gift on the day he was exiled from Zarda. *We should never give up.*

* * *

'Gharra, this is Mai,' they were in the Sanaa tepee in which Adura and Gharra slept. Ghar's paintings adorned the walls, but they weren't his, they seemed more like paintings from the Grand Cave, but with wolf-headed, long-limbed creatures that danced around fires which were fuelled by buffalo bones. Gharra picked a plum from a tree. *There is a tree in here?* Ghar thought. She leaned over from across the tepee and placed it on Mai's tongue. Mai began to wince in pain, her mouth shut, her eyes filled with panic. Ghar tried to reach her, but a tree erupted from her mouth, lifting him up in its branches, up into the sky.

'Ghar, wake up.' Ghar looked around, for source of the voice.

'Ghar, wake up!'

He woke up, his skin uncomfortably slid around inside his moving fur.

'Ghar, wake up, you are having a bad dream,' Mai called out from her cocoon of furs in Ghar's arms.

Ghar sat up, the crackling of the fire and the noises of the forest assaulted his head. He held his hands up to quieten the sound.

'What happened, Ghar?' Mai asked, still on the ground, swaddled in the furs.

'I don't know, you met my mother in the dream, and you ate a fruit and then a tree grew out of you.'

Mai chuckled, still half-asleep. 'Aiy, I wanted to sleep some more,' she complained as she wriggled out of her furs just enough to tilt her face towards the top of the trees, 'but I will have to get up soon.'

Ghar lay back down, 'Let's just sleep all day.'

'Why would you sleep all day? Being here, all day long, that would be so boring.'

'If I were with you it would not be boring.'

'For me it would be boring,' she laughed, 'but thank you for saying I'm interesting.'

'I'm not saying *you're* interesting; I'm saying *I'm* interesting,' Ghar smiled till it hurt. He smiled even more because the puerile humour sounded like something Dun would say.

Mai rolled over on her furs to squint in scorn.

'I'm joking, Mai.'

'I need to go to the Healing Cave, Manar asked me to be there. And I'll have to go foraging later. Maybe you can be interesting while helping,' Mai unravelled the furs from around her.

'That would be great, but I really need to finish altering the moving furs. Dun will be back any day, and I'll have to go back with him.'

Mai returned a sigh and sad eyes, 'Do you have to go? Why don't you let Dun handle it?'

'I proposed this plan with the Gubba; I should complete it.'

Mai turned away, her cheeks losing their vigour.

'But I can come with you to the Healing Cave, can't I?'

Mai gave Ghar a satisfied smile, as she rolled up her sleeping furs to take it back to the caves for storage.

Ghar followed behind her, 'Shall we go now?'

Mai placed her roll with the rest of the tribe's furs, 'You haven't washed yet. Go wash yourself and clean your mouth.'

Ghar walked over to the stream with his tooth-cleaning stick, he liked to give it an extra grind on the rocks to make it more comfortable to use.

Mai sat on her haunches beside him, carrying out her ablutions with form, squeezing the water through her fingers on her face, and rinsing her mouth. 'Zardan, you always forget this,' Mai handed a twig of hairy-back mint leaves, which found Ghar's nostrils even before it was in his hand. 'Smelly mouth, smelly talk,' she stood up and adjusted her moving fur, and then started towards the Healing Cave.

'Mai?'

'Yes,' Mai turned lightly on her feet, in the style of Khazagu.

Ghar laughed at the impromptu dance, but while he thought about what he wanted to say, he toned down and said seriously, 'Just now, when we talked about my going back to the Gubba, I might have sounded like I don't relish every night I get to spend with you, which I do.'

'I know, Ghar,' Mai smiled back. 'The nights of Khazagu, and talking about Zarda, and learning to paint and sculpt. We should do something tonight, shouldn't we?'

There was something incomplete about what she said, it was not only about Khazagu, and painting. 'It's not just that, Mai, I do like being with you; we could do nothing, and I still couldn't choose a better place to be than with you.'

Mai threw her hands up and stared with narrowed eyes, muffling the chirping of the birds and rustling of the leaves, 'What do you mean, Ghar? I like you, but sometimes you do things that make me think you *more* than like me.' She sighed and looked away, 'What do you want, Ghar? Do you want to be my mate?'

Ghar felt like the deer, who was peacefully grazing, only to suddenly realize the tall grass was alive, and a quick furtive glance would not be able to avoid the imminent terror. He put his hand over his mouth trying to hold in the words, but his eyes betrayed him.

'That's crazy, I can't give you a child, Ghar. Why would you want that?'

'Why are you fighting?' Manar called out from behind them.

'I think the Zardan has a fever, and needs to be put in the Healing Cave,' Mai turned away and strode towards the Cave. Ghar just stood there, his words trapped in his chest.

'You can fight with her later, she needs to clean the Cave and go with Mu to find some herbs,' Manar chided. 'I met Tan just now, he wants to talk to you.'

Ghar couldn't speak. Manar put her hand on his forehead, 'Are you okay? Did Mai really want to put you in the Cave?'

Ghar looked down, 'I don't have a fever,' he said, *but I may as well be sick because I'll soon be dead.* 'Is seeing Tan urgent?' He wanted to follow Mai and explain, but he somehow dreaded it at the same time.

'When was it not urgent? Tan calls you, you go.'

'All right, Manar,' Ghar turned towards Tan's cave. He was sad at Mai's reaction, he looked back hoping to see Mai around the corner to the Healing Cave, but she was not there.

* * *

Tan was on his perch, his long legs dangled, untroubled by recent events.

'Tan, Friend of the Spirits, Manar told me you wanted to talk to me.'

Tan replied with a throaty cough, 'Bear with me, Zardan, I am not well today, so I will take a little longer to get where I want to go,' he climbed off the rock face, which was unusual as he usually jumped off, and he clutched his chest, visibly in discomfort.

'Is this why Manar was with you? Why don't you go to the Healing Cave?' Ghar instinctively went over and slotted his shoulder under Tan's arm.

'I am too old to be healed,' he smiled with a certain mischief in the corner of his lips. 'I have never gone to that place in my life; I am not about to go there now.' He looked Ghar in the eye and chuckled, 'besides I would have to tell Manar that she was right if she cured me.' He leaned more of his weight on Ghar and nudged him into his cave.

'I don't understand?'

'She wanted the cave, she thought sick people made other people sick, so it was best to keep them apart.'

'Also, it helps them to rest, away from the tribe,' Ghar remembered another reason that Manar had for the Healing Cave.

'I wanted the cave to sleep there, flowing water, and no endless jabbering from the tribe.'

'Don't you get that here?' Ghar helped Tan on to a stack of furs.

'I do, but the Healing Cave would have been nicer.'

'You should still go there; Manar and Mai can help.'

'That reminds me about the reason I called you here,' Tan lay back releasing Ghar's shoulder. 'It made me uncomfortable to see you interfere in Mai's issue. I know I have supported you to prepare the tribe for challenges like water powder storms, but this was an issue within the tribe. The Elders discussed your interference.' Tan stopped to roll on his side, while he coughed, the phlegm fell beside his furs. His eyes were partially closed, and his pursed mouth looked as if he was trying to hold back some foul-tasting food. 'But I disagreed with them. When I was a new hunter, like yourself, I could see there were ways we could improve; maybe don't kill what we don't need; or save more dried meat. We were so confident on the hunt, even the occasional night of hunger would not scare us.' Tan smiled, 'I grew old, and more accustomed to keeping to the same old ways,' Tan glanced at Ghar, 'until the water powder storm came, and you attached that man up. Then I thought, the time has come to let the new Tans do something.'

'Tan, wise leader, both the old and the new Tans can make changes.'

Tan smiled again, 'If you hadn't interfered, Zardan, we would have punished Mai, and no tribesman would have even questioned our ruling.' He cleared his throat, 'I decided today that that would have been wrong. It took an outsider to see that. Maybe an outsider is the best person to take us through these difficult times.'

Ghar bowed. He was already overwhelmed by his argument with Mai. There was this strange sense of respectful obligation that Tan seemed to place on Ghar, considerate, yet a commitment he could not refuse.

'Yan will lead the tribe; you will need to help him make the right decision.'

Ghar did not like the idea, but Tan was to be respected, at least in this conversation, 'I will try my best.'

'Then Zardan, you have finally become a Khamman.'

'By the Fathers!' Ghar exclaimed incredulously in Zardan, 'I mean, thank you, Tan, I hope I can live up to this honour,' Ghar was thrilled with the proclamation, but inside he felt a resurgence of his Zardan origin as when he had been reunited with Dun. He felt the need to share the news with Mai.

'You may go now,' Tan continued to cough.

'Tan you must come with me, please listen to this outsider, this new Khamman.'

'This is your first order as a Khamma—leave me and go out and help the Khamma.'

* * *

'Ghar, we have to go now,' Dun reminded Ghar, the morning sun was uncomfortably breaking through the chilly air. The Khamma were already well into their day, cleaning out hearths, arranging stacks of firewood, washing out dirty hides and moving furs.

An ordinary day in Khamma, but for Ghar it was elation mixed with chest-blocking despair. He was a full Khamman tribesman now, but at the same time he feared he had lost Mai, 'I need to see her, Dun.'

'If we stay here any longer, we will have the night wilderness as mates,' Dun retorted.

He couldn't help being amused at the thought of some nocturnal creature taking Mai's place. 'Listen, Dun, I asked her to be my mate, and she got angry at me and walked off.'

'Why would she reject you, you are not overly ugly?'

'You're not really helping,' Ghar was too overwhelmed to spar.

'When can we go, Ghar? When can we go? When can we go?'

'Dun, it doesn't help to repeat the question.'

'Can we go? Can we go? We go?'

Ghar gave in, 'All right, Dun, but at least let me leave something for her.'

Dun yipped his appreciation, 'I will get ready.' His gratification and urgency to leave was suddenly abated by curiosity, 'Wait, what are you giving her?'

Ghar felt his face warm up and his eyes get fuller. 'The first time I saw Mai, I started to paint in shadows, and I did a depiction of her.'

Dun interrupted, 'Shadows?'

'Yes, instead of drawing a nose, I draw the shadow the nose makes. Do you want to see?' Ghar led Dun to the cave where he hid his paintings. 'I showed her the initial painting and she really liked it, but I was never happy about it.'

'Why not?'

Ghar was glad that Dun had asked this question. He was proud of his thinking, 'When we paint, we tell a story of what we see. What I wanted to do with this is tell a story of what I feel,' Ghar rolled out the thin hide.

'It's like Mai's face, she's there, but the colours, I've never seen some of these colours!' Dun gazed at Ghar, his tongue visible in his open mouth. 'It makes me feel, Ghar, like a sunset, or fresh meat on the fire.' His eyes met Ghar's just for a moment before returning to the painting. 'Adura would fight to put this up in the Grand Cave.'

Ghar teared up. He thought about Mai again. *Help me out, painting. I need you to help win back Mai.*

* * *

Ghar knelt at Gharra's grave. *She's down there; I feel like digging her out.* She was much taller than the grave she was crammed into. Ghar thought this was symbolic of how the Zarda had treated her, 'Mother, they made me a Khamma,' he said in a soft voice, 'Tan made me a Khamma because I stood up for Mai. Mai is better off now that she does not have to listen to Yan's rants, but she is also angry with me. I asked her to be my mate. I gave her a painting. I hope she will like it,' Ghar wept, the tears stayed in his eyes although he quickly wiped them with the back of his hand. 'I would give anything for you to be here, Gharra.'

Ghar walked out into a busy hum of Zardan song while a group stitched new moving furs along the markings that had been made by Ghar and Dun while at Khamma.

Kara was with Dun, 'This buffalo fur makes me want to sleep all the time.' Her cheeks seem to always have a shade of red. A small mouth with corners permanently slanted upwards gave people the impression that she was always happy, which made her a bit unpopular, especially in the harder times. But now it suited the tribe, with the steady supply of meat and furs. 'But I think this is even better,' she pulled out a moving fur made of rabbit hides, 'it's only for the upper part of the body; it took us ages to gather enough rabbits.'

'It's so soft, I think you should attach it on me,' Dun laughed.

Ghar held it up to get a better view. The moving fur was so thick that it was hard to see any stiches. Somehow it seemed lighter than the buffalo hides. Ghar called out to Bena, 'Hera, do you think Das would let us back into Zarda if we gave them some of these rabbit moving furs.'

'The problem with Das is, he would kill us first and then ask what the moving fur is for,' Bena replied. There was an uneasy chuckle from some of the Gubba.

'What do you think would be a suitable trade to get back to the tribe?'

'All the buffalo on the plains?' Bena again offered in a tone of indifference. 'I think most of us don't even want to go back.'

'At least to finish the Hunter's Walk?'

'That's for young Sanaa; I can only see you.'

Dun put a restraining hand on Ghar's shoulder, with big eyes asking him to stop this conversation.

Ghar nodded. 'That's fair, Hera,' he declared to Bena. He returned to the moving fur he was going to help with.

Dun sat quietly next to him and whispered, 'They don't actually want to go back; partially fear, but I think it's mostly pride.'

'But don't they want to be near the Fathers?'

'The Fathers expelled us, and even if I were to accept your accusation that it was Das and the Elders who decided against the Gubba, the Fathers did nothing to stop them.'

'I don't know . . . I don't think that's how the Fathers help.'

'How do you think they help, Ghar?'

The moving furs had ceased and the group had grown quiet, listening in on Ghar and Dun's conversation.

'The wolf eats the deer, which helps the wolf, but doesn't help the deer; it's not as simple as getting help. Help for us sometimes means a punishment for another.'

Kara joined in, 'So when we eat the buffalo, it's a help for us, but not a help for the buffalo?'

'I am sure the buffalo does not enjoy becoming moving furs,' Dun kept up his jovial attitude.

'Would it be better to think of trouble as a test, like the Hunters Walk?' Ghar felt like he had caught on to something.

'So, if it's good the Fathers are good, and if it's bad the Fathers are testing us?'

'Somehow I think the Fathers would be more consistent. What if the good is also a test?' Ghar felt like his feet were on firm ground, 'and what if this is all the Hunter's Walk?' The eyes that were on Ghar, drifted away, lost in the suggestion that everything they did was part of the test.

'So, shouldn't all of us do the Hunter's Walk, since we are already doing it?' Kara had a cascading thought, 'the Gubba and the tribeswomen as well?'

Dun went serious, 'I think we've already started.'

Ghar nodded, 'Now we just have to complete it.'

* * *

On the way back to Khamma, Ghar discussed with Dun the many ways they could try to get back into Zarda.

'I think we should walk around and pretend we were never away,' Dun had the most entertaining plan.

'I think they might notice a fair skin.'

'You could paint me the right amount of brown!'

'I still think we could offer moving furs in trade; buffalo hides are so much thicker and warmer than deer,' Ghar tried to be serious.

'I could see Adura again, that would be something to appreciate.'

Khamma's tree-laden rocks were a gracious sight for Ghar, 'Even though I was here only a few days ago, I am always happy to come back.'

They stepped into the flowing water and waded through the rocky, frothing stream. A few moments later the green giants hove into view, and after a few more, they were in Khamma. The heavy loads on their backs felt even heavier for the last few steps.

'Mai . . . she doesn't look happy,' Dun alerted.

Ghar turned in time to see a brown roll hit his forehead.

'What do you think this is, Ghar? You put this in my belongings and then leave?'

'But Mai?'

'I am not talking to you,' Mai turned to Dun, 'you can ask your friend what he wants? I can't give him a child.'

Dun looked at Ghar with terrified eyes.

Ghar translated.

Dun looked back at Mai and smiled, 'He wants you.'

Ghar felt the words hit him in the chest and looked down while translating Zardan to Khamman, 'He says that I want you.' He turned his eyes on hers, 'I want you.'

Mai had an expression like she had caught herself before falling. Like she had realized some thought but didn't know what to do with it. She moved into Ghar, her hands in between them. She punched his chest with the heel of her fists while losing her face in his furs.

Ghar quickly dropped the moving furs that he was carrying and wrapped his arms around her; she was still punching, but to Ghar the pain on his aching bones were like the cooling reward of rain drops at the end of a hot day. Each blow let his arms enclose her a little more, until his hands met. He pulled her in, making every moment he was close to her, a footstep that took him to the top of a mountain. Suddenly nothing mattered, Khamma could wait, Zarda could wait, the Hunter's Walk could wait. All that mattered was this precious being cradled in his arms, the light gentle movements of her breathing, the soothing soft sweat on her neck. 'I want you, Mai. I want you. I want you.'

'Then don't leave me, Ghar.'

* * *

'This tribe seems to have taken a very different path lately. Not punishing Mai, working with outsiders, and now you and Mai wanting to become mates,' Manar checked through the collection of dried herbs, berries and pastes that were arranged neatly on the wall.

Ghar smiled, his face was sore from smiling, but he couldn't help indulging himself. He didn't really care that this was not normal, why be normal when he could be Mai's mate? The sound of her name seemed to take on a new meaning, she was no longer a girl he knew, but a girl who was intrinsically connected to him, he could share her pride for her healing, he could take care of her just as he would take care of himself, and he could introduce her as his mate—although that would be meaningless to the Zarda. But, somehow, he could feel that Gharra and Adura would be happy for him, to have a girl treat his needs as important, as well as him having to treat her needs as important, 'Manar, is that a yes or a no?'

'Say yes, Manar, we need you to push Tan,' Mai had a look of mischief, 'Especially since Tan is sick, this is the best time to ask. He will probably say yes to anything.'

Manar chuckled but then went serious, 'It's not nice to joke about his illness. And he refuses to come here and let us take care of him.' There was a concern in the longness of her face. 'I will see him before going to the forest. Can you behave until I get back?'

'By the Spirits, we are the best Khamma,' Mai still had a hint of uncontainable happiness.

'Did you talk to Manar about travelling over to Gubba Zarda to start a Healing Cave?' Ghar asked Mai, as they watched Manar's lanky gait turn around the corner.

'I forgot, Ghar,' Mai slid under his arm. 'Let's go do something.'

Ghar felt like there were a lot of tasks to complete before going back to Gubba Zarda, especially since Mai was coming along. But then he looked at the little bounce Mai had in her walk. *We can always stay here for another day.*

They walked down towards the entrance stream, to find a tribesman announcing in sorrow, 'Tan is dead.'

14

A fight for Khamma

Tan's passing just the day before hung over the Khamma like the lull before a storm.

'Yan calls for the tribe to meet at the main campfire,' Yan's friends moved around the camp passing the message.

'Yan calling a meeting to impose his ways, I suppose. I heard the Elders disagreed with everything he asked for,' Manar glared at the powdered herbs as if they had done something wrong. There came another call for the tribespeople to gather around the main campfire, 'They should have told us about this meeting yesterday, then more of us could have attended,' Manar grumbled. 'There are many out hunting with the wolves or exploring the forest. Just trying to think of something other than Tan.'

'Maybe their intention was to avoid having full attendance?' Mai suggested.

'What do you mean?' Ghar was unhappy with the situation, but he was fascinated by the way the Khamma was changing.

'If they are not here, they can't oppose anything he says,' Mai said.

'Does it matter even if they are?' Manar asked.

Ghar remembered Kara standing up in Gubba Zarda, 'It could matter, if enough people stand up.'

'What would it matter whether people stood or sat, or even lay down?' Manar was getting impatient with Ghar and Mai.

'It's something a Gubba did. When the Gubba Elders proclaimed that they were not going to make the moving furs in exchange for meat and furs, Kara stood up and said she agreed with my plan. Gradually the whole tribe agreed.'

There was another call for the meeting to start, this time with more vehemence. Manar stopped the conversation, 'Let's go, before Yan inaugurates his leadership with our punishment.'

What is 'enough'? Ghar thought that was the best question to ask.

* * *

'My brethren, by the way of the Wolf.'

Ghar was surprised to see Yan and his friends not in moving furs. They had reverted to the older Khamman style of wrapping the furs around the shoulders and around the waist. They looked like outsiders. *I would like to see how they fare in another water powder storm without moving furs.*

'In this gathering I will reflect on our wise leader, Tan, and how much he means to us.'

The tribe collectively called out their praise, 'May he lie among the stars.'

'How much he has guided us through difficult times. How he kept a vigil on the outsiders, how he got us the moving furs, and how he started the Healing Cave.'

Ghar, glanced at Manar and Mai, to make sure he had heard the praise right. There was another call for Tan's ascent to the stars.

'He did much for this tribe,' Yan looked around, meeting the gaze of some of the tribesmen, pausing for their adoration, 'but, as we look back at Tan, we must also look forward with some important decisions for the tribe.'

Ghar noticed some of Yan's friends strategically position themselves beside Manar and Mai, and then beside him. *I think Yan wants us to keep quiet.*

'There are new dangers we face. Outsiders near our hunting grounds, even outsiders within our tribe. When the cold storm killed some of our tribesmen, it gave us a message: the Spirits are not happy with us.'

Ghar remembered that this was a similar argument that Das had used.

'There is also a feeling that we have less buffalo this warm-time, another sign that the Spirits are unhappy with us,' Yan stopped to look around at the tribe. 'We have decided, with the Elders,' Yan graciously bowed to the Elders, 'that we need to follow these plans. We will not tolerate any more outsiders in Khamma,' Yan took a moment to glare at Ghar. 'To help with the hunts we need more men. The women in our tribe will stop participating in hunting. We want tribeswomen to keep their bodies ready for making more Khamma.'

There was a commotion around the tribe as the women looked incredulously at each other. Ghar felt the former idea was insulting to him, Dun and the Gubba. They had done a lot towards providing more Khamma with moving furs and preparing meat. But the idea that women had to stay in camp to make more Khamma for hunting did not make any sense.

'Yan, by stopping tribeswomen from hunting you are taking away hunters, how does that solve your problem?' Ghar felt a sudden smack on the side of his face. He lost the next few moments. He was on the ground with Mai yelling. The next moment, he was in the air; all he could see was the night-black sky.

* * *

'What happened? Is Mai all right?' Ghar wasn't sure where he was, or how he got there.

'You're all right, Ghar, you're talking in Zardan,' Mai reassured him, 'I'm all right, Ghar, just stay still and don't exert yourself. You're in Khamma, in the Healing Cave.'

Ghar felt the cold wet fur on the side of his face, the water dripping down his neck. The pressure was too much to bear, 'Mai, that hurts.'

'All right, Ghar, we need to make the bump go down. But I can do it softer.' Mai poured more cold water out of the waterskin on to the fur. 'Is that better?'

'Yes, Mai,' Ghar caught up with his breathing, he felt like he was trying to keep up with Nara in the forest, 'What happened?'

'You interrupted Yan's speech, so his friend hit you.'

'In front of the whole gathering? Did the tribe do anything?'

'They shouted at Yan's friends, but they too were scared to do any more.'

'The Elders are not happy with this behaviour at all,' Manar announced from somewhere near the cave entrance.

Ghar remembered what he said, 'They want to stop tribeswomen from hunting! I think Yan is going crazy.' Ghar found it painful to talk, but the pain from Yan's ideas hurt his head even more, 'We need Kara,' he said in Zardan, gazing at Manar.

'What?' Manar knelt beside Mai in Ghar's sight. 'I think you are going crazy as well.'

'Sorry . . . Kara . . . I told you about her, she stood up and led the decision to make the moving furs.'

'So, do you want Khamma to do the same?' Mai asked.

'Yes.'

Manar advised, 'There are some who will support you, but most believe Yan.'

'Khamma has to say no to this. This is too important,' Ghar fell back into darkness.

* * *

'Gharra, here are the fish we caught.' The fish left his hands and started to swim into the pine trees, but then they seemed to get irritated by the prickly pine needles and bounced between the trees.

'I wish I could give more for Dun. We have food for the Sanaa,' he pointed to a pile on the ground that erupted with streaky dried meat, colourful berries and dripping honeynest.

'It's all right, my son, just make sure that you have enough to eat,' Gharra replied.

Ghar woke up, his head still throbbing from the swelling, 'Gharra, are you here?'

Mai walked in from the front of the cave. 'Ghar, I am here. How are you?'

'My head hurts, we need to help the tribe take a stand against Yan.'

'Yes, yes, we can do that when you are better, Ghar. Try and sleep.'

'We could see which group is bigger: tribeswomen hunt or tribeswomen don't hunt.'

Mai pushed Ghar's shoulders down flat, 'I talked to some of the tribeswomen about that. I think we are happy not hunting.'

'What? What about the outsiders? Is the tribe all right not accepting outsiders?' Ghar had only just woken up and he wanted to do nothing but stick his face into the cool crisp stream outside the Healing Cave.

'You are already Khamma, isn't that all that matters?'

'But what if there is another boy or girl out there who can bring new ways to Khamma.'

'I am happy you are Khamma. We are together now, and that's all that matters.'

'Why are you arguing with me about this?'

Mai gazed, big-eyed at Ghar, 'We can fight Yan, but if we lose, we will be banished from the tribe. And what Yan is proposing is not so bad.'

Ghar remembered how Das changed the status of the Gubba from being impure and forbidden to stay close to the Sanaa, to thieves to be banished from Zarda. 'This won't end here, Mai. We have to stand up.'

'I want to sit down, let the other Khamma stand up,' Mai raised her voice, frustrated.

Manar walked in, 'What is all this noise about?' Ghar explained what they were arguing about. 'I have to agree with Ghar,' Manar told Mai, 'I talked to Udor; they're discussing the idea of converting the Healing Cave to an abode for Yan and his friends.'

Ghar was about to appeal to Mai again, but then it occurred to him, that Manar had changed the outcome of the argument. 'Manar makes me stronger.' Ghar got up from his fur, to the quick reactions from the healers to put him back down. 'I'm all right, let me show you what I'm thinking.' He reached into a pouch of beetle berries and laid them on the flat rock floor. He picked up a berry, 'This berry is me, and this berry is Mai. If we place them together there is nothing different.' Ghar looked up at their clueless faces. 'But if we put Manar next to me, there is a difference.'

'So, we give the tribe berries?' Manar laughed.

Ghar popped a berry into his mouth, to an admonishing slap on the back from Manar, 'The berries are not important. It's giving the decision-making to the Khamma, and not to Yan. Not even to the Elders.'

'So, each of us gets to decide,' Mai looked impressed.

'I think it is truer to say that each of us gets to say what we want. What we get depends on whether the other tribespeople want the same thing.'

'Yan will not agree,' Manar warned.

'That's true.' Ghar gazed out the cave entrance for a way out of this problem. 'Yan won't, but maybe the Elders will.'

'But wouldn't they lose their remaining control if they handed it over to the tribe?' Mai asked.

'I think they already know they will eventually lose control to Yan. It is only time.'

'I'll talk to the Elders,' Manar offered.

'We will come with you,' Ghar stroked Mai's hair, 'but first, there's something I must do.' He walked out and plunged his face in the creek.

* * *

'So, you're saying the tribe is wiser than us?' Udor was not happy with the proposal, the drone of his voice and his lack of eye-contact conveyed his lack of interest. He was lean, but tall. He had narrow shoulders that blurred any distinction between his torso and his neck. He had a large scar across his cheek that disappeared into his hair. Some of the tribesmen had noticed similar scars going down as far as his chest. There were rumours that a bear had bitten him but Udor's head was so stubborn that the bear gave up.

Ghar was very aware of the unsightly bump on own his head and had this overwhelming suspicion that it made him look abnormal, which did not help that the Khamma viewed him as a new Khamma, an abnormal Khamma. 'Wise Leaders, that is not what we are saying; the tribe does not have more wisdom than you. Tan told you that Yan would take over because it was going to happen. Yan has the support of his friends, and the respect of the tribe.' Ghar pointed at the bump, 'And he is willing to act if we don't agree with him.'

Tura was a smaller Elder who seemed to get lost in her own moving fur. She had wide calm eyes that perched on high cheekbones, somewhat like Manar and Mai. Her face had pronounced wrinkle lines that disappeared and reappeared around her face, creating an impression that they were all connected somehow. Her hair was short in the front and in a tight knot at the back. 'You are telling us to step away from leading the tribe.'

'No, we need the Elders to help lead the tribe to make the right decision. But, by giving the power of the decision to the tribe, we can block whatever bad Yan is doing,' Manar pitched in to aid Ghar in the argument.

'Why would Yan agree to this? If you take away power from us, then you're taking away power from Yan as well,' Tura further questioned the idea of the tribe doing the decision-making.

'He still needs your support; he knows that if you don't support him the tribe won't either,' Ghar advised.

'He would still lose his power over the tribe.'

'No, we will give him the chance to lead after the decision is made. He will not make the decision for the tribeswomen to hunt or not, the tribe will, but if the decision is for women to hunt, then he will lead them.

Udor looked at Tura with a fond smile, 'I wish Tan were here. He would usually know what to do.'

Tura replied, 'He would tell us to go along with Ghar's plan, it sounds strange.'

'We have done what we could, leading the tribe, I can't even remember most of it,' Udor sighed, but still with a smile, 'I think it's a nice gesture to give the responsibility back to the tribe.' Udor motioned to Ghar with a wave of his fingers, 'Now, tell us more about these *decision berries*.'

* * *

'I don't like Zarda, I don't like Zardan ideas, and I definitely don't like Zarda and their ideas that make it hard for me,' Yan scoffed at the proposal that the group offered. 'Why should I take this?'

'We will tell the tribe that we do not support you,' Udor said, nonchalantly.

To Ghar, Udor's demeanour seemed surprisingly effective. Udor had a way of delaying the end of his words, that made him seem like he did not care about any reaction. Fighting back would be futile. Yan's mouth stayed agape. There was a moment of anticipation, the only sounds that Ghar could hear were the birds in flight over the lake, the wind rustling through the trees and the air that gushed out of Yan's mouth.

'You have already supported my leadership, you can't just take it away,' there was a slight conciliatory note in his tone.

'We can, and if you don't accept this plan, we will.'

There was more silence. Yan did not step back or seem to get disappointed. He turned around and whispered to his friends, then turned back to the Elders, 'Wise Leaders, let us talk away from the ears of the Zardan.'

Ghar had had a feeling that this would happen and had hoped that the Elders would insist on including him, but he knew there wasn't much hope of that happening.

'I think that is a fair request,' Tura motioned to Ghar to leave.

'Also, the mother-killer and the cave-waster,' Yan asked.

Cave-waster, that's a new name. Ghar couldn't help but think that was funny. But he stiffened his face. Mai and Manar followed him to the lake's rock bank.

'If that boy ever comes to me for healing, I'm going to send him to the Spirits,' Manar was not amused.

Ghar and Mai smirked quietly, not wanting to seem disrespectful to the Elders. 'He is going to restore some decision-making power to the Elders,' Ghar quickly surmised what Yan was trying to do.

'I thought so too. Right after he makes our expulsion part of the deal,' Mai replied.

'It has been nice living here, but maybe we can live with your friend, Dun?' Manar said with a wry smile.

They looked out at the water, the green-brown giants standing, watching over the tribe, heralding the cold-time to come. The sun cutting through the cold morning air, a breeze drifting a sensuous aroma of smoky fat from a meat-smoking fire. The unworried laughter of children playing on the banks.

Ghar turned to Mai and Manar, 'Let's hope the Elders stop Yan from ruining this place.'

* * *

'Yan offered us a share in making decisions; we would take turns on every issue,' Udor had a slight lift to the right corner of his lip.

'We did not even get that with Tan,' Tura was happy as well.

Ghar was felt his chest tighten, 'Did you accept?'

'Yes, we did. Also, we will send you back to Zarda,' Udor added indifferently.

Ghar felt like shaking the Elders. He stood there speechless.

'You're right, that was funny,' Tura told Udor with a laugh.

'So, you're joking?' Ghar was relieved, but also a bit cross with the Elders for being so cavalier about the situation.

'Yes, Ghar. Yan did offer the decisions,' Udor put his hand on Manar's shoulder, 'but, as I said before, I think it is time that we stepped out of the way.' He shrugged, 'Honestly speaking, I like the moving furs, I like your paintings,' Udor complimented Ghar and then turned to Manar and Mai, 'you have helped me keep comfortable when I was sick.'

Manar immediately grew teary-eyed at the recognition, 'Thank you, Wise Leader.'

Udor nodded, 'We would lose all this if Yan were to decide. I would rather the tribe chooses.'

Ghar bowed; what he really wanted to do was jump, but he remembered to be respectful. 'Thank you for your confidence in me.'

'The *decision berries* are to be tomorrow. There will be a short discussion before this, but you can start talking to the tribe any time you want,' Tura advised the group. She took in a long breath and put her elbow on Udor, 'This already sounds good, no need to decide anything.'

'I agree, it should be interesting to watch them fight tomorrow.'

Ghar was already planning out his arguments.

* * *

There was a thrum of excitement that flowed through the camp. Only dried-and-smoked meat sustained the tribespeople; they were supposed to hunt and replenish their stores, but they had all stayed in the camp to make sure they could attend the gathering.

Ghar had changed the decision berries to making marks on an old hide. *There might not be enough berries for the tribe, and also the berries could get eaten before comparison.* He had painted a female Khamma hunting buffalo on the left and on the right, tribeswomen sitting around a campfire. The Elders and Yan had agreed that a mark would be made for every decision by the Khamma tribespeople.

'My brethren, by the way of the Wolf, may Tan find his place in the stars,' Udor started with a remembrance for his friend. 'We made some decisions at our last gathering,' Udor said, with a tone that mimicked Tan.

Mai whispered to Ghar, 'Udor looks uncomfortable.' Ghar didn't have time to respond. *This was Tan's role,* he thought.

'But we felt that you did not have a say in those decisions,' Udor stopped. He looked at Tura and then Yan. 'This is the way it was, when Tan was here, when we were little children, when our parents were little children.' Udor's poetry calmed the excited murmurs in the tribe. 'Khamma has changed. There are strange new voices in the camp,' he looked at Ghar, 'there was the even stranger water powder.' A dull hum of worry broke out in the tribe. 'But this strange outsider brought us moving furs and even stranger, the attaching of men.'

Ghar noticed the eyes on him; he looked around, worried initially that they were suspicious, but the glances came with nods of appreciation, which Ghar could only return with graciousness.

'Khamma has changed, the way we decide should change too,' Udor said, 'the new Khamma has created a way for you to choose. Each of you gets a say in what the Khamma will do,' he paused, tugging at the top of his staff. 'This is important that you all try to understand the problems, and the solutions that Yan and Ghar will talk about.' He nodded at Yan to start.

'My brethren, by the way of the Wolf, my wise Khamma, we have angered the Spirits.' The tribe broke out into adulation for the Spirits. 'There are outsiders in the camp,' Yan pointed at Ghar. 'In punishment, they sent the water powder. In punishment, they have taken away our buffalo.' He paced between the tribesmen. 'We must appease the Spirits . . . by casting away the outsider.'

Ghar noticed the many confused faces in the crowd. *Is this a decision that will happen today?*

'In order to prepare for the hard time ahead, we need more babies, who will grow into able-bodied Khamma. We need the women to focus on that. We all know how Mai could not give me a baby, because she is too busy as a healer.' There were some Khamma that seemed to agree, Ghar reached over and placed his hand on Mai's. 'Now she wants the outsider as a mate. If women stayed in the camp, we would not have these problems.'

Ghar looked at Manar, *did you ask the Elders about us being mates?* He looked down at his hand on Mai's. Maybe it was obvious that Mai wanted to be his mate.

'But all these problems started with the outsider. These are the issues we must decide on today, we must expel the outsider, and ban the women from hunting. Khamma needs you to make the right decision.'

The tribe had started to talk, most were whispers, but there were some loud calls for Ghar to be removed.

Ghar got up. He had not prepared for this decision, but in a way, being an outsider, he was always ready with reasons to be allowed to stay. 'My brethren, by the way of the Wolf, you are the tribe that accepted me when I was lost. Tan made me a Khamma,' Ghar waited for the tribe to quieten down. 'Tan made me a Khamma.' Ghar pointed at Tuya, 'Tan made me a Khamma because I helped heal Tuya.' He tugged at the moving fur he wore, 'Tan made me a Khamma, because I brought moving furs to Khamma. And when the water powder hit us, we had the moving fur to protect us.' Ghar mimicked Yan's pacing around the fire. He felt a confidence building within him by placing himself in Tan's affirmation. He had thought that talking about the Spirits and their satisfaction might get misread by the tribe, he could almost hear them say, *the Zardan shouldn't talk about the Khamman Spirits.* 'Tan had confidence in me, the Elders have confidence in me, and Manar and Mai have confidence in me,' Ghar gazed out at the crowd, and remembered that it was their choice, 'but now you have to choose. When the hunts get harder, we need the skills of the women. When the water powder storm comes again, we need all the help we can get, from outsiders, from the Gubba, from any tribe out there. We have to be ready to change to face the challenges.' He walked to Udor, 'Are you ready, Udor?'

Udor was not ready to answer, 'Yes?'

'Udor, are you ready?' Ghar urged.

'Yes!'

He walked over to a tribeswoman, 'Are you ready?'

'Yes!'

He asked a few more tribespeople, and then urged, 'We are ready, we need to choose the right path, choose to keep the Khamma women in the hunt, and choose to keep our tribe open to outsiders, open to help,' Ghar bowed and went back to Mai. His limbs were shaking, and he felt a weakness in his chest. 'That was more difficult than hunting a buffalo!'

'You did well, Ghar, you have to go make the marks,' Mai reminded Ghar.

'Aiy,' he made the same sound Mai usually made, 'Khamma, please stay on this side, when you have voted, walk over to the other side of the fire.'

He took the pieces of charcoal he usually powdered down to make paint, and sketched a figure standing in Khamma and another leaving.

The first tribesman approached Ghar. 'Women should hunt. But outsiders should leave.'

Ghar flinched, *not a good start,* he thought to himself. He made the marks and called out, 'Next?'

* * *

Ghar held up the hide for the Elders to see. Marks for women hunting were cancelled against marks for women not hunting, until no more marks could be cancelled. The remaining marks were the winner. Yan elbowed Ghar out of the way to get a better look.

'Looks like the tribe has chosen that women should hunt.'

Yan groaned. Ghar felt relieved in the first choice. He compared the tribe's choices for the expulsion of the outsiders. As he cancelled every mark that was similar on both side it became apparent that the decision was close. He held his breath with the marks. There was a solitary mark that was the difference.

'This decision is only split by a mark. Khamma has chosen to keep the outsiders.' Ghar had not anticipated that the vote would be quite so close, his eyes began to well up, he missed Mai, he walked over and embraced her, 'I nearly lost you.'

'I would have come with you, Ghar.'

* * *

'I talked to some of the women, all of them voted to stay hunters,' Mai announced.

'All of them?' Ghar thought about the result, he did remember seeing a lot of women asking to mark on the 'hunt' side. But all? That made him feel like this really was the right decision for Khamma.

'All, and they're happy that we did this. The hunt is tiring and dangerous, you could get killed, but it makes you feel like part of the tribe,' Mai raised her nose, 'the meat just tastes better.'

'Khamma is a little more unsure about me . . . just a mark of difference.'

Mai had a reassuring shimmer in her eyes, the same as he remembered in the forest when she sheltered him from the rain. 'I want you here,' she sat down with him on the rock ledge, 'and if Khamma doesn't want you, they will learn to want you.'

* * *

Ghar took a walk on the lake shore to help settle his mind. The last few days had been like a tumultuous storm, each gust could have potentially been the end of him. *By the Fathers, if not for your grace and guidance, I would have been finished.*

Tur joined in, with Ulan in tow, 'Zardan, that was an impressive performance yesterday!' Tur said heartily. 'I think you did something great for Khamma.'

Ghar smiled and reached out to embrace them, 'Thank you, my brothers.'

'Now that you are so important, you don't have time for us,' Ulan said.

Ghar couldn't tell whether he was joking, 'Of course, I do!' He knew this was not entirely true. Between Mai, Dun, moving furs and this ongoing fight with Yan, he hardly had any time to do anything else. He replied to Ulan with some courteous obfuscation, 'It is you and Tur who are too busy.'

'The Zardan is quick with words,' Tur cut in. 'It's all right that you are too busy, just remember to greet us occasionally.'

Ghar had come to the same conclusion that he was quicker with words than the truth. 'Listen, you and Ulan were among the only Khamma to give me a chance when I was brought here; I will always remember that even if I might seem to be busy these days. How about we go hunting together?'

'I would like to make some moving furs actually,' Ulan requested.

'Me too,' Tur said, 'also, you are a terrible hunter.'

'Agreed, then you should come to Gubba Zarda; they make moving furs out of rabbits!' Ghar said.

'Agreed!'

The original moving fur group continued their walk, reminiscing and joking.

* * *

Mai laughed with delight, her eyes glimmered like the lake in moonlight during a clear night, 'Thank you, Ghar, for making Khamma better,' she pulled him in closer, he could feel her warm breath on his neck, their feet started to get in the way of their Khazagu movements.

Ghar felt his cheeks warm at the compliment, which was rare from Mai. 'Thank you for making Ghar better,' he smiled, his tone softened by words. He led her out of the group, whispering, 'Let's talk, just us?'

'Yes, Ghar,' Mai accepted Ghar's inviting hand.

'Just that there's always a tribesman around, we can't talk about us when they're around.'

'I know, mates should have some time alone,' Mai giggled.

Ghar thought for a moment, he grinned with her, his natural smile, but also a deliberate, full, deer-eyed adulation, 'I feel like we are not just mates,' he knelt on his right knee.

'Why are you showing me respect for the Spirits? You should look to the stars.'

'I don't know Mai, I don't know how to describe this feeling in my chest,' Ghar held her hands, tears in his eyes. 'I like you, the way I like Dun; I respect you, the way I respect Tan; I feel you, the way I feel Manar; and when you are away, even when you have just turned away, I miss you, like I miss Gharra and Adura.' Ghar sighed, he could not take his eyes off Mai. 'Except, it's all combined.'

'I am beginning to understand what you mean, Ghar. It's like a painting with all the colours.'

'All the colours,' Ghar smiled. 'I lost Zarda, but then found Khamma; I lost the Gubba, then I found them; but when I found you, I was really finding myself.'

They lay down, the Spirits floated above them, glimmering at their shared words.

'I found myself.'

15

Another Beginning

'Mai, I think we should get into the caves,' Ghar felt the wind nip at the skin on the tip of his nose through the small gap in his moving fur. The cold-time had brought on a few of these windstorms, each with debilitating rain, but without the water powder. He motioned the other tribesmen out on the banks to follow him. Ghar tugged a wall of hide, reinforced with harnessed sticks like the tepees, and closed the entrance of the cave. The largest cavern in Khamma also had the advantage of a small opening, which Ghar and a few tribesmen could seal quickly with the aid of a few well-positioned rocks.

Ghar walked with Mai, past some of the mothers with their younglings, past the Elders. The children and the Elders stayed close to the entrance of the cave, where there was a little light streaming in through the gaps of the cave's doorway. Any of the tribesmen who were not well, were to remain at the Healing Cave, in small tepees that would provide shelter. The healthier, older tribesmen and the wolves moved to the back of the cave, which branched out into the darkness. To keep the younglings happy, Ghar and Mai gave the tribesmen paints and small pieces of scrap hide, to draw images of objects. The younglings were especially interested in making impressions with their hands.

Ghar watched a youngling blow the paint through a grass tube leaving the silhouette of her hand on the cave wall.

He brought his fire brand closer, he wanted to paint, not for himself, but for the tribesmen in the cave, especially the younglings who had taken an interest. He used charcoal to gently get the shape of his depiction, and started to fill it, with red ochre, with white limestone, with more charcoal. He had gained an audience behind him. The image slowly formed, the large hooves, the muscular shoulders, a midriff that sloped up to the hind legs, a long hanging nose.

'That's a big-nose buffalo,' a tribesman called out.

A child started to cry. Ghar thought, *I forgot! The younglings have never seen a big-nose buffalo,* 'Youngling, this is only a painting,' Ghar held out his hand, beckoning the child to come closer.

'Do another!' a tribesman asked earnestly.

Ghar looked at a group of hunters huddled together with little heads of children sticking out from the furry mound. *It's so cold.* Ghar had not noticed his cold, shaking fingertips, which somehow stopped shivering when stroking the paint to life on the rock face. *My fingers want me to paint, Zarda wants me to paint.*

* * *

The wild wind, whistling through the heavy, rattling hide-wall had kept the Khamma away from the cave entrance. Ghar braved the cold, unyielding wind to inspect what was happening outside. Freezing-cold water powder revealed itself in the light of Ghar's firebrand. The closer he got to the hide wall, the more belligerent the wind seemed to get, he could hardly look through the gaps, the cold air scratching at the skin of his eyes.

He made his way back into the cave where the tribe had grown from anxious to exhausted. 'The storm still lives,' Ghar knew the tribespeople knew this, but still thought a confirmation would be a distraction from the ordeal.

A youngling sleepily left the fur-laden bodies that were trying to sleep and reached out to Ghar. 'Big-nose buffalo,' she pointed at

Ghar's paintings. Ghar was delighted she remembered, he picked her up and tried to prompt the other names, 'How about this?'

'Tree-antler deer?'

'Yes, and this?'

'Long-face deer.'

'And this?'

'Calm bear.'

Ghar had himself not seen some of the animals. The calm bear was a depiction in the Grand Cave. He had heard from the hunters that it was a bear that did not really mind the hunters, but if threatened would attack. 'Very good, little girl, now you should get some rest, so that when the storm stops you can go outside and play,' he gave the child back to her mother who had woken up at the conversation.

Udor was partially asleep, the whites of his eyes flitting in Ghar's fire light. 'Udor, the water powder storm is still really bad.'

Udor sleepily responded, 'I can hear the wind.'

'Yes, but I worry about the hunters still outside.'

Udor awoke abruptly, 'They should be near the Whispering Caves, that was the plan, yes?'

Ghar had planned with Yan to hunt close to locations where there was a cave in case of a water powder storm, 'Yes, Udor, but we did not plan for this. This storm started the day before yesterday, and it's still so strong,' Ghar pondered. 'If we are nearly out of firewood, then what about the hunters? What about Manar and the Healing Cave?'

'I understand,' Udor looked away, almost uninterested. 'We will have to just wait and see, unless you want to go find them in this storm.'

Ghar could sense the frustration in Udor's tone. Ghar, along with the Elders, Mai and Manar, had tried his best to prepare the tribe for the storm, but the storm had had other plans, 'I don't; we will wait.'

'Then stop wasting that fire stick, and join a pack,' Udor went back to sleep.

Ghar obliged, he fumbled his way back to Mai, who seemed to roll around in her furs, asleep.

He put out the flame and and lay down beside her. *I hope Dun and the Gubba are all right.* He suddenly remembered Adura, with a feeling of shame that he had not thought about her during the storm. *By the Fathers, let Adura and the Zarda survive this storm,* he thought as he fell asleep.

* * *

'The paintings have to tell a story today, to teach us what happened yesterday and, if we consider carefully, what will happen tomorrow,' Adura coaxed Ghar's hand to complete the depiction of a hunter hurling a spear into the chest of a round-horn deer. The bristles of hair that he pressed against the bare hide seemed to create the image on its own, Ghar's fingers only guiding it to the location.

The figures jumped off the skin into the cave, the hunters running after the terrified speared deer. Ghar found the hunters' screams and the animal's yelps amusing. 'Hera, I don't want to paint only what I see, I want to paint what I feel.'

'Then be careful, my son; what you feel may not be what the tribe wants to see.'

'Ghar, wake up.'

Ghar heard the appeal, the more he listened, the more the cave and Adura seemed to drift away.

'Ghar, the storm has nearly ceased; Udor wants us to go out.'

Ghar could feel the warmth from Mai's breath on his face. He nodded as he got up, the cold dulling the sensation in his joints. He was unsure of his limbs' intentions as they seemed to move without much attention to where he wanted to go.

'Relax, Ghar, warm up first,' Mai advised, holding Ghar's arm.

Ghar took a deep breath, and started to jump in place, 'All right, let's go.'

The cave entrance exposed the tribesmen to a blinding white that blanketed the camp up to the lake's shore.

'The green giants have become the white giants,' Ghar explained, immediately regretting removing the fur cover from over his mouth to make the joke. The tribesmen and the wolves left trails in the water powder that Ghar thought would be best to follow, his moccasins plunging into the fresh holes.

They trudged through the water powder; each step felt like a separate journey. To Ghar's dismay the water powder seemed to be sliding down his legs and creating a pool of water inside his moccasins. *Maybe sealing it against water from the outside in not enough. We could fix this by making it taller,* Ghar debated with himself as they came into view of the Healing Cave.

'Manar, what happened?' Mai called out as she leaped through the water powder to get to the Healing Cave quicker.

As Ghar got closer, he could see hunters tending to the fires. A tepee had collapsed. He could hear the commotion, Manar calling out to get more hot water, and the hunters urging their cohorts to stay conscious.

There were tribesmen on the floor, wrapped in furs that were replaced with warmer furs that had been hung out to dry above the fires. He immediately recognized a hunter as Yan's friend, and next to him, Yan. Mai was beside him, consoling him, while warming his forehead with fur dipped in hot water. Ghar felt a twinge of jealousy at Mai reuniting with her former mate, but immediately felt shame at the pettiness of the thought. He took a cold fur that had been put on the ground and placed it by a fire to be warmed.

Tur was seated near a fire; his hands hidden deep in his furs. He was shivering but still clung to the large fur wrapped around his body.

'What happened, Tur?'

'We were out, when the storm hit,' Tur replied, heavy tremors accompanied each word.

Ghar thought he could hear Manar telling him to get Tur to rest. 'Tur, rest, we will talk about this later.'

Tur looked at Ghar in the eye and continued past Ghar's concern, 'We knew where the Whispering Caves were, but the storm made everything move around.' He slouched, a heavy sigh interrupted his shivering. 'Then we lost some of the hunters.'

'Did any die?'

'I'm not sure. We found Yan and Nula under an outcrop near the entrance of the Whispering Caves. They kept each other warm,' Tur glanced around at the injured. 'They gave each other warmth until they could only give each other cold.'

Ghar cringed at the morbid humour in Tur's account, 'Rest, Tur, I think you should save your strength to recover.'

Ghar went back to warming up the furs, occasionally looking at Manar and Mai to see if there was something more he could do. The storm had lasted longer than they had planned for. The firewood in the Whispering Caves would have run out before the storm ended. *That's why the hunters had to make the push to return to the camp.*

There was a small clump of water powder sitting on the rock face; he picked it up and rolled it in his fingers. *It's so delicate, and it becomes water. How can it cause so much harm?* Ghar was left to ponder the contradiction as the tribe worked to save Yan and Nula.

16

Outsiders of the Storm

'Nara!' Ghar called out to the Khamma scout.

Nara walked briskly through the rock cave entrance, with Uru trailing behind him, panting.

Even Uru can't keep up with Nara. 'Nara, you look worried.'

'Outsiders,' Nara said, out of breath. He stopped, his toes meeting Ghar's, he rested his right arm over Ghar's shoulder and slumped. 'Outsiders hunting in our forests.'

He can't be talking about the Gubba? 'Do they look familiar? Have the People of the Tall Grass returned?'

Nara straightened up and stretched. His arms flexed and contorted back but the extra bulk that Nara had built up by eating more with the Gubba made Ghar's wince less painful. 'It's not the Gubba,' he looked up with a knowing glint, 'they are a people I have never seen. They are not the same as the People of the Tall Grass.'

'Did you try to talk to them? Or try to make an offering?'

'I don't approach danger; I try to understand danger from a distance so I can outrun it.'

'Where are they now?'

'I waited and watched them; I was up on a mountain watching them stalk a herd of buffalo. But then the herd ran away and they followed, out of my sight. I decided it was more important to tell the tribe.'

'Could you tell whether they would be aggressive to us?' *Maybe we can make an arrangement as we did with the Gubba.*

'I don't know. But I think the Khamma might choose to be aggressive towards them if we see them again.'

* * *

The Khamma had chosen to look for the new outsider tribe to chase them off their territory. Yan's call for a decision-marks gathering ended in almost all of the tribe agreeing with him. Only Ghar, Mai and Manar opted to try to contact the tribe and decide what to do after.

Yan had recovered from his encounter with the water powder not only in body, but also in stature in the camp. He was the saviour that fought the water powder and brought Nula back to the tribe.

Ghar withheld his respect for Yan, but nonetheless appreciated that he had saved Nula. *It was Yan's fault that they did not have a moving fur, but he could have just left Nula there in the water powder to die; it took courage to save him.*

The wind still held the chill of cold-time, and a warning of another water powder storm, which caused Nara to lengthen their journey to include caves and rocky outcrops of refuge. The pace was frantic, and their footfalls as they trudged through the leafy, forest floor were the only accompanying sounds to the panting wolves.

The forest seems strangely quiet, Ghar thought, 'Has the water powder storm killed all the birds?' he asked, in Mai's direction, but he did not really look for an answer.

'It does sound quiet,' Mai had retained the look of worry that she had at the decision-marks meeting. 'This whole journey sounds too quiet.'

Ghar could only guess what the other tribesmen were thinking. He had heard stories about previous altercations that usually ended with the outsiders running away from the restrained wolves.

They stopped at a stream to drink and rest their burning leg muscles. Ghar watched Yan and Nara walk on. Ghar sat down and took off his moccasins and prodded the soreness on his big toe.

'The skin is going to come off,' he complained to Mai.

Mai smirked, 'Stop being a child.'

Yan walked back to the group, with Nara, 'Hunters, I want you to remember what Tan taught us. If the outsider tribe is too big, then let's try to win without fighting.'

Ghar had heard this before from Tan, the usual lesson at the gatherings, was to show strength, spread the wolves wide, seem bigger than you are, *like the bear who stands*. But, as he got to know Tan better, Ghar understood it was not only looking bigger but thinking bigger. Getting moving furs for the tribe, preparing stores of dried meat for water powder storms, making Ghar a Khamma. To Tan, it seemed the fight was not only from the outsiders, but from insiders as well.

Yan continued, 'When we see the outsiders, we spread out, with the wolves in front, but our hands on their collars. Make sure they see the wolves. And don't let any of the wolves go until I say so.'

Ghar was curious, 'Mai, have any of these men and women fought before?'

'No, most of them have never seen an outsider until I brought you to the camp,' she squashed her lips to their corners. 'Now we have the Gubba; very soon they will know Das himself,' she grit her teeth.

Ghar retreated from the questions. Mai had seemed irritable over the last few days, which made it difficult for Ghar to talk about how he was connected to the outsiders. He was an outsider, hunting outsiders. It was his duty as a Khamma, but he did not want to be responsible of killing another Ghar expelled from another tribe.

The hunters had resumed their journey again; Nara reassumed his position at the helm. Ghar caught up with him; he wanted to talk, reassure himself that the Khamma was making the right choice.

The wolves suddenly grew antsy. They put their noses up, sniffing the air, mostly facing a direction directly ahead of them.

'Everybody, keep quiet, keep the wolves quiet,' Yan hissed, 'Keep low.'

The tribesmen crouched to the ground on their knees. Ghar felt the food in his stomach try to crawl back up his gullet. He was now right in front with Nara, the last place he wanted to be.

An animal came into view from behind a dense clump of trees. A big-nose deer, part trotting, part walking with a spear in its right rump. It noticed the Khamma and bolted.

The tribesmen began to stand up, but Yan commanded them to stay down. The wolves seemed confused—some were focused on the deer, but the others still looked out to the right.

'What are they looking at?' Ghar whispered to Nara.

'Whoever put that spear in that deer,' Nara answered, a calmness in his voice that terrified Ghar.

They waited; Ghar's body began to feel the wait; he was too scared to make a sound that, instead of shifting to the other knee, he rolled from side to side.

The sounds of the forest broke to reveal an outsider, bare-bodied with only a small animal hide across his groin, running through the grass, at a pace that did not seem desperate, but had purpose. He was of small physique, Ghar thought, the same as Nara. He was too far away for Ghar to make out his features, but he did have short hair, brown skin, and scars across his body.

The man slowed, searching the ground, and then headed off in the direction that the animal had taken.

He is tracking the animal, Ghar thought.

'Nara, take Uru and follow him; keep far enough so he won't notice you,' Yan called out in a low voice. He turned to Ghar and another Khamma, Mura, 'Try to keep up with Nara, and give him support.'

Ghar grimaced at the thought of running through the forest, trying to keep up with this mysterious outsider and Nara.

Nara was already disappearing into the thicket.

'Come on, Ghar, let's go,' Mura urged. He was a youngling Khamma, who was known to be fast, his lean body, his strong nose and whipped-back hair all seemed like they were shaped by the wind as he ran.

Yan chose me on purpose; he knew I would get stranded behind Nara and Mura. He looked back at Mai, wincing a parting gesture. He took his spears and followed Mura.

* * *

Ghar lost sight of Mura, he knew this was going to happen. Somehow, he had managed to keep track of Mura's faint shape for some part of the distance, but now he had lost him completely. The pain in his chest felt like it was slowly burning his flesh from the inside; his leg muscles were appealing to him to just stop, rest, it did not matter where Nara and Mura were, they would be all right.

He halted for a moment, his hands on his knees. He looked up again to search for any sign of the Khamma he was supposed to support. He saw a symbol up on a tree, lines crossed. *That's not Khamman, maybe the outsider made it.* He walked quickly looking for another mark. A plant was broken at the stem, still green and moist. He continued in that direction. He saw Nara and Mura crouched behind a fallen tree, Nara holding down Uru on the ground.

Uru greeted Ghar with a flapping tongue.

Ghar stooped low, keeping himself behind the log. The outsider was quickly skinning the deer.

Nara looked at Ghar with a smile, 'The deer gave up, he was too tired, so he just knelt and waited for the outsider.'

Mura continued, 'It was something I have never imagined, he embraced the deer before taking the spear out, and then sliced its neck.'

They were interrupted by the man, who got up and looked in the direction of the Khamma.

Ghar quickly ducked behind the log. He could see Nara looking back the way they came for an escape.

'He's walking towards us with his spear,' Mura warned.

'Did he hear us? Why did he look this way?' Nara's tone held a hint of accusation.

Ghar glanced back at the route they had taken. *Was he going to clean it up and carry the dear himself?* 'He was waiting for his tribe to help.'

Mura stood up, his spear ready.

Ghar peered over the log, to see the man still advancing.

Ghar stood up beside Mura, 'Stand up, Nara,' Ghar hissed. He could tell that Nara was doing what kept him alive all those times he was threatened by the forest's fiercest creatures, find a tree to climb, or in this case, don't move, 'Get up, Nara. If he sees all of us, he might run away.'

The man had progressed to within a spear's throw. He barked foreign threats at the Khamma, his spear tip leading his demands. Nara finally stood up, which discomfited the hunter. He started to retreat to the deer.

Ghar vaulted over the tree trunk, and called out to the outsider, going into a hunched pose, trying to look nonthreatening. The outsider stopped.

Ghar shrugged out of his moving fur and placed it on the ground at his own feet.

The man squatted, his spear still tilted towards the Khamma. Ghar got up slowly with his head bowed, picked up the moving fur and walked towards the man, each step stopped the trembling in his knees. He tossed the moving fur at the man and motioned to him to put it on.

The outsider glanced back at his deer.

He is making sure we haven't stolen his deer, Ghar thought. He made a gesture to put the moving fur on.

'Don't worry, we won't hurt you,' he could not hear Nara and Mura say anything, so he continued.

The man put his spear down and peered around cautiously. He picked up the fur, a hesitant smile erupted across his face. He was a deeper brown than Ghar had ever seen. He had a thick tuft of hair on his head.

Ghar could tell that the man had never touched this kind of fur before; he let the man experience the soft fibres.

'Ghar,' he patted his chest. 'I am Ghar.'

The man looked up at Ghar and returned his eyes to the fur momentarily, 'Woyatcha.'

Ghar had trouble pronouncing the sounds, they were not like the sounds used in Khamma or Zarda. 'Boi-at-ta?'

The man shook his head, 'Woyatcha.'

To Ghar it sounded even faster this time and it hurt his tongue to even try and pronounce these sounds.

Nara called from behind, 'Ghar, get the man to go back; we were supposed to watch him, not learn his name.'

Ghar had a sudden idea, 'Nara, he doesn't seem a threat; let's take him back and see if he has anything we want.'

'That's not what Yan wanted.'

'We can still banish him, but at least we can see if he's useful,' Ghar tried to make the suggestion more appealing. 'We still have to ask the outsider,' Ghar motioned to the man to follow him.

The man took the fur and retreated, walking backwards to the deer. After some gestural negotiation they helped the man carry the partly skinned deer back.

'I honestly think Yan will skin us along with that deer,' Nara said nervously.

'Well, if it makes you feel any better, you have put on some meat on your body, so the Khamma will be happy eating you,' Ghar tried to lighten their heavy thoughts. He continued with the outsider pointing at himself, 'We are Khamma. You?'

* * *

Nara led the group on a faster route than they had taken chasing Woyatcha as he pursued the injured deer. Ghar had asked the man if there were more of his tribe following, but he did not seem to understand the question. He seemed nervous of the Khamma, mainly Uru; any movement by the wolf towards him would trigger a quick jog behind Ghar. *Uru wants the meat,* Ghar thought as he restrained his humour. Nara's pace had taken him well ahead of the hunters.

The man marked a rock with a piece of burnt wood, balancing the lower portion of the deer on his shoulder.

Nara walked back to the group, 'We can see our tribe over that ridge. But I have a feeling our outsider will not want to see this.'

'What do you mean?' Ghar rushed towards the ridge.

Nara held on to the outsider.

Ghar looked down on the Khamma. He could not understand what he saw at first; there were more people like the outsider, but with more furs on. They were all lying down. 'Where are their heads?' His eyes began to fill with tears, and his knees felt like they had been replaced with hairy seeds.

Mura tried to grab him, as Woyatcha broke free of Nara's grip. He ran towards the ridge, and almost immediately grabbed Ghar's spear and stabbed Mura in the neck. Ghar struggled to pull it out, but before he could, Nara ran over and pushed his spear through Woyatcha's neck.

Ghar drew his spear out of Mura's neck, but he immediately knew that Mura was dead. He held the deep cut together with his fingers, there was still blood gushing out, each swipe of the red liquid revealed parts of Mura that Ghar never wished to see. *Should I attach? What do I attach?* He gathered Mura in his arms and sobbed. He did not know him that well, but to see the young tribesman cut open in front of him, Ghar felt it was no end for any man.

The commotion had attracted some of the Khamma below. They arrived with cries of anguish at the sight of Mura. Some stabbed at Woyatcha's corpse.

'What happened here?' Yan appeared over the ridge. Ghar and Nara stood there, looking at each other, Ghar too scared to look at anything else.

Nara spoke up, 'We captured the outsider and brought him back, but he broke free when he saw the bodies down there.'

Mai climbed over the ridge. Ghar ran weeping into her arms; he was crying like a child, the way he had cried when he hurt his knee as a youngling, or when he was banished from Zarda, but he never felt like the tears were due, until now. Every drop that streamed down his face felt like the blood of Mura.

'What happened, Ghar?'

Ghar wanted to tell her that he had made a mistake; he had disobeyed and his actions had killed Mura, but all he could say was, 'I am sorry.'

* * *

'What would you do if the water powder storm lasted long enough to kill your prey?' Ghar answered Yan with a question.

'If all the animals were killed, how did the tribe survive?' Yan pointed out, brash and unyielding as usual.

'I don't know; maybe they hid in caves, maybe they have stronger tepees, I don't think all the animals need to die. Fewer buffaloes make it hard to hunt. Fewer buffaloes have fewer offspring which means next warm-time we see even less of them.' He was reminded of the events that happened in his former tribe, 'I think this is what could have happened in Zarda.'

'Your reasoning doesn't explain why they are invading our territory.'

'They are looking for prey. I think the storms are forcing outsiders to move from their territory.' Ghar cringed at Mura's gruesome slaying; he could still feel and smell his blood, but he still thought it was best to see the outsiders as he saw himself.

'They should still not come here,' Yan was adamant.

'What are you going to do? Surround our territory with thorny bushes?'

Yan stared at Ghar coldly, 'That is why I put all those heads on sticks. That should warn off any outsider,' he said, with a note of threat in his voice.

'So far all the tribes we have encountered are small and no match for the wolves. But can we do the same with a bigger tribe?'

'We'll see when that happens, but let's treat the smaller tribes this way,' Yan was getting more confident in his speech.

Ghar realized the futility in arguing with Yan and decided to seek out Mai's comfort.

She was at the Healing Cave, they had a woman, Tabu, and her youngling who looked like a younger version of Mai. They were sneezing, and their faces wore the tired wetness of a hunter just back from the rain. Ghar knew to stand at the entrance so he would not catch their sickness.

Manar approached Ghar, 'Mai has something to tell you.'

Ghar was happy that Mai wanted to talk to him, 'That's nice. Usually she's busy.'

'I think you should be happier than that.'

'What is it, Mai?' Ghar asked her, as she emerged from the Cave.

'Lately, I feel my body changing, and I get angry with you, sometimes without reason.'

Ghar shrugged, 'That happens sometimes, right?'

'Yes, but this seems different. Remember yesterday I was telling you that I felt like I ate too much? Manar thinks it is something else.'

Ghar was confused by her smiling, 'Are you sick? What is happening?'

'Manar thinks I have a baby.'

'What?' Ghar felt like he looked—scared. He had no control of his face, but there was a happiness on top of disbelief collecting behind his eyes.

'This bump here, Manar thinks that's a baby,' Mai looked away from Ghar, with brimming eyes and trembling lips. Not a happiness that comes with reward, but a gratefulness that comes with the end of a long arduous journey. It was the kind of joy that was tempered by effort and loss.

'The Fathers, the Spirits, thank all of them,' Ghar reached around Mai, his arms ached with a mixture of joy and anxiety that the news brought. Happy that he would have a child, and anxious at the physical challenges of pregnancy. He suddenly thought he was holding Mai too tight, 'I am sorry, I should not hold you so hard.'

'I am not sick, Ghar, this might be a baby, but I still want to do what I want.'

Ghar bit his tongue; he suddenly understood all her changes in temper lately 'Yes, Mai, anything you want,' he felt her midriff, it did not feel like there was a child inside. He looked at Manar, 'shouldn't a bump be bigger?'

'It starts out small, but over time, the bump will grow.'

He knelt to put his head against her belly to listen for the new being. The water powder had brought death to the tribes, but in the mysterious ways of their existence, the water powder had also brought him Mai, and now this little child.

17

Back to Zarda

Ghar knew this day was coming. Each storm, each confrontation with the outsiders brought Khamma closer to Zarda.

These were Zardan hunters, lying lifeless on the forest floor. The symbols on their shoulders and the style of fur wrap, these were all Zardan, Ghar thought. He might have even seen these men before.

The birds chirped and the grasshoppers sang, completely oblivious to the bodies that were arranged the way Manar's collection of tongue-bite roots might be arranged. Yan had the Khamma hunters follow the same gruesome treatment as before, placing their heads on stakes as a warning to other tribes.

Arud, a Khamma hunter was also dead. His wounds were attached up and his body cleaned of the excess blood. They would have to drag him back to Khamma; with every movement some blood would escape the badly sewn gashes.

Ghar wanted to cry, to share his grief with the hunters and ask the Fathers for their guidance. But out here, in front of Yan, in front of the Khamma, he could not do that.

'Did you really have to kill them?' he could not stop himself from confronting Yan.

'They were on our territory, and they did not run away, we had no choice,' Yan grabbed Ghar and yanked him away from the tribe. 'I have seen the signs on their hands in your paintings. Killing them felt like vengeance for the dirty trick that you and Mai played on me.'

Yan has blamed these hunters' deaths on Mai and our baby. He clenched his fists, but he knew Mai needed him to show restraint. He let him walk away.

He felt a hand on his shoulder to find Nara, 'You are Khamma.'

Ghar looked up at him. *What makes me Khamma? Tan's declaration? Das banishing me from Zarda?* Ghar shuddered at Das's memory. Das was not a youngling like Yan, striking out of a need to be seen as a leader. Das was of Tan's stature, but with a misplaced pride in the Zarda, and in the Sanaa, 'Das will not take this lightly.'

'Das . . . the Elder from Zarda?' Nara asked.

'Yes, the Zardan who speaks to the Fathers,' Ghar did not believe that Das spoke to the Fathers but it was a common belief among the Zardan tribe. 'The hunters would follow Das to their deaths if he told them to.'

'But he doesn't know it's us?'

'I think he will be angry enough to kill any tribe here.' *The Gubba. He will finally have a reason to kill the Gubba.* He walked over to Yan, 'Yan, Tan asked me to advise you; this is my advice, bury these bodies, don't let the Zarda come to know what happened here.'

'And then they will come back and take our meat. They are like you, they come here to take things. You outsiders only understand the tip of a spear.'

Ghar turned his attention to the headless bodies. This could not be changed; he could not attach their heads back on. But he could think of a plan to help the Gubba. He had to.

* * *

Ghar and Nara had started at the break of light in the night sky. The nocturnal sounds of insects and animals along with the wind in the leaves and Uru's panting were the only sounds that accompanied them. The warm-time warmth comforted their journey.

After a long, but fruitless, discussion with Mai, Manar and Nara, they decided that the most immediate concern was the preparedness of the Gubba. Ghar would travel with Nara to the Gubba Zarda. They trusted Nara, he had forestalled Ghar from shouldering the blame for Mura's death.

Tan had asked Nara to help me, Ghar remembered Nara explaining his actions. 'Do you know why Tan asked you to help me?'

'Why is not a word I like to use. Most of the time knowing less is better.'

Ghar thought that was curious, 'I think knowing more makes you better prepared.'

'I know more, I worry more,' Nara wore his enigmatic look. 'I want to focus on what I am told to do.'

Ghar thought there was some wisdom in that. All the worrying he did after being banished from the Zarda did not help him get to Khamma. Had he known where the Gubba were, he could have gone to them. 'What about you, Uru?' he asked the wolf.

'The more I know, I eat, the less I know, I eat,' Nara answered on Uru's behalf.

'That sounds like something Dun would say,' Ghar thought of his brother. 'He doesn't know what news we bring; I hope they will not panic.'

'I still think they should move,' Nara held on to their decision. 'I know of places that are accessible only through hidden paths.'

'I think they may have to, but moving the entire camp—the Elders, children, pregnant women—it will be just too difficult.' Ghar thought of Mai again; he would not want her to go anywhere while she was pregnant.

They walked quickly through the forest, which made talking difficult. The cliff caves of Gubba Zarda were a welcome sight. There was still enough sky light to make out the ridges of the cliff, and the dark caverns below. Through the trees the flickers of campfire broke through.

'Ghar,' Dun called across the rock ravine, his voice echoing. 'Nara, what are you doing here?' Dun carefully picked his way across the small stream. 'Come to collect moving furs early?'

Ghar laughed, Dun always seemed to have something cheerful to say, 'Early is better.'

'Give us the fur, and we will give you the moving fur,' Dun smirked back, 'Maybe some buffalo meat would help too.'

Lately the hunts were not as bountiful. Ghar focused on Das, 'Dun, we are here because Yan killed Zardan tribesmen.'

'What?' Dun stopped. 'You mean hunters from Zarda? Where? Why?'

'Hunters, in a field near Animal River.'

'Like he killed those other tribespeople?'

'We have done it a few times; after the water powder storms more seem to be hunting in our territory.'

'Was Das among the dead?' Dun asked; he looked hopeful.

'No,' Ghar shared Dun's disappointment, 'I am ashamed to be disappointed.'

'I know,' Dun looked down shamefacedly, 'even if I were to drive the spear into his chest myself, I would still be sad. Come let's go to the campfire, you must be tired.'

'We realize that Das will want vengeance.'

'Will he think it was us?' Dun's face emptied of colour.

'We don't know, but we think it is best you prepared yourselves; either protect your camp or leave.'

'Leave? And go where?'

'Nara knows of places that are hard to get to except by hidden paths.'

'Kara has a baby in her.'

'What?'

'We are doing what the Khamma do, it's only us together, so the baby must be mine.'

Ghar was elated, but also scared, 'I am grateful to the Fathers!' Ghar exclaimed. 'I am so glad to share this path with you.' He remembered Mai again, he would not make her move while carrying a baby. 'Let's try to think of another way.'

Dun, backed by Ghar and Nara, approached Bena who was sitting with the other Elders, 'Bena, the Khamma hunters have killed some Zardan hunters. Das may blame us for this, and they may look for us to take revenge.'

Bena's face went from fear to anger with every word. 'This is too much! We cannot take the blame for this act.'

'I agree, Hera,' Ghar spoke up. 'We need to keep you safe.'

'The best way to keep us safe is to make sure Das knows this is the Khamma, and not us.'

Ghar realized he had not considered this thorny path. 'But that would put the Khamma in danger.'

'Did the Khamma kill those men?'

'Yes,' Ghar conceded.

'Then the Khamma should bear the consequences and this danger.'

'How would you even tell the Zarda of this?'

'We will send some of our men to inform the Zarda.'

With his focus on the Gubba's safety, Ghar had overlooked the Khamma's. He was sure that Nara had an idea about what Bena was arguing. He thought it best to give Nara the full translation, 'Bena says that they will go and tell Das that it was the Khamma that killed the men.'

'I understood that,' Nara said, stroking the bristle on his face. 'Has the tribe decided that?'

'That's right; the tribe has to decide,' Ghar turned to Bena, 'Hera, I advise you to think of some other solution.'

'This is the best way; this is the only way.'

Ghar sighed, he didn't want to go up against Bena, but really had no choice. 'Bena, you will have to call a decision-marks gathering,'

Ghar and Nara had just arrived in Gubba Zarda, but it seemed like their journey was only just beginning.

* * *

The decision-marks gathering had not gone the Khamma's way; Gubba tribesmen were already on their way to Zarda.

'We can't tell the tribe that the Gubba are going to Zarda to report against the Khamma,' Nara sounded worried, but there was an underlying calmness in his demeanour that spoke of long years of experience with challenges like these.

'I'll tell them that it was I who told the Gubba; you don't have to be part of this,' Ghar was not going to let Nara take the blame. He felt a void in his chest that only grew; only it seemed to grow inwards, collapsing like a tepee supported on stalks of grass.

'You, me, it doesn't matter. Also, they will ask why I was with you,' Nara gazed into the distance, the morning lighting their path back to Khamma. Nara continued, 'We have to come up with a story.'

Ghar felt his misjudgement of the situation was unforgivable. 'What's worse is I did not give the Khamma a choice about what to do. I chose on their behalf. They should at least be given a choice to punish me.'

'Stop moping, Ghar. We made a decision. It was never going to be easy either way. Now we have to do something,' Nara had resolution in his voice.

'But we can't go back and lie; this is too important.'

'How do you think I have managed to sustain my role in the tribe for so long, not hunting, not collecting firewood, only exploring the forest?'

Ghar stopped. He had assumed that Tan was behind Nara's role. He questioned Nara with full eyes.

'I sometimes make the truth more interesting,' Nara smiled.

Ghar was still despondent, 'What can we tell the tribe?'

'I think more important is what do we do? I would assume your Zardan friends will be coming here soon.'

'I can try to talk to Das,' Ghar knew he would get speared before he said anything. 'Nara, I don't see a way out of this. I think the the Zarda will come after us.'

'All right. Then we have to think of what to do.'

* * *

'We went to Gubba to warn them, but on the way back we found a Zardan scout. Ghar questioned him and discovered that they were looking for tribes in this area. He escaped, slashing Ghar's arm.' Ghar and Nara were hoping that the Gubba's inability to speak the Khamman language and vice versa would shield their story from the truth.

Ghar showed the tribe his shoulder, the cut across the skin was a detail needed for the story, it was better than being punished for betrayal. Also, it satisfied Ghar's need to be punished for his lapse.

Udor questioned, 'Wasn't Uru able to run the man down?'

Nara quickly answered, 'We called Uru back; we didn't want the wolf to get injured and I thought it was best to come back immediately and inform the tribe.'

'This is distressing news. Yan, this has something to do with your ill-judged actions, what is your solution?'

'My solution is always to protect the Khamma. We killed those men so that they would serve as a warning. If the Zarda does not heed our warning, then we will feed them to our wolves.'

'Yan, the Zarda is not a small tribe, we might be able to kill some of them, but I think they will overpower us,' Ghar warned.

'They may have men, but we have wolves. Or are you scared we will harm them; are you protecting your Zardan kind?'

Ghar did feel discomfort at the idea of harming Zarda, but there was more a feeling of a lost opportunity to prosper. 'I think we should give them something; maybe they have something Khamma needs. Like what we have with the Gubba. The Zarda is good at making tepees.'

Udor interrupted, 'You and Yan can argue until the Zarda are in our camp, but this needs to be decided by the tribe. I will call for a decision-marks.'

Ghar knew it was solely his actions that had brought things to this pass. What used to be a slim chance, was now a grim reality, and he would have to face it. He looked out at the Khamma; they did not have Maraza, all they had was wolves. Uru was lying belly up beside Nara, enjoying the warmth of the campfire. *We warned the Gubba; maybe if they had stood by us, the Zarda would have desisted.*

* * *

Ghar and Nara made their way back to Gubba, the walk again was too fast for talking. The decision-marks had again gone against Ghar's pleas.

'I can't believe Yan said that I did not believe the stars were not the Khamman tribespeople.'

Nara himself rushed through without breath, jumping from rock to rock and back to the ground.

'But it's true, right? You believe the stars are just other suns.'

Ghar could not manage a sigh, he was so out of breath, 'I *think* that's what they are, I don't *believe* so. But why bring that up. It had nothing to do with fighting the Zarda; to me none of the Khamma even looked like they wanted to fight.'

'Seems like the Khamma decided on whom they trust, not on the argument they trust.'

'I hope the Gubba agree to stand with us.'

'I don't believe they will. I am only running with you right now because this is what I know to do.'

'Thank you, Nara,' Ghar pushed out the final words he could muster from his burning chest. The cliff caves of the Gubba hove into view. *Fathers aid me in my appeal to the Gubba.*

* * *

'I don't think Bena will agree to this. I know he will not agree to this.' Dun huddled with Kara, the night cold was upon them.

'Why aren't there more fires around, it's so cold,' Ghar put his arms around Uru to keep warm.

'We want to conserve; if Khamma is gone, we will have to spend more time looking for food.'

'I don't think that will happen, especially if you stand with us.'

'Let me correct what I said: the Gubba will not agree to this.'

'We have to try and get all the help we can get. Surely the Gubba see the advantage in keeping the Khamma alive.'

Dun sighed, he looked to Kara for advice.

Kara shrugged, 'I don't know; it's choosing death.'

Dun agreed, 'That's what it is, Ghar.'

'Let's ask.'

Dun left the comfort of Kara and joined Ghar. Nara was with some of the Gubba, conversing word by word.

'Bena, Hera, may the Fathers guide us.'

'I saw you down there with Dun; are you bringing bad news again?'

'Not news, but an appeal. Khamma is still useful to the Gubba, meat and furs, and the protection of the wolves. I ask that you stand with us, against the Zarda. I think if Das sees us together, he will change his path.'

Bena laughed, 'Child, now your youth really shows. The only reason Das did not have us killed before was because the other Elders would not let him,' Bena had the incredulity in his eyes. 'Do you want us to give them a reason to kill us?'

'But there is an advantage in trying to help the Khamma; you get to keep the meat and furs, and can further prosper, make new tepees, more spears, more babies.'

'I think few babies is better than no babies,' replied Bena. 'The choice you give us includes our deaths.'

'Let me appeal to the tribe in a decision-marks.'

'Let it be done,' Bena sighed. 'Dun, have our hunters come back?'

'Not yet, Hera.'

'The hunters who went to inform the Zarda?' Ghar asked.

Dun answered, 'Yes.'

Bena shook his clasped hands in a defeated gesture. 'This is not our fight, but we are already losing.'

Ghar thought, *you sent the hunters; we could never tell what the Zarda would do.* Ghar had a disturbing thought, 'Das might keep your hunters to guide them to Khamma. Maybe even Gubba.'

A heavy silence fell on the group. Ghar realized he was asking all the wrong questions, 'Our answers are only as good as our questions.'

'Adura's advice,' Bena acknowledged.

'Can I appeal to the tribe?'

Bena nodded.

* * *

'The Gubba said no.'

Mai reached around Ghar, 'Don't worry; you tried your best.'

Worry was all that Ghar could do. Yan might have put the Khamma at risk by killing the Zarda, but Ghar, by warning the Gubba made the conflict with the Zarda unavoidable. He watched the Khamma hunters prepare more spears and discuss combat. *At least Yan is trying to prepare them.* He caressed Mai from her hair down to the softness of her face. 'I should join them.'

She looked at him, with eyes that tried to say that he didn't need to, being a new Khamma, but visibly hid a truth that she agreed. He was a new Khamma, this was the time to be a Khamma.

He stepped down the rocky outcrops from the Healing Cave, 'Yan, what can I do to help?'

Yan stopped what he was doing. He was so caught up with preparing the tribespeople, he looked like he had completely forgotten Ghar. 'This is a fight against your Zarda; are you sure you want to be there? A lot of them will die.'

Ghar felt his stomach sink, partly at the thought of the Zarda being harmed, but partly at Yan's confidence. He knew it was misplaced—Zardan hunters could take down wolves in the wild, the Khamma's wolves would be no different.

'Tan made me a Khamma, I would be proud to fight alongside you.' He said it, but his heart wasn't in it, and he was sure the tone of his words betrayed his convictions. 'By the Spirits, by the Fathers, I would rather you let me first talk to Das, to see if we could win this fight before fighting.'

'I have thought about that. You can talk to your Zardan leader, by all means, and we will give you time. But if he is still arrogant, then we will show him the might of the Khamma.'

Ghar noticed a cooling in Yan's posture, like he was stepping back from his need to fight, recognizing Tan's wisdom in avoidance.

Ghar explained, 'If you lead with the wolves you take away their main advantage, the surprise of their speed.' Yan's yielding freed up Ghar to think about the fight. 'The wolves would be best positioned behind the Zarda where they won't expect them.'

Yan looked at the wolves. 'How do we get behind the Zarda? We still don't even know where they are.'

'We should know soon. Nara and some of the hunters have taken up positions on the main passes.'

'If the Zarda decide to come at all.'

Ghar knew there was little hope of that happening. 'That would be best, but we should still be prepared.'

'What if while you talked to Das, we led the wolves to the sides and as far behind them as we could.'

This would be the ultimate betrayal, something the Fathers might not forgive, but Ghar had already begun to place the blame on Das. This had all started with the expulsion of the Gubba.

* * *

'They are at Backbone Mountains,' Gan, a hunter, ran into the camp, the evening sun revealing the fear-stricken expression on his face.

Yan called out to the tribe, 'I need all of you to get ready to meet at the campfire.'

Ghar was fitting knapped flint to complete new spears for the hunters. He dropped them on the ground, and quickly ran to the Healing Cave to get Mai and Manar. 'The Zarda, at Backbone Mountains, Gan just said so,' Ghar announced, his breath catching up.

'Let's go and see what Yan, Udor and Tura want to say,' Manar replied, arranging some of the hide packs of berries as she started to walk.

Mai followed; she didn't look entirely comfortable, 'Ghar help me.'

The tribe had assembled around the fire. Yan was talking to Udor and Tura, their demeanours spoke more clearly than their words.

Yan turned to the tribe, 'Khamma, my brethren, the time has come. The Zarda are setting up camp near Backbone Mountains. We will be ready tomorrow morning.'

Ghar could tell that none of the hunters were looking forward to the clash with the Zarda. Even Yan was not at his most assured.

'Khamma,' Ghar shouted, 'I may have been Zardan, but today I choose Khamma, and Khamma will prevail,' He quickly glanced at Mai, before letting loose a loud battle cry, with his fist high in the air.

The tribe went up in a roar.

'Khamma, today we eat to our fill, for tomorrow, we feast on the Zarda,' Yan shouted to even more cries from the crowd.

Ghar roared, but he held back a sigh for Zarda as he held Mai's hand. This could be the last time he would hold her hand.

18

The Fathers

Every step had a rush of feeling; they had embraced their kindred back in the camp with the full knowledge that they might never see them again. There was the chant to keep the Khamma alert to their cause, and the constant reminders from Yan, as he strode back and forth between the ranks of hunters, 'Remember, no spears will be thrown until I say so.'

The walk felt so unfamiliar; they had been in these forests before and they knew its most intimate secrets, yet the walk felt like they were doing it for the first time. Their green trees and grass were back, with new shoots peeking out of the branches.

They were arranged in groups, a middle, a left, a right and a wolf group lead by Nara and some of the other tribespeople who were fast. Ghar lead the middle group. When the time came, he was supposed to approach the Zarda and seek out Das to discuss whether there was a possibility to trade instead of killing each other.

Yan approached Ghar, 'I hope your idea works.'

Ghar nodded. The night before, he had remembered the buffalo near Backbone Mountains, 'The wolves are better at herding the buffalo, so let's use that. If there is a big enough herd, that will be enough to scare any tribe away.'

Yan grunted his approval. 'You had better hope that Tur and Ulan can keep the herd of buffalo under control.' There was something about Yan's actions that made Ghar suspect that there was more to the plan. But Ghar needed to concentrate on his talk with the Zarda.

A hunter in the vanguard issued a warning cry. The groups started to arrange, left flank, middle, right flank. Ghar moved to the front from where he could see the smaller tepees that were used on Zardan hunts. He started to sing loudly, as loud as he could while still enunciating the words.

As he learns how the cold gives birth to the warm,
And the night gives birth to the day,
And the dead gives birth to the living,
Be sure his tracks will be different,
But his path will always lead back to Zarda.

He made his way through the new grass and shrubs, as he got closer, he could see the Zarda tribesmen, spears raised, uncertain about what was approaching them, 'I want to speak to Das.'

Das emerged from the tepees at the back, picked up a spear that was leaning against the tepee and walked quickly towards Ghar. Ghar thought about running away, back to Mai, back to his unborn baby, but this was the only chance for the Zarda and the Khamma to come out of this unscathed and without needless death.

'So, you survived,' Das recognized Ghar, 'son of Adura.'

Ghar realized that Das had deliberately not acknowledged Gharra, but this was not the time to argue about that. 'Hera, I come to you to find an alternative path to bloodshed. My new tribe, the Khamma, we have plentiful access to buffalo meat and furs which we can trade for something that you are willing to give. This will help sustain both our tribes.'

'You killed my men, put their heads on stakes; I will take your buffalo meat and furs, and I will take your wolves, but only after every Khamma is mounted on a stake.'

'Hera, this is not the time for vengeance, your men trespassed on to our hunting grounds; don't make their blame a cause for all our deaths. Our tribe is strong, and we have the advantage with the wolves.'

The ground began to rumble, Ghar knew it was the wolves herding the buffaloes. 'The Khamma control the buffalo,' he pointed at the source of the sound. He looked past Das, at the Zarda who were clearly taken aback, 'Now is the chance for you to run away.'

Das brandished his spear at Ghar, who dodged it, but still stood his ground. The shaking ground gave him the reassurance to continue.

'Zarda, ready your spears.'

That's not good, Ghar thought, the ground was shaking even more, he turned around to see a herd of panicked buffalo stampeding towards them. *Yan betrayed me!* He noticed a huge log behind which he could seek refuge; he ran quickly and ducked down just as the powerful hooves of the beasts rocked the log as they vaulted over it and into the Zarda camp. The desperate Zardan hunters tried in vain to spear the beasts which galloped on in a fear-crazed, headlong rush, taking the spears and the hunters with them. The thundering of hooves abruptly gave way to the snarling of wolves and the chivvying cries of the Khamma hunters. The Zardan hunters, who were fortunate enough to not be trampled by the buffaloes, were being mauled by wolves; the Khamma quickly spearing the injured.

There were a lot of the Zarda and just as quickly as the Khamma had the advantage, the Zarda retaliated, killing wolves, hacking away at the less-trained Khamman warriors. Ghar was still cowering by the log, when a hunter started towards him. He ran over to the closest body he could find and picked up the abandoned spears. The hunter who chased him was seemingly uninjured, except for his shoulder bleeding. Ghar threw the spear into his chest. He ran to the fallen hunter, yanked the spear out of his hand and stabbed him in the neck.

Ghar sank to his knees in exhaustion. The air all around him was filled with cries of pain and sounds of struggling combat. He looked up to find Das running towards him. Ghar grabbed the spear and jumped up, and ran to a clump of pine trees.

'I should have killed you in Zarda,' Das shouted as he walked into the cluster of closely spaced trunks, his spear leading his steps.

Ghar did not say anything as he desperately looked for an escape route out of the spinney. In a fight alone with Das, Ghar knew he was sure to lose. A spear bounced off a tree after hissing past his head. He realized he was moving away from the Khamma, who were his only hope. He ran behind a boulder and quickly climbed to the top. He needed to see where Das was and then make a run for the aid of any Khamma. He could see Das stalk to the other side of the rock, expecting Ghar to continue running.

Ghar jumped from the boulder, losing his footing, but the fear kept him moving; his knees and elbows skimmed across the forest floor while running. Ghar realized he was no longer carrying a spear.

Another hiss flew past his ear, the spear lodging in a tree. He ploughed back into the fighting, men with their arms around each other, punching, gouging, biting. There were bodies everywhere.

His felt a smack on the side of his face; his ear, his hair, the corner of his eye, all erupted in pain that he could not contain, and suddenly he was on the ground. He crawled, turning just enough to see Das nearly upon him. *Mai, I am grateful for you.*

Ghar turned away from Das; he would not give him the satisfaction of seeing the fear on his face or hearing the whimper in his voice. It almost felt like the earth was opening up, embracing his return, he could see Gharra and Adura in the distance. They hurled their spears. His eyes closed slowly; his fingers squeezed the earth, relishing it for a final time.

* * *

'Gharra, Adura,' Ghar held them close, his face lost in their bosoms, 'I tried, I tried to complete the Walk, and be of pride to you.'

Gharra laughed, 'The Walk isn't something you complete; it's the way you live your life, the way you treat people, the way you remember the Fathers in your tasks.'

Adura ran her fingers through Ghar's hair, 'And for this we are so proud of you, our son.'

'Ghar, wake up!' Dun's voice floated into his head, 'Ghar, wake up! the fight is over.'

'What!? Am I not dead?' Ghar exclaimed, his eyes still closed. He opened them to see the forest pines reaching for the evening sky.

'Ghar, wake up!' Dun pulled Ghar up, his arms around his shoulders.

'What happened?'

'I killed Das, that's what happened.'

Ghar looked around to find Das's body, a spear lodged in his mouth, 'Adura and Gharra—'

'Adura and Gharra?'

'It doesn't make sense,' he looked at Dun, he was still not sure if this was real.

The field was strewn with bodies, a lot dead, but some were still writhing in pain. There were the Zarda and the Khamma and the Gubba, sitting, standing, talking to each other, tending to their wounds.

'Why are you here, Dun?' Ghar shook his head, 'Is this a dream?'

'I may be a Gubba, I may be a Zarda, but before all of that, I am your brother, Ghar,' Dun took steps, nudging Ghar's legs along with his knees. 'Besides, I wanted to see if my Maraza actually works.'

'Why are they sitting around, and not fighting?'

'It takes a field full of corpses to realize fighting is stupid,' Dun offered his thoughts. 'But it could be that after Das and Yan fell, there was no more need fight.'

'Manar, I can see Manar,' Ghar said.

'Yes, let's go see her. Mai is here too.'

Ghar limped over to Manar, as she knelt, bandaging a cut of a Khamma hunter. She turned her eyes just enough to notice it was Ghar. 'Wait a moment,' her words were weakened by the tears in her eyes. She secured the hunter's arm and turned to Ghar, sobbing. 'I am so happy you are alive, Ghar,' she gestured to the bodies in the field. 'I was so scared we would find you out there.'

'Dun saved me,' Ghar smiled through his exhaustion. 'Das was about to kill me,' Ghar began to cry, he had not realized he would not see Manar again in his final moments with Das. 'Where is Mai?'

Manar stopped, wide-eyed, 'Mai, she is over there.'

Ghar saw her on the opposite side of the field. He ran to her, stumbling, running, he could hardly see through the tears in his eyes. As he closed in, he realized that the man she was tending to was a Zardan.

Mai turned around at the loud footsteps on the leafy forest floor and stopped.

To Ghar it was like seeing her for the first time all over again, lingering over the shape of her eyes, pondering about her long unwavering nose, and relishing the firmness of her caring hands.

She held up her hand to stop Ghar, while she finished up with attaching the man's wounds, who looked in pain, but also seemed confused about what was happening. She continued working steadily, her tears falling, she turned away to make sure her teardrops did not enter the man's wounds.

'Ghar, just looking at you seals up this hole in my chest that opened when you left Khamma.'

The man whimpered in pain. 'I am sorry,' Mai wiped her face. She motioned to Ghar to soothe the man, 'What happened to your face, Ghar?'

'Das, he was so close to killing me, but Dun showed up at the right time.'

Mai cut the thin sinew to close the wound. She washed the awl with water and put it back into a wrap. She laid her knapsack on the floor and walked around the man and jumped on Ghar. The pain that Ghar felt was excruciating, the impact of Mai's face on his, the clash of her knees with his shins, the weight of her chest on his, but he did not resist, he flinched, but he would not push Mai away. This pain was a part of his life, and the more he succumbed to the reality of his near death, the more alive the pain made him feel.

They lay there intertwined, until they heard Manar calling out, 'This is no time to rest, there are people that need healing.'

Some of the men put up the tepees, that were felled by the buffaloes. The injured were moved in, and cared for, Zarda and Khamma alike. Fires were started and water collected. Ghar thought it was fitting that the Zarda's preparation to attack the Khamma was now being used to heal the tribes.

The surviving Khamma wolves protected the neatly arranged bodies. It was only the next morning that Dun pointed out Yan's body. He had a large cut in the back of his neck. Mai closed it, asking the Spirits to accept him to the stars.

* * *

'The Zarda Elders have invited us to complete the Hunter's Walk,' Dun said excitedly.

'It was more negotiated by yourself, than "invited", from what I hear,' Ghar scoffed.

The Elders, even in the current circumstances were trying to maintain the Zarda tradition. Ghar had temporarily excused himself from the discussions. He was just glad to be back in Zarda, in the tepee in which he grew up.

'They were a bit stubborn at first, but we did save so many Zarda that night. If that does not give us the right, then I don't know what would.'

'I wonder what the Fathers would say,' Ghar thought out loud.

'They have kept their silence for so long, I have a feeling they will remain silent on this too.'

Ghar cringed at insulting the Fathers, 'Don't say that, or we'll get expelled again.' He looked up, 'Fathers, please accept this as humour, nothing else.'

The Zarda and the Khamma were merged, still maintaining their locations and hunting grounds. The tribes were to meet regularly to share resources, tools, and healing techniques. The fight had somehow brought the tribes together, Ghar eloquently attributing the strange outcome to the Zarda Fathers and the Khamma Spirits.

But importantly, the Gubba had moved back to Zarda, with the Zarda Elders agreeing that the Gubba and the Sanaa were equal—the discussions ongoing between the Gubba and the Sanaa were about what 'equal' meant.

'When Das struck me down, I saw Adura and Gharra.'

'Really? As in a dream?' Dun asked.

'They threw the spears that killed Das.'

'I killed Das,' Dun asserted.

'I know that, but I saw them, and then after that, I apologized to them for not completing the Hunter's Walk.' Ghar drew closer to the fire. 'They told me that the Walk was not something you complete—it was life, living the way of the Zardan hunter.'

Dun's eyes watered, 'They are dead, but they still live in us.'

'Adura could still be alive,' Ghar said tearing up. 'She came looking for me.'

'Don't do that, Ghar. They found her belongings, her ripped furs, her spears, her paints,' Dun did not want to relive what had happened to his birth mother.

Mai and Kara entered the tepee. 'What are you doing?' Mai asked.

Ghar glanced at Dun, 'We are living.'

Kara volunteered, 'How about we "live" some Khazagu; I think we should teach our Sanaa brethren.'

Ghar smiled at them, 'Yes,' he turned to Dun, 'and yes.'

* * *

They had completed the dawn ceremony to start the Hunter's Walk. Ghar was especially thrilled that they had managed to convince the Elders that Mai and Nara should be allowed to complete the rite as well.

The songs led them through forests, ravines and across rivers. They moved slowly, Mai and Kara were both carrying new Zarda Khamma.

'I hope it doesn't turn out to be something boring,' Dun exclaimed.

'Don't call it boring and anger the Fathers,' Ghar said, but he too secretly hoped that it was worth the trek, and also worth the risk to Mai and Kara. The Zardan hunters had all been sworn to secrecy on what was at the end of the walk.

Nara and Uru were not leading from the front, which was refreshing for Ghar, but they did on occasion, by their natures, push the group to move faster.

Dun reminded, 'No need to rush anymore, Nara,' in broken Khamman.

'Is that it?' Ghar called out.

The rock mount will reveal its secret,
Only when you travel around it,
This is the life of a Hunter,
Taking the path of hardship,
But that hardship does reward,
And return the Hunter back to the Zarda,
Back to the Fathers.

'What is that?' Mai caught sight of a figure emerging from the rock.

'That looks like a giant man's head.'

They had to journey all the way around, each new view eliciting yelps of excitement. The grey-rock mountain was shaped like men's heads. There was the original head that they had first seen, a similar character was next to him with a long sharp nose, and then another character with hair on the upper lip and a final figure with hair on his chin.

'This is why some Zardan hunters have similar face hair,' Dun felt the bristle on his own face. 'Should I try some hair on my chin?' he asked Kara.

'That has been carved from the rock, look at all the rock pieces at the base,' Ghar thought out loud. The ache in his limbs, and the sweat pooling in his moving fur were vindicated. This was something that would stay forever with any Zarda, or any person who viewed it. 'These are the Fathers,' Ghar smiled, he had never imagined that they would have a form, that they would have been knapped from a rock mountain. The song started to play in his head.

And return the Hunter back to the Zarda,
Back to the Fathers.